CW01636216

Death at the Yumbo Centre

D.M. Pickersgill

Death at the Yumbo Centre

ISBN: 978-1-0684280-2-9

Cover Design by More Visual / bookartwork.com

A Note to the Reader

Welcome to *Death at the Yumbo Centre*—my second novel after my debut, *Followers*.

If you've read *Followers*, you might recognise Dan, our reluctant, introverted, and occasionally disastrous hero. If you haven't, don't worry—this isn't a sequel in the strictest sense. There are no major spoilers from *Followers* hidden here, and you can absolutely enjoy *Death at the Yumbo Centre* without reading anything else first.

You'll notice a few references to "what happened last October." That's a nod to the events of *Followers*—so if you're curious about Dan's earlier misadventures, you might want to dive into *Followers* either before or after your trip to Gran Canaria.

Whichever way you choose, thank you for picking up this book and spending time with these messy, complicated characters. I hope you enjoy the ride—and maybe you'll need a stiff cocktail afterwards.

See you by the pool!

Chapter 1

Lying back, letting the warmth of the sun seep into my skin, my body sinks into the ground like it belongs here. Above me, the sky stretches out, impossibly blue, the kind of blue that feels endless, untouched, a colour that only exists in places like this. The clouds move lazily, slow and unbothered, drifting without purpose, without urgency. I watch them shift, morphing into soft, shapeless figures that my brain half-heartedly tries to turn into something recognisable.

The heat is perfect, that deep, golden warmth that makes everything else fade away. My limbs are heavy, my breathing slow.

I close my eyes for a moment, feeling the weight of the sun pressing down on me, the lazy hum of summer wrapping around my body like a second skin. When I open them again, the sky is still there, still endless, still moving in its own quiet rhythm.

There's noise nearby, chatting maybe, I can't quite tell.

Such a peaceful day.

The kind of day I came on holiday for.

So calm.

So relaxed.

My palms are damp, but not from sweat.

No, it's from the blood that covers them.

Chapter 2

DAN

4 days earlier

Stepping off the bus with a groan that would make a pensioner proud, my back clicks back into place after that soul-crushing airport transfer. At 6-foot, there's limited appreciation for the battery hen seating and, naturally, we were the last stop on a 75-minute joyride marathon around the island.

The driver, tired and sweating, chucks our baggage out of the bus to the side of the road with all the delicacy of a sledgehammer, one after the next.

"Come on!" cries Hugo, my faithful travel companion, bursting with unfathomable Labrador energy. Bounding ahead with his arms out, he's through the automatic doors in record time.

Clocking 1:25am on my watch, I sigh and wipe the sweat from my brow with the shoulder of my t-shirt. As I lug my overstuffed baggage up the steps of the hotel, every single one of the 23kg allowance tinges my soul with aches and regret. For one week in Gran Canaria, where I will predominantly be wearing swimming shorts and unlikely much else, the excess of unnecessary items weighs my suitcase down like a small museum. Enough underwear and shorts to last a lifetime; four pairs of shoes I'll never wear; toiletries to make a Boots sales assistant weep with joy. Even that crop top no self-respecting forty-year-old man—homosexual or otherwise—should ever be seen wearing, made the cut.

And a travel iron. A travel iron!

What was I thinking?

As the automatic doors to the Hotel Maspalomas Oasis hiss open for me, Hugo, already in reception, looks back grinning, "We're here!" And while I'm fully aware we're here, I can't but love his unwavering enthusiasm for life, even if mine left me somewhere around passport control.

The flight from Bristol was only meant to be four and a half hours. Try telling that to my spine after three hours of delays, an overcrowded gate full of shouting toddlers, cackling hen dos in matching t-shirts, and rugby lads testing the limits of Lynx Africa.

The flight itself was not much better. More screaming kids. The vibe of the hen dos and the rugby lads, now significantly drunker after three hours more beer than anticipated, escalated quickly to loud singing and chanting and I'm pretty sure the maid of honour getting finger blasted by the scrum half in the back row. All this while the woman next to me wanted to chat about her cat's separation anxiety, which resulted in me nodding uncomfortably for 25 minutes. Eventually after an opportune break in the flow, my headphones went in and my only other need to speak was when asking for the four gin and tonics I consumed to support my journey.

After further delays on arrival waiting for our luggage, the transfer to the hotel was enough to send me spiralling, leg room limitations aside. As expected, the bus was packed with a selection of young families, tired kids screaming or talking nonsense, like nails on a chalk board at the early hours, their parents given up on them.

Hugo, ever the hostess, was gleefully chatting to all and everyone about the holiday ahead, the king of small talk, effortless and entertaining. His immediate rapport with a very loud lady with three kids called Kelly, gave me anxiety. Her screeching voice, unnecessarily hysterical laugh combined with her excessively crude humour, which she comfortably displayed in front of her young kids, was enough to make me want to pound my forehead against the window to make it stop. *Please don't let her be at our hotel, please*, I silently pleaded, envisioning a week of having to sit by her and her rabble every day by the pool. The thought sent shivers down my spine. Fortunately, she got off two stops before our hotel, which put a thankful premature end to their blossoming friendship.

As I enter the lobby however, even with my overburdened baggage and bleary eyes, all is forgotten as I can't help but marvel at the place. Hugo's choice has certainly paid off. The hotel is like a slice of a tropical daydream—a colonial-inspired façade meets modern décor, where the marble floors gleam, and the walls are adorned with serene images of local landscapes.

The reception is surprisingly welcoming. A concierge, who looks as if he were plucked right out of a glossy travel magazine, greets us with a theatrical flourish: "Welcome to the Maspalomas Oasis!"

Hugo, ever the extrovert, claps me on the back and announces with booming enthusiasm. "Hi there! I'm Hugo, and this is Dan!" he says, like the concierge and us are all pals on a night out. His voice rings out as he chatters, effortlessly blending humour and charm, while I stand slightly behind him, clutching my suitcase like it's a lifeline.

It's times like this that I love having Hugo as a friend. As a self-confessed introvert with bludgeoning social anxiety, making small talk in the early hours, while exhausted from travel will never be successful or comfortable for anyone involved. It's second nature to Hugo, and allows me to switch off into survival mode, where I'm borderline functioning and very little else.

After the standard passport exchange, a lengthy explanation of the eating arrangements, and the scrawling over the hotel map, that will no doubt end up in the bin in less than 5 minutes, we are presented with our keys.

In no time, we're on floor 6, outside our room, with the concierge valiantly attempting to haul both our suitcases through the corridor, like a reluctant human forklift, despite looking like he might pass out any second. Once again, I feel a pang of guilt for packing my travel iron.

As Hugo darts into the room to check out the balcony, my guilt exacerbates as the lack of cash means the only reward the concierge receives for his efforts is a sheepish smile and a closed door.

"Dan, look! We have a great view of the pool!" Hugo screams like an excitable child. "When I stayed here last time, the best seats were over in that corner," he says pointing into the darkness.

Stepping into our twin room, I head over to the window to see the pool, lit up from below, shimmering like a siren calling me to dive in. Our home for the next seven nights.

"I can't wait to get out there tomorrow!" Hugo says, checking his phone. "Looks like it's going to hit around 28 degrees in the afternoon."

I sit down on one of the beds. "Sounds perfect," I say, the vision of lying in 28-degree heat, sipping a cocktail, in October, after the twelve months I've had is exactly what I need. Rubbing my hands across the bed linen, it's crisp enough to make me question what I have done to deserve this much freshness in my life.

"Well, I'll grab the other one then," Hugo announces, diving on to the spare bed next to me, wriggling around on it gleefully. Letting out a joyous moan, he says, "Dan, this bed is like a marshmallow! I am going to sleep well tonight!"

"Yeah, same here," I agree, closing my eyes for a moment.

It's been years since Hugo and I spent any quality time together, and this is our first holiday together since our twenties. Hugo and I are the kind of friends who pick up right where we left off, no matter how many years have passed. We met back in 2003 at university in Exeter, where we bonded over our love of musicals, men and strawberry daiquiris. Living together in our twenties was chaos, a fabulous blend of clutter, cheap spirits and ineffective cleaning rotas.

Even though we don't see each other as often now, him in London, me in Bristol, a single text or phone call is enough to whisk us back to those days of carefree banter and spontaneous hijinks. Hugo has this uncanny ability to make even the most mundane topics sound epic. Whether we're dissecting the strategic brilliance of a Beyonce setlist or debating who would survive longer in a zombie apocalypse, his spirit is infectious.

Our friendship is built on years of shared secrets, laughter, and a mutual willingness to be brutally honest. Although now it's more about perpetually reminiscing the glory days of our relationship, before real adulting took over.

And here we are, two forty-year-old, single, gay men, sharing a room like we are in Uni again. There aren't many people I would be prepared to do this with, but after twenty plus years, Hugo has seen me in every conceivable low, passed out in my underwear in a pool of sick with a KFC in my hair kind of low, so sharing a room with him is no big deal.

Hugo, ever the optimist, is busy unpacking his bag of travel oddities with the flair of someone opening a treasure chest. "I've brought my Bluetooth speaker and this nifty microphone, so we can do karaoke before we go out."

"Definitely won't be doing that," I say.

"You will. And I've got us a facial mist spray each for the poolside to help us keep cool."

"Practical and appreciated."

Hugo nods. "I freestyled and chucked some hyaluronic acid in there too to keep our skin hydrated so don't spray it in your mouth."

"Of course you did."

"And, the best part, I've got us some pool hammocks!" Hugo says excitedly, whipping out a bit of plastic and waving it around like it's a winning lottery ticket.

"Pool hammocks?"

"Pool hammocks. They will change this holiday and your life for ever."

"Great," I say, lacking any level of enthusiasm.

"They have little drinks holders in them too."

"Ooh okay, I'm invested."

"Told you."

Still laying on the bed, I'm too tired to unpack and itching to sleep. However, after marinating on public transport all day, I feel like I've trudged through a swamp of grime. A shower is non-negotiable. "I'm having a quick shower before bed," I announce to Hugo, rummaging for my trusty washbag.

"Okay, Loverboy," Hugo replies, nonchalantly resuming his own unpacking antics.

I flick on the bathroom light switch to find the modern shower is a delight: sleek, stylish, and promising a rejuvenating experience. Just what I need. The shower fires up and I start to undress.

I place my phone on the side and out of habit, click into Grindr. The grid lights up instantly with chiselled faces and headless torsos. The first twenty or so profiles are within 50 metres of my location and instantly, my phone starts to ping:

Hey?

Horny?

What's up?

Looking? sent you a picture

What you into?

Welcome to Gran Canaria, I think with a raised eyebrow.

Overwhelmed by it all already, I shut my phone down. This is one side of the holiday I can't bring myself to investigate at this time of night. The lure of the shower and impending sleep is far more appealing than anything the Maspalomas gays can offer me right now.

Stepping under the warm cascade, the water washes away not just the day's grime but also the existential dread of my travel choices. For a fleeting second, I imagine a week of sun, relaxation, cocktails, and maybe even a dash of fun. And honestly, what could possibly go wrong?

Chapter 3

DAN

Despite getting into bed around 2.30am, I wake up feeling surprisingly refreshed, finding Hugo already up, grinning like a man who's discovered the secret to eternal youth. Throwing on some shorts and a T-shirt, we shuffle out of our room, me still half-asleep, and head down for breakfast.

The day is glorious: the sun's shining, the air carries a hint of salt from the ocean, and I'm already daydreaming about the relaxing day ahead.

"Is it frowned upon to have a cocktail for breakfast?" Hugo ponders as we approach the dining area, his eyes sparkling with mischief.

"Bloody Mary?" I offer.

"I'd rather drink vomit than alcoholic tomato juice. I was thinking more like a Bucks Fizz?" Hugo says, scratching his chin.

"Oh okay, Cheryl Baker, I could do a Bucks Fizz," I second.

"Then, Bucks Fizz it is!" And before you can shout Making Your Mind Up, we're sitting at our table justifiably drinking at 10.30am. This is what we came on holiday for.

After breakfast and a swift return to the room to shower and get our necessary items for the sunbathing ahead (sunglasses, sunscreen, of course the pool hammocks), we make our way to the pool area. As soon as I step outside, I'm hit by a blast of vibrant energy.

The pool deck hums with chaos—a circus of tanned bodies and echoing laughter. A swarm of young singles fill the pool, their laughter and splashes blending into a contagious, upbeat vibe. I spot a few token old folk too—those who, bless them, seem to have missed the memo that Maspalomas Oasis isn't a retirement home. One elderly gentleman is sunbathing with a floppy hat and oversized sunglasses, clearly not having done his research on local climate conditions. And then there's the odd oblivious straight couple with kids, struggling to keep their little ones from cannonballing into the deep end while the parents exchange exasperated glances.

Hugo and I stake out our little slice of paradise by the pool. We find a prime spot under a generous umbrella, and I set down my essentials: my Kindle, which has seen better days but is packed with a selection of trashy mystery and romance novels to work my way through, plus my trusty headphones.

I close my eyes for a second and listen—the water lapping against the tiles, a distant whoop of someone winning at table tennis, and the soft hiss of lotion being applied too late.

Our spot is perfect—just far enough from the chaos to relax, but close enough to judge whatever antics unfold across the day. Hugo, who never met a moment he couldn't turn into a game show, immediately launches into a plan for the day. "Dan, my man," he declares, "we should definitely try out every cocktail at the bar today. I need to whittle them all down to my Top Three."

"Okay, cool, kind of like The X Factor."

"Yes exactly, you are the Louis Walsh to my Simon Cowell and we will spend the day sorting out our Sam Baileys from our Tesco Marys."

"Which sounds like a productive use of our holiday, so I'm on board," I nod.

"Perfect, I'll get us two Tequila Sunrises to get us through boot camp," Hugo says, jumping up.

"Okay sounds like a plan. Can I be Dannii Minogue rather than Louis Walsh though?"

Hugo ruffles my hair. "How about Sinitta?" he says, before winking and prancing off to the bar on a mission.

"Deal."

Smiling, I watch Hugo walk away from me, pulling his powder blue swim shorts up further around his waist. He's a short, stocky guy with sandy brown hair, which is delightfully tousled, complementing a round face that lights up with an effortless smile—one that seems permanently set to "easy" mode.

As he arrives at the bar, his full cheeks and soft jawline make his expressions irresistibly genuine, as he greets the Mediterranean barman with a wide smile. Instantly, he's chatting and laughing as he does, quick to make friends with anyone and everyone. It's his innate gift that I wish I had.

Physically, Hugo carries a bit of extra weight around his belly, adding to his solid, dependable build. That little bit of extra fluff is just another part of his charm, a badge of honour from countless hearty meals and even heartier laughs.

Before I can relax in the moment, one of the poolside entertainers—a woman with a dazzling smile and an overabundance of enthusiasm—approaches our spot. "Hi there, Mr. handsome! You fancy pool game? It's all good fun!" she chirps, in a thick eastern European accent, her tone practically bursting with excitement.

"Oh, no, thanks," I say as an immediate response, my tone firm yet polite, served with a forced smile. I'm not in the mood for any impromptu games that might involve overly competitive water volleyball or synchronised cannonballs with strangers, preferring my relaxation untainted by the chaos of forced fun with people I don't know.

"You sure? Will be lots of fun," she assures me. I shake my head and smile. Not missing a beat, she winks and trots off to find another unsuspecting guest to entertain.

Thank God Hugo isn't here; he's the kind of maniac that would force me into doing something like this. I still haven't forgiven him for the time we had to play in a pool noodle jousting tournament with a bunch of drunk students while in Majorca in 2008. I make a mental note to keep Hugo away from the entertainment staff for as long as possible.

Hugo swiftly returns with our cocktails, complete with paper umbrellas and unnecessary decorative fruit. "Voila!" he cries, presenting me with our first poolside drink.

"Fabulous," I say, taking the long glass in hand and having a glorious sip. "Ooohh nice."

"Very," Hugo says in agreement.

"So, you're now best friends with the barman?"

"I just said hello," Hugo replies, waving his hand as a denial.

"And know all his backstory?"

"No, well, I mean, he's called Raul. That's all I know. And he's over here saving up to go to university to be a vet. And he's a salsa dancer."

"Well, how you do this, I'll never know." I say, shaking my head in amazement.

"It's called actually talking to people. You should try it sometime." Hugo glares at me wickedly.

"You know I don't talk to strangers."

"Stranger Danger," Hugo winks.

"Exactly, Pippin taught me well."

"Oh, I enjoyed your 80s education safety video reference there," Hugo nods to me.

"Thank you, I try my best."

Just as we're settling into our sunbathing routine, the hotel cranks up the volume on some thumping dance music. The pulsating beats echo around the pool, and my stomach churns in protest. "Seriously? It's not even 11am," I mutter under my breath, trying to drown out the insistent bass that has nothing to do with my mellow mood.

Hugo, however, seems unfazed. He bobs his head to the beat, declaring, "It's all part of the holiday vibe, Dan."

I lean back against the lounge chair, letting the warm sun soak into my skin as I reapply sunscreen—twice, just in case.

Across the pool, I spot three handsome men deep in conversation, each one a mirror image of the other. They share the same sun-kissed tan, tousled sandy hair, and striking, identical eyes that seem to wink in unison. Dressed in sleek swimwear, they laugh and gesture in perfect harmony—so much so that it's impossible to tell where one ends and the next begins. Their synchronised smiles and repeated banter create an almost surreal vibe, as if the poolside had been commandeered by a trio of perfectly cloned models, each one doubling down on that irresistible, doppelgänger allure.

Sighing, I look down at my own belly smiling up at me. How it had grown over the last 12 months. Self-consciously pulling my swimming shorts up higher, I tuck the bulge under the waistband.

After a difficult year, overcoming the trauma of last October, alcohol and chocolate had become the main crutches to get me through the day. It wasn't uncommon for me to down a bottle of wine each night to help me sleep, the visions of that final fateful evening still replaying in my mind most nights. I shake my head, reminding myself of the promise that I made that I wasn't going to dwell on it at all this holiday.

Instead, I focus more productively on my ever-diminishing self-esteem, comparing the pecs of the Adonis clones to my ever-expanding bitch tits. I shake my head, knowing that none of this thought process is productive. Only one thing can resolve this. I turn to Hugo, "Another cocktail?"

*

About an hour later, we're working through our third cocktail, a "Morning Mirage." No idea what's exactly in it, but it tastes like a mixture of orange juice, pineapple juice and enough coconut rum to make you forget what country you're in.

While I'm happily sat with one eye on my Kindle and another on everyone else around the pool, I am starting to feel relaxed, despite the heat of the midday sun rising.

As much as he loves a holiday like this, Hugo gets itchy feet and wants to wander around to meet people. In the last hour, he's already befriended a German woman on her honeymoon and an older gay couple who are sitting across from us.

"He's called Terry and the smaller one is called Robert. I think they're having relationship issues. I was getting an odd vibe. Terry was being sarcastic about everything Robert was saying. Robert was saying not so positive things about Terry's mum. It was getting uncomfortable," Hugo fills me in on the situation, which I am actively invested in.

"Ah, interesting. We don't have to go out for drinks later with them, do we?"

"Oh no, this is just to keep us abreast of our neighbours. I won't inflict them on you."

"Excellent."

Across from me by the pool, something immediately catches my attention. Four new guys appear, and I can't help but notice them all at once—they're a perfect picture of confidence and effortless cool, like they've stepped straight off the cover of a magazine. The first guy has dark, messy hair and a grin that's a little too charming, like he knows something no one else does. The second one leans back in his chair, sporting a long beard. The third one is the kind of guy who looks like he was sculpted in a gym—perfectly chiselled jawline, abs that probably have their own fan club—and doesn't seem the least bit concerned about this poolside world. The fourth one is just as impossibly handsome, with a type of smile that seems to invite people into whatever conversation or inside joke he's already got going.

Once again, it's hard for my 40-year-old self not to feel a little self-conscious; my stomach does its usual anxious flip as I adjust my towel around my waist, feeling simultaneously out of place and strangely captivated by their effortless charisma. I can't help but stare, feeling every inch of my insecurities ripple through me. It's funny how they're all just chatting, laughing, and lounging while I'm observing from the sidelines, a bit overwhelmed by how they seem to possess a kind of energy I will never match. For a moment, I wonder if they know how good they look and if they have ever known what it's like to feel so unremarkable.

"Wow, the Chippendales have arrived." I nudge Hugo with a teasing smile. Hugo, in return, tilts his sunglasses down to take a peek.

Glancing over, I'm expecting his usual sparkle of appreciation for attractive men. Instead, Hugo's expression sours—his nose turns up ever so slightly, and he shoots me a look that's hard to read. "Hmmm," is all he can say, dismissing them as if they're nothing more than an annoying distraction.

"Hmmm? Is that all you have?"

"Oh sorry, let us marvel at these perfect specimens of gay beauty. Just what we all need more of in the world," Hugo takes a sip of his cocktail.

I can't help but quip, "Jealous, are we?"

That seems to hit a nerve. Without missing a beat, Hugo straightens up, his face tightening with a mix of irritation and something else I can't quite place, and he strides off toward the bar. "I'm getting a drink," is all he says.

I watch him go, a mix of amusement and concern twisting in my gut. His reaction is so unlike his usual self—we've always been ones for co-objectifying any local talent that's out of our league.

Furrowing my brow, I squint in the sun as I watch Hugo walk past the four men, looking straight ahead. I clock one of them looking up at Hugo as he passes, his eyes following him to the bar. As the sun continues to blaze and the vibrant chatter of the pool fills the air, I'm left wondering what really set him off—and whether there's more to this unexpected mood shift than meets the eye.

Chapter 4

HUGO

Hugo ambles away from the pool, his mind swirling with memories and quiet insecurities as he makes his way toward the bar.

Chewing on the inside of his cheek, he knows he shouldn't have snapped at Dan. It was only banter—but it struck a nerve, and Hugo had to walk away.

After over twenty years, Hugo has always joked that his relationship with Dan is like that of an old married couple—equal parts endearing banter and stubborn disagreement. Yet, beneath the teasing and occasional squabbles lies a bond forged over years of shared adventures, late-night confessions, and a mutual appreciation of the Real Housewives franchise that no one can take away.

As he moves further from the lively pool area, the thumping dance music and laughter fade into a soft background hum, as he arrives at the bar. He flashes that signature smile—warm, crinkly-eyed, the kind that usually earns him free shots—from across the bar to Raul.

"Raul, my friend, what's next on the list?" Hugo beams as he speaks.

"How about a Long Island Iced Tea?" Raul suggests.

"Make it two!" Hugo applauds the suggestion, smiling wide, as Raul nods and gleams back. People often remark on Hugo's ability to light up a room with that smile, how his deep hazel eyes crinkle in genuine mirth. In the eyes of many, Hugo is the embodiment of approachability and good humour—a steadfast, dependable presence. But there are times when he wishes he could be seen as more than that.

Looking back over at the four handsome men, lounging by the pool, he feels smaller than his actual 5ft 7 frame should allow. Pulling his shorts up at the back to hide his love handles gives him a temporary reprieve from the self-judgment, but one that will only last so long.

Compliments come and go—something about his "dad bod" being cute or cuddly—but none of it sticks, especially when he's shirtless by a pool, trying not to catch his own reflection in the sliding glass doors. As a forty-year-old man, it's almost absurd caring so much about his body shape like some insecure teenager, especially when it's never looked any different. His rational brain tells him his true worth lies in his achievements, deep friendships, and the life he's built. That said, here he is sucking his stomach in like everyone else.

"I need to get some more triple sec," Raul announces, snapping him out of his indulgent daze.

"Of course, no hurry," Hugo smiles back.

Raul disappears off, leaving Hugo stood at the bar alone.

It was two years since he was last here. That visit had been filled with a kind of heady optimism—a belief that he had found love. He remembers the way his heart had soared, the electricity in the air as he shared secret smiles and lingering glances with someone who seemed to understand him completely. But that was two years ago and the world had moved on since then.

Now, he's happy that Dan will be by his side during this holiday. In more recent years, their paths have diverged slightly—each caught up in the whirlwind of adult life, careers, and responsibilities. Hugo has always admired Dan's unflappable calm and the way he seems to accept life's absurdities with a shrug and a smile. That said, Dan's brain goes into meltdown over enforced small talk with strangers, so they each bring different strengths to the table.

Sometimes, though, despite Dan's own irrational anxieties, Hugo can't help but feel a twinge of envy. While Dan appears content with his own quirks, his quiet strength and authenticity are a balm to Hugo's self-doubt.

"So, who do you have to blow around here to get a drink?" a loud female voice screeches from behind him.

Momentarily startled out of his daze, Hugo spins around to find a small brunette woman glaring at him. Her curvy body rocking a neon-bright, figure-hugging one-piece swimsuit that screams she's not here to blend in. Decorated with sequins that catch every stray ray of sunlight, she's giving off a vibe of both defiant confidence and a touch of desperation to recapture her youthful glow, and Hugo is here for it.

"Well, your talents would be wasted on me, but Raul the barman would probably make you a great Mojito in return for a quick hand job," Hugo says, tilting his sunglasses down to her.

The woman screams with laughter, her oversized, glittery hoop earrings jingling with every chortle.

"Then Raul better get his pants down, I'm ready for my cocktail!" she shrieks across the bar. "I've already polished off a bottle of prosecco over breakfast and I'm gagging for some more."

"Excellent news. I'm working my way through every cocktail on the menu today," Hugo says proudly.

"This is exactly the kind of challenge I came on holiday for! I'll be dancing on the bar with my tits out in no time."

This woman is one trashy minx, Hugo thinks, but the kind of car crash he wants in his life this holiday.

"Well don't hold back on my account," Hugo signals to the bar.

"Oh, I never hold back, babe," she says with a wink. "It's my brand."

On that note, Raul returns to the bar with a bottle of triple sec in his hand. "Sorry to keep you waiting."

"No problem," Hugo says, as Raul returns to finishing off the cocktails. "I'm just ordering a couple of Long Island iced teas," he says to his new busty friend.

"A couple? My style of drinking!" she giggles, then makes an unfortunate snorting sound, which she doesn't seem to care about.

"Well, one is for my friend," Hugo nods over to Dan, whose head is down buried in his Kindle. "But he's also joining me on today's challenge."

"I better catch up then!" she screams. "Raul, babe, get me a Long Island iced tea too. And a mango daiquiri on the side." Raul nods, apparently fine with being called "babe".

The woman rearranges her sheer patterned sarong, wrapped around her waist, then pulls her oversized sunglasses up on to her head. "I'm Jessie. It's my first day here."

"Yeah same, mine too. I'm Hugo, it's a pleasure to meet you."

"Oh, nice babe. So, excited for a week of sun, cocktails and sex?"

"Well yes, although not sure how much sex I'm going to be getting."

"Just flip your Grindr on darlin', it'll probably explode, you'll have no problems," she says with a cheeky grin. Whilst not exactly taken aback by Jessie's assumption of his sexuality, clearly her credentials as experienced fag hag have served her well. "My problem is I'm on holiday with a bunch of gays. No one'll want to eat my fanny out here, it's gonna be a challenge." She frowns like she's facing climbing Everest.

"I'm sure you'll rise to it," Hugo nods.

"Oh, I definitely will. I'm not going a whole week on holiday and not getting any cock, that just wouldn't be fair!"

Hugo giggles with her. This woman is an experience that he is instantly drawn to. "So, you're here with friends?"

"Yeah, I'm with my boys!" She points to the four guys by the pool.

"Oh."

"Yeah, just for a week. Lads!" she shouts at them to get their attention. They don't look up.

"Lads!!" Again, they're too engrossed in each other. "LADS!!!" She screams across the pool. Still nothing. "TOMMY!!!!"

Finally, one of them looks over. He's lean and tattooed with messy, thick hair. "Just getting a drink, will be right over!!"

Jessie cries out. Tommy, presumably, just nods and turns back to his conversation with limited interest in her statement.

"Aww, they're a bunch of cuties!" she says.

"Aren't they just," Hugo says, as Raul presents their drinks across the bar.

"Oh, I'll introduce you to them!" Jessie screams with enthusiasm.

"Uh, no really…" Hugo is momentarily lost for words which is very unlike him.

"Yeah, yeah babe, I definitely will."

Jessie bounds off, Long Island iced tea in one hand, mango daiquiri in another, beckoning him to follow. "Come on!"

Hugo grabs his drinks and wanders over, a sinking feeling in his stomach. As he approaches, his chest tightens as the four men turn in his direction, a collection of eyes he did not want on him.

Chapter 5

DAN

Lounging by the pool, book in hand, a cocktail in the other, I savour a certain degree of quiet, as the dance music has been turned off in favour of a game of pool volleyball. The entertainment staff are screeching and hollering, their collective victims thrown in the pool to start the enforced holiday merriment.

Turning up the volume on my noise cancelling headphones is enough to drown out the furore, as I work through a playlist of musical classics.

The sun is a tyrant today, pounding the pool deck like a personal vendetta, turning everything into a shimmering hallucination. Having done my best to ignore its heat by diving into my novel, I am in need of a break. My mind is on Hugo; seeing him stood alone by the bar, I wonder what had irked him so much.

The last sip of my Morning Mirage, now diluted by the melting ice, lacks the punch of its first joyous taste. Despite our mini to-do, I took comfort knowing that Hugo would return with two drinks in hand for us, and no doubt some more gossip around the dynamics of the hotel guests.

To give me respite from my book, I pick up my phone and have a flick through the news. All the standard miserable headlines you would expect that I choose to ignore as I'm on holiday.

One catches my eye. "LOCAL BUSINESSMAN FALLS TO HIS DEATH IN MASPALOMAS." I see a reference to the Yumbo Centre in the article, so I scan it through. It's in English from a local news source. A guy somehow fell off the roof at the Yumbo and died yesterday. Not the most glamourous of deaths.

With my interest dwindling in the news, I open Grindr, my first time since last night. In the app's flickering screen, hundreds of profiles flash before my eyes. Being less than a ten-minute walk from the Yumbo Centre, the app is on fire as ever. Once again, reams of men, all shirtless, horny and looking, all less than 500 metres from me. I'd be lucky if I get a handful within 1 kilometre back home, but like any all you can eat buffet, it's a lot to stomach.

The immediacy of Gran Canaria's hookup culture is overwhelming. It's as if every handsome specimen in this sun-drenched paradise is just waiting for a chance to have a roll in the hay. Already fourteen messages. All unread. All shouting "Hi" into the void. Just looking at them makes my chest tighten. It's like being smothered by digital thirst.

Flicking through them, the content is very similar: most just say "Hi", a few more start with "Looking?", then the odd "Activo?". There's a wide selection of penis pictures on offer, all of which, after a decade of these apps, I'm completely numb to. A couple of bumhole pictures also bless my retinas, which make me feel as confused as ever, especially the second one that looks particularly angry with me.

A new message pops up from a handsome Mediterranean guy named Luca. His profile picture shows a rugged grin and a backdrop of cerulean water. Hmm, I think to myself, flipping through his pics and having a read of his profile.

I read the message:

Let me guess, you're by a pool, playing with your phone sipping a cocktail?

So, you're either psychic or really good at stalking?

Definitely stalking. I'm hiding behind the parasol in the corner.

Oh exceptional work, I couldn't spot you at all.

Thank you, it's years of practice. I can spot a handsome Englishman a mile off ☺

The compliment leads to a wave of discomfort, knowing full well all my pictures are over a year old, prior to twelve months of trauma binging. Again, I pull my shorts over my belly as if Luca is actually watching me from behind the parasol.

Well thank you, are you sipping cocktails too ☺*?*

Sadly not my friend, I'm working today, no cocktails for me ☹

I will drink some for you then!

Please do! Or perhaps I could share one with you later tonight?

Before responding, I glance up from my phone for a moment. Across the pool, in what seems like mere seconds since I last had eyes on him, Hugo is now holding court amongst the four stunning specimens of man beef across from me.

How the fuck does he do this? is all I can think, watching him chat and laugh, unfazed by the presence of a million gorgeous people around him. This was a classic Hugo scenario, in a blink of an eye, he's the centre of attention, all eyes on him, lapping up every moment. It's a gift that I wish I had.

Amongst the group of men, there's now a woman too, curvy, vibrant, commanding attention with a laugh that rings out like a challenge. I wonder if Hugo has met his match. Or his soulmate?

With one eye on the unfolding action and another on my Grindr chat, I ponder Luca's invitation. Not normally one to jump on the date bandwagon so quickly, Hugo's social butterfly aura has inspired me to take the bull by the horns.

Sure, I'd love that!

"Dan, come join us!" I hear Hugo holler in my direction.

Fuck.

My natural reaction to look up at the call of my name means I've skipped the opportunity to feign selective hearing.

Hugo is waving two drinks at me, presumably one is mine, as the remaining five of the party stare straight at me.

My heart does a little flip, as does my stomach.

I'd love to say I've matured, become more confident in myself and integrating with others over the preceding twelve months, but old habits die hard. Joining a group of beautiful strangers for some ad hoc jollity-cum-small talk is still right at the bottom of my special skills list. Especially after what happened back home last year.

Pushing my sunglasses up on my nose, I shake that thought out of my mind.

Nodding acceptance to Hugo's invitation, I stand up, hoisting my shorts and clicking my back into an upright position, before wandering over.

"This is Dan!" Hugo announces on my arrival.

Immediately, my whole body is man-handled by the excitable woman of the group. "Oh babe, it's nice to meet you," she says pulling me in for a hug. "I'm Jessie." It's an uncomfortable embrace as both of us are dripping with sweat from the heat of the sun, which doesn't appear to bother Jessie. I, on the other hand, could probably leave the glistening boob sweat of a stranger wiped over my chest, but here we are.

"Nice to meet you too," I respond with excess enthusiasm.

"And these are my boys." One by one, she introduces the rest: "This is Dito, Tommy, Reece, and Mason." Their names bounce around as if in a rap.

Dito leans over to shake my hand, his engaging, open manner taking me by surprise. "Nice to meet you Dan." His smile is warm, his eyes friendly. Obviously tall, dark, beautiful and built like a brick shithouse, but with an approachable aura, that *should* make me feel more comfortable around him. But I'm still me, so I struggle to make eye contact with him as I take his hand.

The other three, all sitting down, don't make the same effort and just nod in my direction.

"I was just saying, my plan is to take that concierge for a ride this week," she shrieks across the pool.

"And definitely not in the hire car sense," Tommy says, flipping his perfectly tousled chestnut hair out of his face. With too many tattoos to comprehend, his solid pecs seem to pulsate as he talks, although that may have been in my head.

"No, I'm definitely talking about a ride in my fanny!" Jessie screams as a couple walk past with their young children, appearing not to faze her at all.

Everyone laughs slightly uncomfortably, apart from Mason and Reece, who remain po-faced.

"So, what are your plans for the week?" Dito asks us both, although I let Hugo take the lead on this.

"Well, just plenty of sun, cocktails, naps, cocktails, go to the beach, cocktails," Hugo says raising his current glass in the air.

"And more cocktails!" Dito adds.

"And cock!" Jessie adds, volume turned to ten.

I'm pretty sure I catch Mason rolling his eyes, beneath his sunglasses. His shaved head is glistening in the sun, as is the rest of his tight body, already a glorious, bronzed colour from, I would assume, the regular trips to the tanning salon. Mason is much slimmer than Dito, lean and toned with a thick black beard.

"We should hire a boat for the day," Mason says, his deep, rich voice almost landing like an order.

"Oh well, I'm not too sure about boats. I get seasick. Don't wanna vomit on my tits while I'm out there," Jessie announces.

"I'll be up for a boat trip," Reece says, ignoring her response, pulling his sunglasses down slightly as he responds to Mason. I catch his eye, and, against my better judgment, I let my gaze linger just a moment too long. Those piercing blue eyes—seriously, they're like little sapphires that could outshine a disco ball—completely mesmerize me. His whole face is a masterpiece: an angular, chiselled jawline, freshly shaven like he's been kissed by a razor, and cheekbones so sharp they could double as landmarks. All of this is tied together with a classic, muscular frame like some gay wet dream. He's one of those Insta-gays you see online with tens of thousands of followers, living a picture-perfect city life while you're scrolling at home in your dressing gown.

"Yeah, sounds like a great plan!" Tommy chips in, taking a sip of his beer. "Although not for a couple of days, I wanna go out and get hammered tonight."

"First night out at the Yumbo tonight, so excited for it, got the perfect dress for it!" Jessie shouts.

"Oh, tell me more," says Hugo, snuggling up to Jessie. I know he has zero interest in women's fashion, but her energy is infectious to him, and in typical Hugo style, he's indulging her.

As Jessie regales us with the description of her attire for the night, Reece and Mason start to play on their phones, while Tommy and Dito appear to be listening. "I'm so excited, never been here before!" she beams.

"So, you've never experienced the wonder of Gran Can?" Hugo asks.

"No never! You have then?"

"Yeah, I was last here a couple of years ago," Hugo explains to her.

"At this hotel?"

"Yes, I stayed here last time as well."

"Oh, the boys always stay at this hotel too, don't you lads?" Jessie throws out to the others.

"Yeah, been to this one loads of times. Handy for the Yumbo, nice hotel and food's good, so it's easy," Tommy adds.

"We may have been here at the same time then," Hugo says.

"Yeah, maybe," Tommy replies, rearranging his swim shorts. As he does, I notice a god-awful tattoo of a dolphin wearing sunglasses on his calf, which I internally judge.

Standing there, the only words from me is coming from my internal monologue, reminding me how I've not spoken yet, as I feel increasingly out of sync with this group of dazzling strangers. My mind is a jumbled mess as I try to keep up with what is being said.

While I'm processing all of this, Jessie announces, "We should all go out for a drink tonight!" The suggestion hangs in the air like a challenge. Hugo agrees enthusiastically, and the others murmur their agreement. Forcing a smile, I echo their enthusiasm, though inside, my stomach churns at the mere thought of another social group encounter.

This isn't the first time I've been dragged into a scenario where beautiful, charming people demand my attention—and last time, it didn't end well.

Chapter 6

MASON

Sitting back in his rattan chair, Mason watches the poolside scene with a mix of amusement and thinly veiled irritation. Jessie is in full flow—loud, brash, and insistent on making her presence known. Every screeching laugh and drunken story chisels away at Mason's patience like a slow, dull blade.

Having lost count of the times she's screamed the word "fanny" in his face over the last 24 hours, her desperate need for attention and limelight is draining.

Tolerance for her over-the-top antics is ice thin, yet for the sake of the holiday, he puts up with her. It's just one week after all.

A duo of best friends, who have known each other for years, Jessie and Tommy are inseparable. The story of how they met has been recounted more than once, but he can't really remember it.

Mason, on the other hand, has known Tommy for about three years now. They met at a wild party where flirtation and recreational drugs blurred into one night of chemical-infused sex, and instead of igniting something lasting, they settled into a casual camaraderie. That of an easy and unforced connection, built on the shared knowledge that every weekend is an excuse to drink too much and laugh too hard. This is the third time they are on holiday together, and while Mason appreciates Tommy's laid-back vibe, he often wonders how long he can endure the endless cycles of inebriated revelry.

"We should all go out for a drink tonight!" Jessie screams, like vocal nails down a chalk board.

"Oh yes, definitely!" the little tubby guy she's brought over says. Mason can't remember his name; he has other things on his mind.

Looking over to Reece, who's buried deep in his phone, he senses Reece has similar feelings about Jessie. The difference being, he knows Reece doesn't have the same levels of patience. He may look like a calm and unapproachably cool cucumber, but he's seen the other side of that coin before.

And it's quite a side.

A scary one.

Mason's relationship with Reece is a curious mix of past indiscretions and present nonchalance. In his twenties, Mason shared a one-night stand with Reece   a brief, lustful encounter that fizzled out almost as quickly as it ignites. Yet, through the intricate social web spun by Tommy, all now in their mid-thirties, they have reconnected in recent years. Mason had introduced Reece to some of his work connections to help launch Reece's consultancy business recently too, which appears to have been fruitful for him.

These days, Reece is a familiar face, moving with a cool detachment that sharply contrasts with Jessie's vibrant energy. His handsome features and silent allure are hard to ignore, and despite Mason's inner cynicism, having a night out with him always gets you noticed and into the best places.

"Yes great, maybe a cocktail at Rita's before the night starts?" Dito suggests.

Jessie and the two randoms she's picked up nod wildly at this suggestion, while Mason feels obliged to do the same.

Mason isn't exactly sure how long Dito's been hanging around with Tommy and Reece—maybe a few years. They've crossed paths a handful of times over the last six months, enough for Mason to get a sense of him. Affable, quick with a joke, and dangerously easy to like, he wastes far too much energy indulging Jessie's theatrics, but Mason chalks that up to his open, easy-going nature. Undeniably handsome—broad-shouldered, all effortless charm—Mason insists he's not his type. Or so

Mason tells himself, convincing himself he'd turn Dito down if he ever tried anything. Not that Dito ever would.

"Yes, let's get there early, get a prime spot and judge all the gays as they walk by!" Jessie squeals excitedly.

"Judge them! You'll be best friends with them all by the end of the night," Tommy retorts.

"I can't help it that I'm a magnet to homosexuals."

"Well, the gays do love a tragic and emotionally broken female."

"They do," Jessie agrees. "And I'm a particularly messy bitch."

"And that's just your sex life," Dito quips with a cheeky grin to Jessie, who laps it up. Mason appreciates Dito's presence, though sometimes he feels that Dito's charm is far too effortless—a reminder that some people navigate life without ever having inner demons.

And Mason has his fair share of those.

Beneath the veneer of laughter, teasing, and poolside banter, Mason nurses a deeper, seething anger—a bitterness that has been quietly fermenting for years.

Everything changed last time he set foot on this island, revealing truths that altered him forever and, after the passing years, this holiday is his turning point—a moment to confront not only the ghosts of his past but also the parts of himself he has long denied.

A fierce, unyielding confrontation of the pain and betrayal that has haunted him for so long is finally due.

This is his time, he thinks—to face his past, reclaim his dignity, and make those who disrespected him learn that their arrogance comes with a price. As the promise of new experiences hangs in the humid air, Mason steels himself for the week ahead, aware that every laugh and every clink of a glass is a prelude to a confrontation he has been waiting for.

And when that moment comes, Mason vows, there is one who will pay dearly.

Chapter 7

DAN

Perched at an outward-facing table at our regular starting bar, Rita's, Hugo and I watch the groups of gays rotating around the circuit that is the Yumbo Centre, like some homosexual conveyor belt.

It's just gone 10.30pm, and the night air still clings, warm and heavy. Like most of those around us tonight, we've opted for shorts and vests. The heat beats down, coating everyone with a thick, sticky sheen, but no one seems to care; they're too caught up in the energy that vibrates through this little corner of Maspalomas.

Sitting comfortably in my seat, I take in the beautiful Canarian architecture: the Yumbo Centre is like one of those cheap old concrete car parks that some business has forgotten about, now injected with sparkles, dark rooms and coke. A wild mash-up of gaudy 70s kitsch and modern-day over-ambition. Flashing neon signs, garish splashes of pink and turquoise paint, and cheap concrete structures come together in a way that's both tragically tacky and oddly captivating.

The lower level of the Yumbo is like an athletics track, a circuit surrounded by open bars, where guys either spectate from the outward-facing bar seats or compete by walking laps, knowing full well they're being watched and judged. A kind of cruising Olympics. And I'm very much spectating tonight.

On the upper levels, the place is a labyrinth of winding walkways, filled with bars, restaurants and scattered shops, each corner feeling like it's part of a fever dream left behind by someone who really loved the colour orange.

"Why do I always feel at home when I come back here?" Hugo says to me.

"Is that true or is it your thirteenth cocktail of the day talking?" I reply.

"That's true. But on the plus side, I now know what my top three cocktails are from the pool bar for the week."

"And to stay away from the Dumpster Fire."

"Fuck yes, who would put that much Tabasco in a cocktail?"

"Raul would."

"Ah yes, my new close personal friend, Raul."

"One of the fourteen new friends you've made today."

"I've not been counting but that sounds about right."

"More than I've made this decade."

"Unsurprising," Hugo rolls his eyes.

People-watching here is its own form of art. Everyone's watching everyone, even if they're pretending not to. Every seat from the array of outside bars that surround the lower level of the Yumbo Centre face outward, so you can sip a drink while watching the gays go by. There's something thrilling about it—people-watching like this fills that strange voyeuristic void I always knew I had.

Tonight's clientele, as ever, is a queer kaleidoscope, drawn in by the promise of uninhibited fun, cheap drinks, and a safe space to be themselves.

"What can I get you boys to drink?" a voice says, as I flip around to see our sun-kissed waiter flashing a friendly smile.

"Ah, right on time!" Hugo cheers. "Dan, what can this fine man get for you?"

The waiter faces me and awaits my response, swiping his hand through his shaggy dark hair, which is beginning to whiten at the sides. I do love a silver fox, and there's something undeniably handsome about his understated, comfortable demeanour.

"Um," stumbling with my words, "um well, how about a strawberry daiquiri?"

"A frozen one?" he asks, his eyes warm and inviting.

"Yes, definitely a frozen one," Hugo adds in.

"Great, okay." The waiter nods with a smile.

"And one for me too!" Hugo adds. "It's Jimmy, isn't it?"

Obviously, they're old friends, I think to myself, internally rolling my eyes.

"Yes, it is, how do you know?" Jimmy says smiling.

"I remember you from when I was here a couple of years ago, never forget a face!"

"Or a name, so it seems," Jimmy adds.

"Not at all my friend. I'm Hugo."

"Hi Hugo. Well, welcome back."

"Thank you, and this is Dan," Hugo says, signalling to me.

I smile and say hi, forcing eye contact, where I normally would aim to avoid it.

"Well, it's lovely to meet you Dan, and to see you again Hugo! So big night out tonight?"

"Well, it's our first night out," Hugo starts.

"And we've been drinking since 10.30am," I add in.

"So definitely a big night out then." Jimmy smiles.

"Most likely," Hugo says.

"Well shame I can't join you, but I can definitely provide the drinks! I'll be right back with them."

Jimmy again flashes his glorious smile and swooshes off to the bar.

"How do you seem to know everyone on the planet?" I ask.

"Not on the planet, just maybe at the Yumbo Centre. I did make a lot of acquaintances last time."

Unable to fathom how many acquaintances that could be, I nod. "So, you never really told me about that guy you got it on with last time."

Hugo pauses. "What guy?"

"That guy, you know, your holiday romance, your Gran Can fling. What was his name?

"Oh, that was nothing."

"Nothing, you called me drunk at 2am, crying, saying he was the love of your life!"

"Yes, that may have happened."

I laugh out loud. "Well then tell me all about him. What was his name again? Bobby?"

"Benny," Hugo says calmly. "His name was Benny."

"Ah yes, Benny, of course. Your holiday soul mate," I say prodding Hugo in the arm.

He glares at me. "Well, it didn't work out."

"I mean, clearly, as you've not mentioned him since. What happened?"

Shifting around in his seat, Hugo looks back to the bar, as if to see where our drinks are, before moving in closer. "I mean, we met, we spent a bit of time together, got on well, and then he just kind of disappeared."

My brow furrows. "Disappeared? What, like ghosted you?"

Hugo moves his head from side to side, as if pondering his next words. "I mean maybe, I don't know. Just one day I never heard from him again. Maybe he went home early, I don't know. He just kind of vanished."

"Vanished, how odd."

Before I can ask another question, Jimmy arrives back with our drinks, placing two frozen strawberry daiquiris in front of us. "Voila!" And with a tap of my card, the drinks are paid.

My phone buzzes with a Grindr notification. It's from Luca, the local guy I was chatting to earlier.

Still fancy that drink?

I turn to Hugo. "So do you mind if I meet up with a guy from Grindr?"

"What, for a hookup?"

"No, like a drink."

"A drink? Like a date?" Hugo says, side-eyeing me.

"No, just a drink," I insist.

"Only you would come to Gran Can and arrange a romantic date. Who is he?"

I flash the picture of Luca at Hugo. "This guy."

"Oh, well who am I going to talk to while you're out dating?"

"I mean literally everyone."

"I know, I'll have ten new friends by the time you're done."

I message Luca back and he agrees to meet me at Rita's shortly. "He's on his way."

"Fabulous, just don't agree to blow him until he buys you a drink."

Chapter 8

REECE

Reece takes the long steps down into the depths of the vibrant Yumbo Centre, the pulsating bass of dance music and the clamour of voices washing over him like an unwelcome tide. The air is thick with cheap cologne, cigarette smoke, and the unmistakable scent of desperation. He's here again—this holiday is his first time back in this gaudy palace of nightlife after two years—every time he swears it will be his last.

Walking a few steps ahead, Jessie, Dito and Tommy walk behind him, with Mason trailing behind on his phone. Jessie is holding court, her voice cutting through the humid night air, laughing too loudly at something Dito has said. Having lost interest in her before they even got to the airport, Jessie has already outstayed her welcome. Why Tommy insists on bringing her everywhere is beyond him, but he does, like she's his lap dog.

Walking past the bars, he can feel the eyes on him. The rows of men seated with their beers and cocktails, looking him up and down like a piece of meat, their cocks twitching with excitement. And they can look, but he knows these men could never have him.

He's worked hard to create the perfect image for himself: revered, lusted after, unattainable. Most men would only dream of being near him and he has used this desire time and time again to get what he wants.

In his twenties, Gran Canaria was thrilling. A hedonistic paradise, full of promise—sun-drenched mornings and chaotic, vodka-soaked nights. But the shine has dulled. The cheapness of it all grates against his carefully curated existence. He's so far beyond this place. It's beneath him now, he tells himself.

Catching his reflection in a passing window, he stops for half a second, long enough to take himself in. The precision of his appearance is calculated, as always. Understated designer clothing, high cheekbones, sharp jawline, piercing eyes that shift between blue and green under the glow of light. His skin, smooth, flawless, perfected through a meticulous regimen.

But his hair, normally styled to perfection, has a small curl twisted off in a random direction. He hadn't noticed it before he left the hotel room, maybe from a light wind whilst walking down here. His hand flies up to his dark mane, desperately trying to pat it down, to tame the errant curl.

The others move ahead of him, oblivious to his momentary spiral. His mind races. *Is it that obvious? Has anyone noticed?* They don't know the lengths he goes to, the appointments, the tweaks, the discipline. Perfection isn't an accident, it's a job. A full-time one. And even now, even after all the work, there are moments where it still isn't enough.

"I'm dying for a beer," Tommy says. "Let's just go anywhere, I don't care."

"Yeah, same, as long as there's vodka and a hot Spanish waiter I can feel up," Jessie says, reorganising her cleavage.

"Sure, let's just stop here then," Dito says, pointing to the closest bar. Everyone agrees. "Reece, you okay with that?"

Reece, still fiddling with his random hair curl, not really listening, also just nods. "Tell me again why we came here?" he asks, scanning the crowd with disinterest.

Mason, who's been mostly silent, lets out a dry laugh. "Because we're creatures of habit. And because Tommy said he needed a 'change of scenery', which really just means he needed a different bar to get trashed in."

Tommy grins, unbothered. "Exactly."

How do you describe Tommy? Reckless. Self-destructive. Maybe that's why Reece has always been drawn to him. People assume their friendship is built on a foundation of sex, drugs, and nights of excess, and in some ways, that's true.

But they have unspoken history.

One they both choose to forget.

"Two years," Jessie says suddenly, turning to him. "Since you've been here, right?"

He blinks, surprised she remembers. "Yeah."

She studies him. "Big gap. Why'd you stay away?"

He smirks, deflecting. "Had better places to be."

Dito laughs. "Oh, please. We all come back eventually. The Yumbo has a gravitational pull. You can fight it all you want, but here you are."

Reece doesn't respond. While Jessie orders at the bar, he looks at the mirrored wall to his side. The random stray curl of hair has been tamed, and his anxiety starts to calm.

He looks at his four friends across from him. Can he even call them friends? Acquaintances? Connections? Friends is a stretch. Having always appreciated the transactional nature of relationships, Reece knows when he should call time on friendships. He's used to navigating social circles with a careful strategy—aligning himself with the right people, the ones who could elevate him. He goes to the right parties, making the right friends, sleeping with the right men. Every connection is a step forward to move away from his past.

A past that filled him with shame.

They've all served their purpose in some ways: Tommy's reckless impulsive side has brought him distraction; Mason's work connections have benefited his business; Dito's parents are rich, and he's had many a night out on Dito's credit card. And Jessie, Jesus, she offers him nothing but mental exhaustion.

But he knows this holiday is the end of their friendship. There's nothing more these people can offer him, and being here in this cesspit of a holiday destination just confirms that. Feeling his patience wearing thin, just being with them is exasperating.

Looking again at his reflection in the mirror, he sees the calm controlled persona he portrays, knowing full well the monster that rages within him.

The anger. The rage. He fights so hard to keep it under control.

It's time to set himself free from them. Close them down.

To remove these people from his life forever.

Chapter 9

DAN

Sitting at our table, with my fingertips I nurse the base of the frozen strawberry daiquiri that has been placed in front of me, waiting for it to melt slightly so I can slurp its sweet, icy goodness without getting brain freeze.

Hugo is mid-story about a disastrous date where a man, who had turned up in cycling shorts, tried to split the bill down to the penny. "He pulled his phone out of the front of his shorts and started totalling up what he owed, like it was perfectly normal behaviour," Hugo says, waving his drink in the air.

I'm starting to feel nervous over meeting Luca, after our brief Grindr chat earlier. Why, I don't know exactly. I don't have the best track record with dating, being single and forty is testament to that. However, I've always been comfortable being alone, the introvert in me enjoying the quiet time on tap. With no desperate need to be in a relationship, I shouldn't feel the pressure of dating, but a mild tension is rumbling in my stomach.

Meeting new people, the anxiety of whether we will click or whether it will just be an hour of painful small talk weighs on my mind, making me feel apprehensive.

Momentarily distracted from my self-destructive thoughts, across from us, I spot Jessie and the others—laughing, drinking, basking in the glow of their own fabulousness.

I nudge Hugo and nod in their direction. "Look who it is."

Hugo turns his head, squinting for a moment before his face lights up. "Oh, my girl Jessie," he says fondly. "She's a walking goddess. That one could make a funeral feel like a hen do."

Jessie, true to form, is animated—throwing her head back in laughter, gesturing wildly.

Hugo sighs dramatically. "She deserves better company, though." He tilts his drink toward the men surrounding her. "Look at them. The Holy Trinity of vapid."

I laugh. "Wow, someone's got their judgement pants on tonight."

"Oh, come on, Dan, just look at them." Hugo leans in conspiratorially, lowering his voice even though there's no real need. "Reece? He's basically an AI-generated Instagram model. Perfectly symmetrical, zero personality."

I glance over at Reece, who is looking effortlessly beautiful, drink in hand, all sharp angles and tailored indifference. He's absurdly good-looking, and he knows it. Even from this distance, his eyes are captivating.

I hate myself for being insanely attracted to someone so insta perfect, like as a 40-year-old I've learnt nothing from obsessing over unattainable beautiful men. Although, at least this one was gay, not that it makes him any more attainable.

"And that Mason," Hugo continues. "Just constantly buried in his phone, contributing nothing, like he doesn't need to because he's so pretty."

Mason is indeed sitting slightly apart from the group, leaning back against the bar like he's reluctantly tolerating everyone around him.

"And Tommy," Hugo sighs, shaking his head. "Absolute mess. He's probably already lost his wallet, his dignity, and half his brain cells."

I smirk. "So, you love them all, then?"

"Yes, I'm obsessed with them," Hugo deadpans, taking a sip of his drink. "They're the blueprint for what happens when pretty boys grow up without considering whether they need a personality."

I nod toward Dito. "And him?"

Hugo tilts his head, considering. "He seems alright. Handsome, but not in that soulless 'I'll ignore you unless you're hot' way like the others. Potentially he could hold a conversation without checking his reflection every ten seconds."

My fascination continues as I watch them for a moment longer: Jessie still holding court, the boys existing in their own curated little world. "So, you're not going to go and say hello then?"

Hugo snorts. "Don't be ridiculous, I'm heading straight over there as soon as your lover boy arrives." As Hugo raises his glass for another sip, his eyes flick past me, and he straightens up slightly. "Ah," he says, setting his drink down. "Speaking of which."

Turning to follow his gaze, there he is—Luca. Tall, quietly handsome, a hint of Mediterranean mystery about him. His dark eyes scan the bar before landing on me, and a slow, knowing smile spreads across his face as he walks toward us. He's wearing a bright red t-shirt and shorts.

Without even waiting, Hugo pats my shoulder and mutters, "Enjoy, be normal," and disappears towards Jessie and co, leaving me alone as Luca reaches me.

"Dan," he greets me smoothly, his voice warm but unreadable.

"Luca," I reply, managing a smile.

Half standing up, we have an awkward hug as one arm goes around his shoulder and another stabilises on the chair for balance.

"You seem nervous?" he teases, eyes flicking over me as he takes Hugo's empty seat.

"No," I lie, signalling the bartender for another drink. "I'm perfectly at ease."

Luca chuckles. "Was that your friend? Boyfriend?"

I laugh, "Hugo? Oh no, he's just my friend."

"He seems very protective of you."

"What makes you say that?"

"The death stare he gave me for one," Luca says with a smirk.

I shrug. "He just likes to pretend he's my bodyguard."

Luca tilts his head slightly, and I study him. He has the kind of face you don't forget—sharp but not severe, with dark, expressive eyes that give nothing away. He carries himself with an ease I envy, like he belongs anywhere he chooses to be.

"So," I say, "you live here?"

Luca smiles, a little too knowing. "Something like that."

I raise an eyebrow. "Something like that?"

He takes a sip of his drink. "I don't live anywhere specific for too long. The island suits me—for now."

"And have you been here long?"

"A few years now."

"And what brought you here?

Luca smiles at me. "I just needed to get away, start afresh." He sips his drink.

Get away from what? I want to ask.

"Right," I say, mirroring his sip. "And what do you do?"

He exhales a short laugh. "That depends on the day."

"Wow, you really are the mystery man!" I say mildly exasperated.

"Am I?" His lips twitch like he's enjoying this.

"Yes. Where do you live? A mystery. What do you do? Another mystery. Why did you come here? You don't make it easy, do you?"

He leans slightly closer, his voice lower now. "Would you prefer I tell you something predictable?"

I meet his gaze, something stirring in my chest. "Maybe I'd just like to know who I'm having a drink with."

"You already know. I'm Luca. I saw you on an app, I wanted to meet you, and here we are."

It's a deflection, but after a day of drinking, I'll take it. Ultimately, the most this man will ever be to me is a holiday romance, more likely a quick chat and a semi-drunk snog before I meet back up with Hugo again, so his backstory is neither here nor there right now. "Fine. Keep your secrets, handsome mysterious stranger."

"Handsome?" He flashes his smile, which captivates me.

"Handsome. Although, bear in mind I've been drinking since 10.30am this morning,"

"Well, here's to beer goggles," he says, raising his glass.

"Are daiquiri goggles a thing?" I ask, clinking mine against his.

"Sure."

We both take a sip of our drinks. "So," I say, shifting in my seat. "What's it like living here, however long that may have been?"

Exhaling through his nose, he considers the question. "It's… different."

"Different how?"

Taking a sip of his drink again, his eyes flicker to the crowd around us before answering. "It's slower. More detached. You'd think being on an island, people would be desperate to connect, but it's the opposite. Everyone's transient. Here for a week, a month, maybe a season. Then they disappear. It makes you wonder if it's worth making friends at all."

I watch him carefully. There's something in the way he says it—like he *has* made friends here and he's regretted it.

"So, have you?" I ask.

"Have I what?"

"Made friends?"

Luca smirks again, but there's something tired behind it. "A few."

"And?"

"And," he says, swirling his drink like he's measuring his words, "they don't tend to last."

The answer unsettles me more than it should. I can't tell if he's talking about circumstance, or if he's the kind of person who lets people slip away on purpose.

"Is that by choice?" I ask.

"Not always. I mean, normally they're on the next plane out of here when their money runs out or their holiday's over or there's some drama."

"Drama?"

"There's always drama on this part of the island," he says with a smirk.

"I'm sure there is. So, you prefer keeping people at arm's length?"

His hand moves onto my thigh, exposed from my shorts riding up my legs. "No, not at all. I like to keep people close." Further up my thigh it goes, sending a bolt of electricity through me. "But I have no expectation that they stay around for the long term."

He moves closer. "I like to live in the moment."

And with that, he leans in to kiss me.

Chapter 10

JOSH

Josh watches Luca make his move from the other side of the square. Two bars down, at Rocky's, the Yumbo Centre's premier drag bar, he lingers at the edge of the crowd, watching the show unfold.

Resident drag queen, Ms. Fanny Liquor, is on stage, doing a routine as Susan Boyle singing 'I dreamed a dream', while occasionally lifting up her dress to reveal a hairy merkin.

The crowd screams like hysterical banshees, lapping up every moment, but after watching this routine every couple of nights for the last two years, Josh is beyond tired of it. Taking a harsh drag of his cigarette, the rush of nicotine is what he desperately needs.

Luca is back on form tonight, he notes. It has only been ten minutes since he saw Luca take a seat next to the unsuspecting holidaymaker, and already his tongue is planted firmly down his throat. Playing the exotic mysterious stranger—it always works for Luca. Week after week, a new bunch of horny men looking for a thrilling holiday romance to write home about.

And Luca always delivers just that.

Josh and Luca go back years—a friendship built less on trust and more on shared survival instincts. Despite Luca being ten years older than 25-year-old Josh, their experiences brought them together—nights filled with reckless abandon, where the only rule was excess, and the only currency was how much you could handle. He remembers the way they'd stumbled through the maze of bars at the Yumbo, off their faces, high on whatever was available, laughing, dancing, fucking up in ways that felt immortal in the moment.

But there had been danger, too.

Nights that spiralled too far, when the wrong people got involved, when they got hurt, situations when all they could do was run.

Josh had come out unscathed—he always did—but he knows the same can't be said for everyone involved.

Seven years he had lived in Gran Canaria, but some days, it feels like a lifetime. Manchester was a memory that grew fainter with each year that passed, but it is still there, lurking beneath the surface like an old wound that hasn't quite healed. He had run from that place, from the screaming fights, the bruises hidden beneath long sleeves, the feeling of never being enough. His father had been a mean drunk, and his mother had been too beaten down by life to fight back. So, he left. Got on a plane with barely anything to his name and landed on an island where nobody knew who he was.

At first, he had barely survived—sleeping where he could, taking whatever jobs he could find, clinging to the edges of the island's nightlife like a stray dog. But then he found Rocky's and his first secure job, bartending.

He's built together his life over the last seven years; friends, acquaintances, connections that have helped give him what he wants out of life.

With a flourishing side business, he doesn't need his job at Rocky's anymore financially, but he does it for the escape.

Josh looks back and Luca is still tongue-deep in his latest victim. Behind them, Jimmy is serving drinks. Another friend. Or maybe more of an acquaintance.

Another one he knows all about.

Taking another drag of his cigarette, Josh flinches at the sight of more familiar faces another bar down, which hit like a shot to the chest, a mix of amusement and something darker twisting in his gut.

He hasn't seen them in a while, but he remembers them well.

Eyeing them closer, Josh looks at the group of lads. He remembers one was called Reece; he still follows him on Instagram. Another was Tommy. Another one he recognises too, but can't remember the name. Always good with faces, not so much with names.

Interesting that they've come back, after what happened last time, Josh thinks. Maybe they just thought no one would remember them. But Josh remembers everyone who comes to this island, especially guys like this.

So many secrets he's gathered over the years. The dirt that people want to forget, to leave behind as they fly off home. The shame, the regret. But Josh remembers it all.

And he loves to remind people of it too if need be.

Not right now. These boys are returning customers, so he needs to keep them on side.

Pulling his phone out, he tracks down Reece's profile on Instagram and fires off a quick DM.

I see you're back in town. Anything I can help you with?

On stage, Ms. Fanny Liquor is finishing her act, with the next coming right up.

"Ladies, gentlemen, and everyone in between! Next up we have our very own shining light," Fanny shouts down the mic. "The only thing dirtier than her mouth is her gusset—the very filthy, Miss Candy Chokem!"

Josh takes a final drag of his cigarette and flicks it to the floor. Straightening his wig one final time, he marches his heels through the crowd and up on stage, taking the mic from Fanny en route.

Laughter and whoops fill the room. This is his domain. The place where he rules.

And yet, as he scans the crowd, his eyes flick back to the entrance of the bar up the way, to the guys he recognised outside.

He smiles to the crowd, who smile back up at him. They are in his world now.

Chapter 11

DAN

Luca and I have been talking and kissing for what feels like an hour, maybe more. Time has melted into the blur of drinks, laughter, and the way he looks at me like he's enjoying every second. My cocktail glass is empty again—when did that happen?—and I barely remember ordering another, but here it is, condensation pooling around the base.

After a day's worth of drinking, I've very much checked in to my talkative side, which tends to happen when I'm this intoxicated. It's a side of me I enjoy, despite the requirements to achieve it. We've talked about life on the island, our dreams, our childhoods, embarrassing memories and awkward sexual experiences. I'm not convinced Luca is telling me the truth and potentially making up his own back story as he goes along, but he's funny and charming, which is all I'm after right now.

Luca leans in, his breath warm against my ear. "You know," he murmurs, his voice dripping with amusement, "I think you might be a bit of an alcoholic."

I laugh, maybe too hard. "I'm just keeping up with you," I say, nudging his arm.

He smirks. "Oh, *I* could stop anytime." He pauses. "Could you?"

"Why stop when you're on holiday?"

This is a fair excuse for the week, one that no one would question.

Drinking helps me. It takes the edge off, makes everything looser, softer. It makes me seem funnier, more interesting, and, most importantly, I stop caring so much about how I come across.

Lately, though, it's been more than just a social lubricant. The past year, it's crept into the spaces in between.

But when I do drink, I don't stop at just one. I like the feeling too much. The warmth of it, the numbness. It's not that I drink to get drunk, exactly, but I drink to feel *different*. Less like me.

And the truth—the thing I don't like saying out loud—is that I don't know how to be in social situations anymore without it. How even the thought of being around people, of having to navigate their expectations and energy, makes my chest tighten.

Luca touches my wrist, pulling me out of my thoughts. "You disappeared for a second," he says, tilting his head slightly. "Where'd you go?"

I shake my head, forcing a smile. "Nowhere."

Leaning in again, he presses his lips to mine, and just like that, the conversation shifts. The weight in my chest loosens, dissolving into the warmth of his mouth, the press of his body against mine. Another drink appears. I'm not sure what time it is, and we keep going—talking, laughing, kissing, the night spinning around us.

As we break apart, Hugo is standing above me. "Alright boys, get a room," he says with a sparkle in his eye.

I laugh, although too drunk to feel awkward about the situation. "What's going on?"

"Just been drinking with Jessie and the boys."

"New best friends?"

"Oh, they're alright. Speaking of new friends," he turns to Luca, "I'm Hugo, nice to meet you."

"Pleasure to meet you too, Hugo," Luca replies.

"Are you a local here?"

"I am, yes."

"So, you know all the deep dark secrets of this island?" Hugo says, mischievously.

"Every last one," Luca replies.

"Well, I look forward to hearing all about them this week."

"What are you up to now?" I ask.

"Well, just to say, we're wandering off to another bar, so just text me if you want to meet up later," Hugo says.

"Okay, great, have fun!"

"You too!" he says with a cheeky wink, signalling a blow job to me as he walks out of Luca's eyeline.

I roll my eyes and shake my head, although I feel this is where this night is headed. I'm conscious that my head is feeling woozy from the alcohol, but it's a feeling that brings me comfort and confidence.

Hugo disappears back into the crowd, leaving me alone with Luca again. I settle into my seat, the alcohol humming pleasantly through my system, my inhibitions softening. Luca looks at me over the rim of his glass, his expression lazy, his smile lingering.

"So," I say, tilting my head, "the dark secrets of the island? Tell me more."

Luca smirks, swirling his drink. "Everywhere has secrets," he says, his voice smooth, but a touch slower than before. He downs the last of his drink. "It's just a matter of who's paying attention."

"Oh, I bet," I press, nudging his knee with mine. "So, let me guess—mafia ties? Hidden pirate treasure?"

Luca chuckles, but there's a sluggishness to it now, like it takes him a second longer than usual to react. "Something like that."

"I'm sure the local sexual health clinic probably has an abundance of secrets too."

"I'd say soooooo?" His words are slurring now, the alcohol taking over him.

I nod. "And all the gay drama on top."

Luca leans in, his expression suddenly unreadable. "Bad things happen here," he says softly.

I pause, caught off guard by the shift in his tone. "What kind of bad things?"

He blinks, his focus looking straight ahead. He shakes his head, as if trying to clear it. "People come here to disappear. Some succeed. Some don't."

His eyes are fixated ahead of him. I follow his gaze ahead, which is directly on Hugo, standing with Jessie, with Reece, Tommy, Mason and Dito by his side. They finish up their drinks and begin to walk off to another bar as Hugo had said.

As they walk off, his eyes narrow, like he's processing something he wasn't expecting, as his focus follows them. He goes to place his empty glass on the table, but misses. There's little I can do as the glass smashes on the floor. In the hustle and bustle of the night, no one around notices.

"Luca?" I suddenly feel fifty percent more sober than I did two minutes ago. He doesn't respond. "You know them?" I nod to the passing group, watching his reaction carefully.

Tilting his head, Luca doesn't answer right away. Whatever he's trying to say, it's getting tangled up in his own thoughts. His eyes lose focus for a second before he looks back at me, his pupils slightly blown.

"Doesn't matter," he mumbles. "Old stuff. Bad stuff." He's slurring more, his reactions slower, his movements less controlled.

"Bad people," he adds.

My stomach tightens. "What do you mean?"

Luca looks at me, his gaze momentarily sharp again, like he's assessing me. Then, his expression slackens, his head lolling slightly to one side.

"We're all bad people," he murmurs. "This place is full of them. Full of regrets."

He's losing track of the conversation, with more fragmented words, thoughts slipping away even as he tries to voice them.

Reaching out, I gently rest a hand on his arm. "Luca, maybe we should get you some water."

He doesn't react at first. Then he chuckles darkly, shaking his head. "No water. No fixing it."

My skin prickles. "What?" He's not making sense.

"Too late, it's too late," he chokes.

The tone has changed to an anger now, sobering me up, an uncomfortable feeling in the pit of my stomach.

"He's gone, dead gone, gone," Luca splutters. He pushes himself up and, unsuccessful, stumbles back into his chair.

"Who's gone?" I ask, although I have no idea what he's going on about.

I open my mouth to ask again but, before I can, he mutters something else—so low I almost miss it.

A name.

"Benny," he says.

Chapter 12

LUCA

Benny.

Luca pushes himself up from his seat, the world tilting slightly as he does. His legs feel wrong, heavy, but he ignores it. He just knows—*he needs to go*. His mind is thick, thoughts tangled, disjointed.

Benny

The name pulses in his head like a dull drumbeat, a sound that won't fade. He's not thought of that name for a long time. That name was his past. But now seeing them back, the memories come flooding back like a headrush.

"Luca…" Dan is saying something to him, but it's not going in.

The room shifts too much, the music warps at the edges, like it's pressing in on him from all sides. The heat of the night feels suffocating, his skin clammy, his pulse erratic.

Dan says something again—his voice sharp with concern—but Luca barely registers it. He just needs to get away. Away from the noise, from the neon lights, from the weight of the past clawing at his chest.

Dan reaches for him, his touch grounding for half a second. "Luca, hey—where are you going? You're not okay."

Luca shakes his head, tries to laugh, but it comes out wrong, unsteady. "I'm fine." The words slur, but he doesn't care.

Dan frowns, moving closer. "Let me come with you."

"No!" he says, more aggressively than he would like, but he just wants to get away from this place tonight.

His mind is a whirlwind, flashing images he doesn't want to see—shadows, voices, mistakes, things he buried that refuse to stay dead.

He looks at Dan, really looks at him, and there's something too kind in his face, too patient. Luca can't handle that.

"Stay," he says, pushing Dan's hand away, his own voice distant in his ears.

"Luca—"

"*Stay!*"

And then he turns, stumbles slightly, but forces himself forward.

As Luca stumbles into the open square of the Yumbo Centre, the neon lights bleed into the night, smearing at the edges of his vision. The music is relentless, the bass a dull, pulsating thud against his skull. Everything is too loud. Too big. But at the same time, suffocatingly small, the walls pressing in, the heat thick in his throat.

With legs that feel disconnected from his body, sluggishly he forces himself towards the steps, leading back up to street level. The glow of the bars warp in his vision, twisting into impossible shapes. Laughter crashes in his ears. He blinks, and for a second, it's not the tourists laughing, not the boys flirting by the bars—it's *them*.

And Benny.

That night.

The beat of the music is inescapable, a living thing pressing against his ribs. Gripping the railing, he drags himself up the steps, limbs heavy and uncooperative. Below him, the Yumbo twists into a warped painting—bodies blurring, writhing, faceless against the neon haze.

And then, screaming.

Echoing, piercing through the noise. The crowd is below. Or is that in his head?

His foot slips on a step, nausea rolling through him. Losing track of time, minutes stretch, bend, disappear. The heat clings to his skin like something living.

Suddenly, he's at the top. The other side of the Yumbo. The bars are beneath him now, a churning sea of people still lost in their revelry. Up here, it's empty, the restaurants long closed, their shutters pulled down, chairs stacked haphazardly.

What time is it?

The lights below cause him to squint.

Three? Maybe later.

The metal railing is cool beneath his palms as he leans into it, trying to steady himself. He looks down at the crowd. The drinks. The music. The endless noise.

Benny.

A sharp inhale. His pulse spikes.

Them. All of them.

Gripping the metal tighter, his knuckles are white. The air feels thick, pressing against his throat. The nausea won't leave. His head is spinning, his thoughts unspooling into something messy, broken.

Memories press in—heat, sweat, panic—mixing with the present until he's not sure which is which.

And then he feels it.

A tightening.

Around his neck.

Not hands.

A rope.

His breath catches.

The railing blurs in front of him, his vision darkening at the edges. His fingers claw at his throat, but there's nothing there. Or is there?

He can't breathe.

The crowd below sways, a kaleidoscope of colour and movement, oblivious.

His chest burns.

His vision swims.

No air.

His legs buckle.

Darkness

Chapter 13

DAN

I've been wandering around the square of the Yumbo Centre for a while now. I should probably find Hugo, but even with the alcohol blunting my edges, the thought of spending the night with his newfound friends curdles in my gut.

After watching Luca disappear into the night—unsteady on his feet, swallowed by the haze of the Yumbo—I decided to wander off in the opposite direction.

For a second, I considered following him, but resisted. He had pushed me away—physically, verbally. He didn't want me there. I'd known this guy for a couple of hours tops, so I'm not about to go chasing him into the night. I use the term "known" very loosely; the stories that came out his mouth most likely works of fiction.

Even at this hour, the Yumbo buzzes—bars packed, guys in shorts and vests drifting by in lazy circuits.

The drinks are still humming through my bloodstream, leaving me pleasantly numb, but my mind won't settle.

That moment when I pointed out Hugo and the boys, that flip in temperament, the way his whole body tensed, his expression shifted like a trapdoor swinging open beneath him.

He *knew* them.

That wasn't just casual recognition. That was something deeper, something loaded. His reaction to Hugo had been normal, but to Reece, Tommy, Dito and Mason, something very different.

Bad people.

That's what he had said: *Bad people.*

And then—*Benny.*

My thoughts tangle and snag against each other, knotting tighter with every step.

Luca slurring that name, like it clawed its way out of his subconscious without permission. I turn it over in my mind.

Benny.

A common enough name, but not that common.

Hugo met a Benny here before. We talked about it earlier today: a guy he got friendly with on his last trip, one who then seemingly vanished. It was just a passing story at the time, mentioned between sips of a piña colada. But now, it doesn't feel like nothing.

Coincidence or not, I need to find Hugo. Even with this much alcohol in my system, I recognise that my brain is starting to spiral and Hugo's level head is the counterpart to my overthinking.

Where are you? I text to Hugo.

I quickly get a response. *Burger King. Think I'm going to head back to the hotel.*

Yeah same, where shall I see you?

By the 6-pack zone? Okay, be there in 2.

The 6-pack zone was located in a corner of the Yumbo Centre, a corridor of bars that during busy periods like Pride, turned into a mass of half-naked heaving bodies gyrating to thumping dance music, the thought of which gave me anxiety. At this time of year, it was no more than another collection of packed bars, but a handy location to meet.

As I head in that direction, I see Hugo walking up ahead of me. Chasing to catch up with him, he greets me with a warm smile.

"How was your night?" I ask.

"Yeah, it was fun. Jessie is insane."

"And the others?"

"They're off doing their own thing."

The night is still thick with heat as Hugo and I weave our way through the last stragglers of the Yumbo Centre, the glow flickering over our moist skin. The drinks have left me hazy, my thoughts tangled, but finding Hugo has anchored me, if only slightly.

"More importantly, how was your evening? No end of the night sucky sucky?" Hugo asks with a glint in his eye.

I laugh. "Uh no, definitely not."

"No? I thought it was going well?"

Before I reply, a noise pierces the air.

A scream.

Not the drunken kind, not the high-pitched shriek of some tourist being dramatic. A real scream.

Hugo stops mid-step, his face snapping towards the sound. "What the fuck was that?"

I don't answer. My stomach clenches as another scream follows, and then shouting, voices overlapping, a swell of panic rippling through the usual nighttime chaos.

As we step closer, at the start of the 6-pack zone, hanging from the walkway above, I see:

A body.

Hanging.

A rope tight around its neck, the head tilted unnaturally to one side. Legs slack, lifeless.

Someone is shouting in Spanish. People are gasping, moving, pointing. Some are frozen. Some are turning away.

My breath catches as I step closer.

The red T-shirt.

My vision tunnels to a single, brutal point.

Luca.

Chapter 14

TOMMY

Tommy wakes up to a thick, pounding headache, the kind that feels like his skull is being pried apart with a crowbar. His mouth is dry, his throat raw, his limbs heavy with exhaustion that sleep didn't fix.

The room smells of sweat and booze. There's a metallic taste in his mouth – God knows what he took last night. Or where he went. Or what he did.

That's normal.

Blacking out is normal.

Wincing, a dull ache spreads through his body. Stomach churning, he peels open one eye, the bright morning light slicing through him like a blade. And then he notices the body next to him.

A man. Naked. Facedown, one arm sprawled across Tommy's waist like they belong to each other.

Tommy blinks.

He doesn't recognise him.

Not even a flicker of familiarity.

He looks closely at the tattoo on the man's left bum cheek. "Bite Me," it reads.

You'd think I'd remember that at least, he thinks to himself, but no.

This, too, is normal.

Exhaling, his eyes move in and out of focus on the ceiling. Nights like this are two a penny to Tommy—so many strangers, so many bodies pressed against his, so many names he never asked for or never remembered.

Does it even matter anymore?

The man stirs slightly but doesn't wake. Tommy carefully lifts the heavy arm off himself and sits up, pressing the heels of his hands into his eyes, trying to squeeze out the exhaustion and nausea. Feeling like shit is just the morning routine now.

His body's wrecked. His head's wrecked.

His life's wrecked.

Swinging his legs over the edge of the bed, Tommy plants his feet on the cold tiles, as his stomach lurches in protest, his whole body reminding him of what he did to it last night.

What *did* he do?

Drink, yes. Definitely coke. Maybe G. Who knows?

That familiar emptiness slithers in. He wishes he could feel something other than regret, but it's not even real regret—it's just exhaustion. He's tired of this cycle, of waking up in unfamiliar sheets, next to unfamiliar bodies, with the same gnawing ache in his chest.

The bottle of tepid water on the nightstand has its appeal and he grabs it, chugging it down like it might erase everything. Despite protests internally, he keeps drinking until it's empty.

Forcing himself up, he hobbles, as if he's eighty years old, into the bathroom, flicking the light switch on as he enters. The sharp artificial light stings his eyes.

Staring at his naked 35-year-old body in the mirror, he knows he is paying the price. From a distance he looks exceptional, his body lean and muscular, his face naturally handsome. But on closer inspection, the truth is revealed. His skin isn't what it used to be—too many late nights, too many drugs, too much dehydration. Slathering himself in expensive serums can only undo so much damage, while foundation and bronzer give his cheeks some semblance of colour. But nothing fixes the dullness under his eyes, the way his complexion has lost its glow.

Filling up a glass from the tap, he catches sight of the bottle of PrEP next to the sink.

Shit, did I take it last night before I went out? Maybe, fuck I can't remember.

Tommy, at best, takes his medication event based, but even then, it's hit and miss. He grabs the small bottle and pops two pills just in case, like it will have some magical post-intercourse impact. He's always playing catch-up, always trying to fix things after the fact.

A soft groan comes from the bedroom, as his one-night stand shifts in his bed. Tommy doesn't care though, he's already disengaged. Whoever he is, he's just another notch in a never-ending list.

A list that doesn't make him feel good anymore.

Maybe it never did.

He runs a hand through his hair, sighing. He should shower. He should eat. He should do *something* today, but he knows how this goes. He'll sit in this hangover, let it soak into his bones, maybe sit in the sun later to get some more colour to his body.

And tonight, he'll do it all again.

Because stopping would mean *feeling*.

And Tommy is too far gone for that.

This can't last forever, he knows that. The way he drinks, the way he parties, the way he fucks—it's unsustainable. Telling himself he's young enough to get away with it is a lie that is wearing dangerously thin.

Still looking good, yes. Still functioning, maybe, but the cracks are getting harder to ignore.

The anxiety is always there now, buzzing under his skin like static, creeping up on him when he least expects it. Paranoia, too. And his memory, getting worse as the weeks go by.

The dissociation is the worst part. Sometimes he feels like he's floating outside himself, watching from a distance as he makes another bad decision, drinks another drink, snorts another line, lets another stranger fuck him like he's nothing. There are moments—right in the middle of it all—when he feels completely absent, like his body is moving but *he's* not there. And afterward, when he's alone, the self-loathing hits like a truck.

But he keeps going. Because stopping would mean sitting in the silence.

And the silence is unbearable.

He tells himself he's having fun. That this is the life. That he's young, and this is what being young is about. But he knows it's bullshit.

He knows this is *punishment.*

For all those nights—nights where he was careless, reckless, where people got hurt.

He looks at his hands; they're rough, red, dirty even.

For now, all he can ask is, *did I hurt anyone last night?*

Chapter 14

DAN

The morning feels *off.*

Not just because of the hangover—which clings to my brain like a drunk ex who won't take the hint—but because of *everything else.*

Luca.

His body. The rope. Just hanging there.

I still can't wrap my head around it.

Sitting across from Hugo at a plastic table in the hotel's open-air breakfast area, my plate is practically untouched. The smell of greasy bacon and overripe fruit is too much to stomach, not even a sip of coffee is coming close to my lips.

A group of young kids are running by, giggling and screaming way too loud, and I really just want to throw a piece of undercooked toast at them. The Hotel Maspalomas Oasis, as lovely as it is, has invested in one of those conveyor toasters, where you have to put the bread through about three times, just to get a mildly bronzed result. And I just do not have the time or the brain capacity to wait around for that this morning.

Hugo, meanwhile, is practically glowing. He's tearing into a croissant, his sunglasses perched on his head, already looking refreshed and raring to go. You'd never think he'd witnessed a man hanging from a railing less than twelve hours ago.

"You need to eat," he says between bites.

I shake my head, pushing a piece of marginally toasted bread around my plate. "I can't."

"Eat!" he orders.

I put a grape in my mouth and suck on it.

Every word between us hangs awkwardly in the humid air, heavy and unwanted, like the last guest at a party who doesn't know when to leave. We *haven't* talked about last night. Not properly. I think he's waiting for me to bring it up.

Eventually, I say, "Do you think I should go to the police?"

Hugo looks up, chewing. "Why?"

"He was acting weird before—erratic. Like, *really* off. I don't know, maybe it means something?"

Hugo sighs, wiping crumbs from his fingers. "Dan, what would you even say? That a guy you just met on Grindr was drunk and talking nonsense before he—" He stops, like he doesn't want to finish the sentence. "Look, it's horrible. It's *awful*. But you weren't his best mate. You weren't his therapist. You didn't know him."

"I *know* that," I say, too quickly, too defensively. "But still."

"What do you think the police will do? What, launch an investigation because some guy had a few too many drinks before he…" He trails off again. I see it in his face—he doesn't want to dwell on it.

I look down at my plate, my appetite completely gone. "I just keep thinking about what must have been going through his head," I mutter.

Hugo exhales, leaning back in his chair. "It's tragic," he says simply. "But you can't let it ruin your holiday."

I glance up at him. "Jesus, Hugo."

"What?" He shrugs. "I'm being realistic. People do this sometimes. It's awful. And you can't *fix* it. You barely knew him. You can't be like this for the whole holiday."

I want to argue. I want to tell him it's *not that simple*. But the truth is, I don't *know* what I'm arguing for.

We didn't stay around much longer after we saw the body, it was just too harrowing to watch. The police arrived swiftly to the ensuing chaos, not helped by the hordes of drunken guys nearing the end of their nights, alcohol-fuelled gay hysteria at its finest.

Back in the hotel room, I just wanted to crash, even though my head was spinning out of control. The sensible pre-night ritual of drinking a pint of water and setting up another on the side table was forgotten, as I slumped into bed.

Hugo fell into a deep slumber almost immediately, his light snoring grating in my brain as it was haunted by thoughts of the night.

I couldn't stop replaying those last few moments with Luca. The way his mood shifted, the way his body tensed when he saw them—Reece, Dito, Mason, Tommy. He knew them. One of them. All of them maybe. There was history there, I was sure of it. But what history?

And then there was the name.

Benny.

It slipped out of Luca's mouth, slurred and strange, like a ghost breaking free. Was this the same Benny Hugo knew? The way Luca said it—like it was clawing its way up from somewhere dark—makes my skin prickle.

At the breakfast table, the same thoughts are in my mind. I glance at Hugo, who's busy spreading an unholy amount of butter onto his third croissant, blissfully unbothered by any of this. He looks fresh, glowing even. I look like I've been dragged through a hedge of existential dread.

I want to ask him about Benny, tell him what Luca said, but maybe Hugo's right, maybe I should just leave it. I didn't know him. I can't change anything. It's very sad, but maybe I should just try and enjoy the rest of the holiday.

So, I say nothing.

For now.

"Right, I just need to lie by the pool and not move all day," I say instead.

"Yes!" Hugo says, "And you can definitely do that! After the pool party."

I feel a small bit of sick in my throat. "What pool party?"

"The pool party that Jessie invited us to last night," Hugo says with a grin.

"No, Hugo, no, don't make me do it," I plead, slumping back into my chair.

"Come on, it'll be fun!"

"It won't."

"It will," Hugo insists. "Just think of all the hunks in trunks that we can ogle and judge to make us feel better about our crumbling self-esteem."

“Mine’s crumbling enough today.”

“You won’t be saying that after we work through a selection of Mojitos.”

And while more alcohol is the last thing I need, I know there’s no chance of me escaping either the pool party or this hangover, so hair of the dog is the only solution, as it often is.

“Fine, pool party it is,” I grumble, already mourning my dignity and my liver.

Chapter 15

DAN

With all the enthusiasm of a cow being led to the slaughterhouse, I rock up to the XL Beach Hotel with Hugo by my side.

This place appears to be at least one star down on our own lodgings, a 5-minute walk away, but, by the look of the clientele, no one is here for the spa facilities. Unless it's the sauna and a facial kind.

Upon entering the pool party, which is tucked away behind a row of palm trees via a very aggressive-looking bouncer in tiny shorts, my senses are pushed to overload. The moment Hugo and I arrive, it's like we've been dropped into the middle of a glistening, semi-naked fever dream.

As the music hits me—a relentless thumping bassline that makes my internal organs vibrate—I can feel my stomach churning. The DJ, a shirtless man in oversized sunglasses, is perched on a raised platform, nodding along like he's conducting a spiritual experience rather than just pressing play on yet another remix of Beyoncé's Break My Soul.

The heat suffocates, the air hums with chlorine, aftershave, and the thick, sticky scent of self-importance. The pool itself is an Instagram battlefield, packed with preposterously muscular men clutching a selection of inflatable flamingos like their life depends on it.

"I've never seen so many speedos in one location before," I say with wonderment.

"And so much subtle Speedo adjustment. Why can no one leave their banana hammocks alone?"

"Are you complaining?" I ask.

"Oh, no." Hugo furiously shakes his head.

Scanning the crowd, it's a mix of absurdly beautiful people and their less genetically blessed friends, who got dragged here for moral support. A kaleidoscope of golden hairless gym gods, posing Insta-Gays, some older party veterans in designer sunglasses and a multitude of twinks, already sunburnt from their first few days here.

Hugo lets out a low whistle. "This is a lot, even for me."

The music shifts into an intense house remix of some Gen-Z favoured song I wouldn't know, as a group of men in neon swim briefs erupt into synchronised dancing near the bar. Hugo claps his hands together. "Now it's a party."

Meanwhile, I'm just standing there, deeply regretting every carb I've ever eaten.

"I need a drink," I say, because coping mechanisms are important.

Hugo laughs. "Babe, we all need a drink."

And with that, we push our way toward the bar, past the grinding, flexing, sun-kissed chaos, ready to drink our way through the sheer intensity of it all.

Like a glitter bomb in human form, Jessie appears out of nowhere, shrieking our names and barrelling toward us with all the enthusiasm of someone who had four Red Bulls for breakfast.

"Hugo! Dan! You bitches made it!" she yells, throwing her arms around both of us in a hug that is 80% enthusiasm, 20% headlock.

I make a strangled noise as she crushes me against her sun-warmed skin. Hugo laughs, patting her on the back like a trainer calming a particularly excitable puppy.

She pulls away, beaming.

"Survived the night, did you?" she asks.

"Here to fight another day!" Hugo responds.

I just smile.

Jessie is quite comfortably wearing the smallest bikini top ever engineered—it's effectively a couple of teabag sized pieces of green material covering her nipples, held together by some string. With a light mesh open shirt on, covering up absolutely nothing, her look has been finished off with a gratuitously large pair of white sunglasses.

I marvel at how comfortable she is here, being the only female in this ultra-diverse environment of predominantly white gay men.

"Come on, the boys are over here," she says dragging us over to their sunbeds, and sure enough, there they are.

Tommy and Dito look up to say hi, while Reece doesn't make any attempt to acknowledge us.

"No Mason?" Hugo asks.

"No, he was off his face last night, was a broken man this morning, so just crashing back at the hotel," Tommy explains.

Lucky bastard, I think to myself.

Draped over a lounger, Tommy rearranges himself in his ridiculously small red speedos, which I can't help but cop an eyeful of.

Dito, looking golden and radiant, is also wearing the swimwear of a man who has nothing to prove. "How was your night?" he asks.

"Heavy, but so much fun!" Hugo says.

"Me and Hugo disappeared off to that Coconut place with the poles on the tables," Jessie says, no one really sure what she's going on about.

"I was working that pole like a slut to Slave 4 U, slid my vadge right down it in front of everyone. The gays went insane for me!" she screeches.

"Sounds like a health and safety nightmare," Tommy says.

"That's your STI results, babe," Jessie fires back, giving him an incredibly loud slap on his bum cheek, which Tommy seems to lap up.

Sliding my sunglasses down my nose a notch, I take in the glossy magnificence of them all. Tommy, bedraggled but still annoyingly hot. Dito, effortless. And then there's Reece—lounging in his usual state of carefully curated disinterest, his body lean, sculpted, and resting in a way that says, *I know you're looking, and I don't care. But also, please do keep looking.*

"And how was your night, Dan? We didn't see you," Dito asks.

Being dragged into the conversation, so unexpectedly by a handsome man in speedos takes me off guard and I stumble to formulate actual sentences.

"Um, oh, yeah it was okay," I say, with all the charisma of roadkill.

"Did you hear about the guy who topped himself?" Jessie screams out.

"Yeah, awful," Dito says.

"Can't believe I missed it, I was so out of it," Tommy adds, like he's talking about the latest episode of Eastenders.

"Yes, it was really terrible. We saw him hanging there as we were leaving," Hugo says more sincerely.

"No way! You saw him? That'll give you nightmares," Jessie shakes her head.

"Yeah, it was a bit of a shock. Dan had been on a date with him just before it happened," Hugo adds.

And I want the ground to open and swallow me up.

With a death stare to Hugo, in return I'm met by the eyes of everyone staring back at me in utter disbelief.

"You what?!" Jessie shrieks.

"You knew him?" Dito asks.

"Like an actual date or did you just fuck him?" Tommy sensitively adds.

There's a barrage of questions, and I feel I need to defend myself immediately, but as per normal my ability to string together a coherent sentence under this immense pressure causes problems. "No, I mean, I just… we just met for a drink," I fumble through my words. "We just chatted for a bit and then he left."

"What did he say?"

"Did he sound like he was going to top himself?"

"Did you tell the police?"

So many questions, I feel my face going redder and redder, none of which is due to the searing heat. Trying to answer their questions is a struggle, but they keep firing them at me.

"Did you snog him?" Tommy asks.

Jesus.

The people pleaser within me feels the need to answer, rather than telling Tommy to fuck off. "Yes, just for a bit,"

"So, let me get this straight," Reece enters the conversation. "You met this guy, kissed him, and then he hung himself. Wow," he says rolling his eyes in faux-judgement.

Everyone bar Hugo laughs and all I want to do is curl up and die. "Come on guys." Hugo tries to tone down the conversation, but the situation is getting too much for me.

"Well, he seemed to know you lot," I blurt out.

The laughter stops.

"What?" Tommy asks.

"How do you mean?" Reece asks, knocking his sunglasses down to meet my eyes, his blue eyes piercing my inner soul.

Again, that struggle to find my words.

"Dan?" Hugo says.

I clear my throat. "He seemed to recognise you all, when you walked past us with Hugo. He seemed to get quite anxious about it, in fact, when he saw you."

Tommy screws up his face. "Are you sure it was us? Could have been anyone he was looking at."

I don't answer.

"What was his name?" Reece asks.

"Luca," I say.

There's silence for a moment. I'm trying to read everyone's reactions, but it's like a game of poker; I can't work out what they're telling me.

"Never heard of a Luca," Reece says, pushing his sunglasses back up over his nose.

And then without considering the consequences, I land my final grenade.

"What about Benny?" I ask.

There is a moment of silence.

"Who's Benny?" Jessie asks, looking confused.

No one responds.

"After he saw you guys, he got quite upset. He mentioned the name Benny, before he ran off," I explain.

There's an undeniable tension in the air. It's thick and uncomfortable, but turning the tables on them is giving me an electric buzz, but more than that, I can see in their eyes the discomfort. I know they recognise that name, but no one is jumping to explain.

As if the universe decided to kill the tension in that moment, the booming voice of Ms. Fanny Liquor slices through the air, dragging the focus mercifully away from me and back to the pool party chaos. "Alright, you sunburnt, borderline-alcoholic sex gremlins—who's ready to make some terrible decisions?"

Chapter 16

MASON

Mason sits on the balcony, one hand stroking his dark beard, the other gripping a cold beer, condensation pooling between his fingers. The sun beats down—a relentless, golden weight—but he barely registers the heat. His sunglasses shield his eyes, masking the fact that he's not really looking at anything—just staring over the pool below, watching half-naked bodies glisten in the sun, hearing the distant thump of house music and drunken laughter.

His friends are probably three drinks deep by now, posing for Instagram stories and pretending they're living their best lives. He told them he wasn't feeling up to it, that he was too hungover, which wasn't exactly a lie. His head is pounding, his stomach still unsettled from last night's cocktail of bad decisions and cheap whiskey.

But normally, he'd just push through it. A few drinks, a dip in the pool, and he'd be fine. Normally, he'd be right there with them, faking enthusiasm, flashing that easy smirk, pretending everything is just one big fucking laugh.

Today, though? No.

Because last night, he saw *him*.

Like butter wouldn't fucking melt.

Laughing. Joking. So much fun to be around.

Like nothing had ever happened.

Like the past meant nothing.

Mason squeezes the beer can tighter, the aluminium denting slightly under his grip. *He* was always going to be here, this was no surprise. Still, seeing him—after all this time—sent something through Mason that he wasn't prepared for.

Rage. Raw, unfiltered rage.

The kind that makes your skin burn. The kind that crawls up from the depths of you, from places you thought were long buried. The kind he's spent years suppressing.

Mason mastered the art of shutting down early—a survival skill honed like a blade in a world that didn't want him soft. Detach, stay cold, never let them see weakness.

Learning young that the world is brutal, unfair, and unforgiving, anger was a useless emotion, something his mother told him he had no right to indulge in.

When he was six, his father had left, walked away without so much as a glance back, and Mason had to learn—quickly—that no one was coming to save him. You either hardened up, or you got eaten alive. So, he locked everything down.

No tears. No outbursts. No breakdowns.

Especially as a queer teen, battling with his sexuality around a homophobic family. His family spoke about gay people like they were another species. *Those people.* Said with a sneer, or a laugh, or worse—pity. Like it was a condition, something you could catch if you weren't careful. He learned early to keep quiet. To hide the way his eyes lingered too long on boys in magazines, or how his voice softened when he got excited. Every instinct became a crime. Every glance a risk.

There was no space for softness. No room for instincts or authenticity—only silence and the constant weight of hiding. Just a childhood of holding everything in.

When he was older, he tried girlfriends. He tried working out a lot. He tried praying at one point. And when none of it worked, he turned to the only things that made him feel nothing at all: drink, drugs, sex. Distraction. If you never slow down, you don't have to feel the rot under your skin.

So, he never had a coming out. Not really. Just a slow, grinding rebellion, which created a quiet, simmering resentment, turning to steel beneath his skin.

But last night?

Last night, something snapped.

The anger had surged up, boiling over in a way he never lets it. Not in public. Not where anyone can see, mind.

Over the last couple of years, he's watched firsthand Reece explode —violent, messy, a storm of fists and blood—not once, twice in fact. His calm controlled persona, so easily triggered, no one sees it coming.

Shocking in the moment. Surprising, yes. But Mason was never disgusted by it. Never afraid of it.

He was enthralled.

Inspired, almost.

Because Reece let his rage out.

And maybe, last night, Mason finally understood why.

Taking another sip of his beer to soothe his dry throat, his jaw clenches so tightly it aches.

Mason has spent years keeping his rage on a leash.

But after last night, the leash is gone—and Mason isn't sure he wants it back.

Chapter 17

DAN

Hugo and I weave our way through the crowd toward the bar, the heat still thick, the sound of house music thumping and overpriced drinks clinking in the air. He hasn't said much since we left the others, which—let's be real—is unheard of for Hugo.

I glance at him. His sunglasses are pushed up onto his head, his lips pursed in that very specific "I am mildly annoyed but pretending I'm not" way.

"Okay, what?" I ask, finally caving.

Hugo exhales, dramatic as ever. "Oh, I don't know, *Dan*, maybe the fact that you didn't tell me anything about what Luca said last night?"

I wince. "In my defence, I decided not to because *you* told me to let it go."

"You were holding out on me."

"That too," I admit.

Hugo shakes his head, muttering, "Unbelievable." Like I've just revealed I've been secretly engaged to a woman for the past ten years.

"I wasn't sure whether to say anything," I say, defending myself. "I mean, Luca was drunk, erratic. He was talking about some bad history with the boys, and then he just… blurted out the name Benny."

Hugo stops in his tracks, turning to me so abruptly that a half-naked man behind us crashes into him, spilling his drink. The man glares, but Hugo barely notices.

"Benny?" Hugo repeats. "He actually said *Benny*?"

I nod.

"Not Billy?"

"No."

"Or Bobby?"

"It was Benny."

Hugo's face twists—somewhere between nostalgia, sadness, and mild indigestion.

"Do you think it's the same Benny you knew?" I ask. Hugo doesn't immediately respond. "I mean Benny isn't the most common name."

"Ben is literally the most common name for gay men ever. I know like nine of them."

"Yeah, why is that?"

"No idea."

We ponder this, before I add, "But *Benny*, not so common, right?"

Hugo reluctantly nods.

"Do you think it's the same Benny? Your Benny?"

"He's not *my* Benny," Hugo says. "Well not now anyway."

"But you were quite into him, right?"

Hugo sighs. "Yes, I really was."

I shift on my feet. "So… tell me more about him."

Hugo sighs, putting a hand on his chest like he's about to tell the most dramatic love story of our time.

"Oh, Dan. *Benny was…*" He pauses, his expression softening. "I met him on the beach. Golden hour. Picture it—waves lapping at the shore, the smell of salt in the air, me, looking devastatingly attractive in swim shorts—"

"Oh, shorts on. So, you weren't at Kiosk 7 at this point then?" I interject.

Hugo ignores me. "And then—there he was. Just sitting there, skipping stones like some sort of tragic novel protagonist."

I raise an eyebrow. "Skipping stones? What is this, *Call Me By Your Name*?"

"Shut up, *let me have this*."

I nod, letting him continue.

Hugo sighs dramatically. "We got talking. He was funny, Dan. Like, *actually* funny. Not just *charming-guy-who's-hot* funny. A real, proper, make-you-laugh-until-you-snort kind of funny. He listened. He cared. He liked me. Not in the 'let's get drunk and fuck' way.

"Although, you did do that, obviously."

"Obviously. But in a *real* way." Hugo shakes his head, smiling to himself. "I knew it was just a holiday fling. But deep down, I *wanted* it to be more. I thought—maybe this one's different. I thought we would stay in touch, maybe see each other back home. He lived in London too; we weren't a million miles from each other."

Hugo pulls out his phone and tries to unlock it with his face, but it's not working with his sunglasses on.

"Hang on," he says, typing in the passcode.

"240285," I see him type in, as the phone unlocks.

I roll my eyes. "Hugo, is your passcode still your birthday?"

"Yes, my dear and always will be."

"I thought after all these years, you'd change it."

"Why, are you planning on having a nose through it?"

I laugh. "I've made that mistake before, scarred me for life."

Hugo pushes his sunglasses up on his nose and scrolls through the pictures on his phone, before holding it out to me.

"Here," Hugo says.

And there he is.

Benny.

It's a picture of the two of them together, at the beach laughing. They're kind of an odd couple: Benny is tall, lanky. Clearly not one for going to the gym, he's skinny next to Hugo's stocky frame. He wears thick rimmed Harry Potter style glasses, resting on his prominent nose, his frizzy dark hair badly receding.

"I mean, he's not an oil painting, but we just connected, like I never have with anyone."

I glance at Hugo, who's looking at the photo like a widow in an old Hollywood movie.

"So, what happened?"

Hugo sighs. "We had a stupid argument on the last night. I can't even remember what it was about. He disappeared off that night. And then I never heard from him again.

I frown. "Disappeared?"

"Gone. Vanished. Poof. Didn't answer my messages, nothing." Hugo shakes his head. "I thought he'd text me back eventually, but he never did. I always just thought, he just didn't care as much as me."

I let that settle, staring at Benny's face on the screen. "That must have been hard for you?"

Hugo has been my friend for many years, and I know he wants nothing more than to fall in love, properly, hopelessly, stupidly in love—the kind that makes power ballads suddenly make sense and gives everyday moments a cinematic glow. He craves the kind of connection where lazy Sunday mornings stretch into afternoons wrapped in tangled sheets and soft laughter. It's that big, messy, breathtaking romance he desires, the kind that makes you text your friends in all caps and lose track of time in conversations that never seem to end. But more than anything, he wants to be chosen—not as a fleeting holiday fling, not as a fun distraction, but fully, completely, without hesitation.

"Yeah," Hugo says solemnly. "Wasn't meant to be."

I pause for a moment before asking. "Do you think it's the same Benny Luca mentioned?"

Hugo's expression darkens. "I don't know. Maybe. But I didn't recognise Luca. Benny and I spent so much time together, I never saw him with anyone else."

"Who was he travelling with?" I ask.

"He flew out on his own from what I remember."

I chew on my lip, staring at the image a little longer before Hugo snatches his phone back, tucking it away. "I don't want to dwell on it," he says, voice clipped. "It was two years ago."

I nod, even though I can tell he's still thinking about it.

"But Luca definitely seemed to know the guys, some of them at least. When Reece, Tommy, Dito and Mason walked by, his face dropped and he was rambling about bad people or bad history, I can't remember."

"Hmm, well maybe a hookup gone sour. A night of regret in Bunker can do that to a gal."

"I suppose," I say. "Would it make you want to hang yourself though?"

Hugo doesn't rush to answer this question.

Before I can say anything else, I feel it.

A prickle on my skin.

Like I'm being watched.

I glance across the pool, and there—on the opposite side, lounging like some sort of mafia boss—is Reece.

Cold. Calculated. Unwavering.

Staring straight at me—sharp, deliberate, and cold enough to carve the skin from bone.

Chapter 18

JESSIE

"Alright, you oily *slags*—where's my drink?" Jessie shrieks, tossing her bag onto her sunbed and kicking off her sandals with all the confidence of a woman who's just declared herself as the destination of fun itself.

People turn to look—as they tend to—but whether it's amusement, intrigue, or mild horror, she can't tell. She would like to think it doesn't matter which. But it does.

Throwing her arms around Tommy, she plants a deliberately aggressive kiss on his sunburnt cheek. "You look like a beautiful lobster," she announces.

Tommy groans, swatting her away. "Babe, I'm *hanging*."

"You're *hanging*? It's only day two. You need to push through it." She turns and shouts toward the bar, "Someone get him a drink before I have to put him down!"

People laugh. She feeds off it, throwing in an exaggerated eye roll and a dramatic sigh. She knows the role. Plays it well. The loud, brash, funny one.

It's fine. It's *fine*.

Downing half the cocktail next to her, Jessie scans the crowd and feels the familiar prickle of awareness. She knows what this looks like. The one larger woman in a sea of gorgeous gay men: the fag hag, the plus-one, the sidekick.

Surrounded by no one who would ever be physically interested should make her feel less insecure. She's hyper-aware of her body, her thighs pressing against the sunbed, her stomach hanging out of her bikini. But being surrounded by all these handsome men, regardless of their incompatible sexuality, still makes her feel self-conscious, uneasy.

So, she compensates. With volume, with theatrics, with jokes that land just on the right side of self-deprecating before they become tragic.

Throwing an arm around Dito, she gives him an exaggerated up-and-down. "Dito Beato, I'm loving your trunks. Makes your bum cheeks look like melons." Jessie gives his left one a quick squeeze.

Being the polite guy he is, Dito laughs, charmed, affectionate. He always at least acknowledges her. Unlike Reece or Mason, sometimes they didn't even say hello. "Going to get a drink," he says before wandering off.

She feels it again—that dull ache of being a supporting act in everyone else's movie.

Her stomach gurgles. Breakfast was only an hour ago, but she's thinking about food already, as she so often does.

Food has always been more than just sustenance. It's company. It's what she turns to when she feels invisible. When she gets home to an empty flat and no messages on her phone. When she watches her friends pair off, fall in love, build lives while she remains stuck in the same loop of shallow friendships and fleeting nights out.

Food fills a void. A box of chocolates is a distraction from loneliness. A tub of ice cream on a Sunday night is a soft, easy hug in a world that doesn't always feel welcoming.

Jessie came here hoping it would feel like old times, like when she and Tommy were inseparable, when she wasn't just an add-on to his life but *part* of it.

They've known each other since school, where they were the class clowns, the school's Ant & Dec; she loved it back then, she felt seen and admired. But nearly twenty years on, it's not the same. Tommy's one of the few friends she's kept in touch with from those days.

They've been through it all together: the drunken nights out, the drug experimentation, the bad dates and failed relationships. Jessie was Tommy's biggest supporter when he came out at 17. It strengthened their bond and connected them forever.

Over the years, neither of them really grew up. While their other friends settled into careers and relationships, Jessie and Tommy clung to their party lifestyle and to each other. Jessie felt safe with Tommy, and Tommy liked having Jessie around as his ride-or-die best friend.

But things had changed recently, over the last couple of years, she's felt it more and more. The distance between them. The connection is still there, but it feels like it's hanging together by a thread.

Tommy's lifestyle has become more and more reckless these days. More parties, more drugs. The kind of parties, as a straight woman, she will never be invited to. They joke about his wild behaviour, make light of it, but she knows he's not happy inside. He's broken. And she can't reach him, can't fix him anymore. She doesn't know how.

So here she is on holiday, with her best friend, feeling so alone.

Taking another sip of her cocktail, Jessie takes a big sigh, which no one around notices. She just wants him back—wants *them* back—like it used to be, when they were loud, stupid, and inseparable. This is the holiday that will bring them back together.

She'll do anything to make that happen.

Chapter 19

DITO

Dito steps away from the bar, a cold drink in hand, condensation trailing down the plastic like it's trying to flee the heat. The bassline thumps behind him, a deep, steady pulse that vibrates through his chest. Instead of heading straight back to the group, he lets his feet take him on a slow, meandering path through the crowd.

He passes a pair of men dancing like they're in a music video—shirts off, sweat glistening, hips doing things Dito's sure require regular stretching and possibly chiropractic support. Everyone's either flirting, posing, drinking, or pretending they're not doing all three at once. It's theatrical. Artificial. A little ridiculous.

It's why he likes these holidays. Everything's turned up to eleven. You can be a little louder, a little glossier, a little looser. You don't have to be yourself and you know you'll get away with it.

For the week at least.

Sipping his drink, he takes in his surroundings. The sun is bright but slipping, casting gold over the crowd. Somewhere across the pool, he sees Reece, all cheekbones and aloofness, radiating that curated detachment he does so well.

A year or so has passed since they became friends. Not close, exactly—Reece isn't close with anyone, not really—but they move in the same circles. Dito still isn't sure what Reece actually does for a living, other than looking expensive and somehow always getting into the kind of bars where you have to give a secret password. But he's useful. Always knows someone. Always knows something. He's like the human version of an exclusive mailing list.

Without any deep connection between them, conversations with Reece are often surface-level and sharp-edged. But he's interesting. And Reece always makes sure something's happening. That's fine with Dito—he didn't fly out here for soul-searching.

There's also an appreciation of all the work that Reece has done on himself. The teeth, the filler, the hair transplants, who knows what else—none of this he's open about, but it's plain to see. Dito's not averse to a nip/tuck here and there to get the best out of himself, and Reece's perfection is his trademark.

Tommy, on the other hand is messy, ridiculous, and absolutely the kind of person you'd want next to you when you're downing tequila shots you'll regret in 45 minutes. Dito likes people who don't pretend to have their shit together. And Tommy's chaos is refreshingly honest. If you're going to spiral, at least do it in a Speedo with a smile. It serves a purpose for now. Meeting through Reece a while back, again, theirs is a shallow but entertaining friendship.

Mason is still a bit of an enigma. Dito's spoken to him at a few parties before—pleasant enough, but there's always been this undercurrent, like Mason's holding back, constantly watching the room like it might betray him. Still, Dito's intrigued. There's something there. Something behind the beard and the brooding. Maybe this trip will crack that open. Holidays have a way of stripping people back.

Then there's Jessie.

There's a genuine affection for her. More than he expected to feel, actually. She's funny, sharp, and absolutely doesn't care what anyone thinks—on the outside, anyway. But Dito sees it. The little cracks behind the big laugh. The way her eyes flick towards Tommy when he's off with someone else. The way she keeps throwing out jokes like lifelines, hoping someone grabs on.

Being the outsider is a role he knows, to be the side character, he knows it all too well.

Taking another sip of his drink, he exhales slowly. He's glad he suggested this holiday for them all, a time to get under the skin of these people he refers to as friends. There's something charged humming beneath this group—like a circuit close to blowing. As if everyone's performing, trying to keep their storylines straight. Like there's a script no one wants to admit they're following. But he's not buying it. Not all of it.

They're hiding something. All of them.

And Dito, well...

He's charming, but not stupid.

Everyone's got secrets.

Especially this lot.

By the end of this trip, he's going to get to the truth.

Chapter 20

DAN

I follow Hugo back to the group, clutching my drink like it's a life raft, already regretting every decision that led me to come here today.

I could be back at our hotel right now, flicking through a book or having a power nap but, no, I'm immersed in the thumping beats and enforced social interactions of the pool party.

Back with the group, Dito has disappeared, while Tommy is sprawled across a sun lounger in a near-death-like snooze. Jessie—bless her chaotic, tequila-powered soul—is holding court, chatting away, like she's hosting her own talk show.

And then there's Reece.

Sitting up, perfect posture, expensive sunglasses, with the exact air of a man who's above all of this. He's scanning the pool area like he's expecting paparazzi, completely ignoring the conversation happening around him.

"Huge Nuts!" Jessie screams, christening Hugo with a nickname no one would ever want.

We both smile. Fortunately, I don't receive a similar nickname.

"That drag queen was well funny!" she shrieks, showing her respect for the talents of Ms. Fanny Liquor. "I was laughing so hard at one point, my nips nearly flung out of my bikini!"

"You'd have someone's eye out with those beauties," Hugo adds.

"Yeah, they do get me all the boys to be fair," she says, juggling her massive breasts around in her hands.

"Completely wasted here, mind," Hugo says.

"Well yeah, they could be wrapped around my head and tied in a bow, no one here would blink an eye. Much more exciting things for them to look at here," Jessie says, perusing the half-naked men around her.

"Well indeed," Hugo says, tilting his sunglasses and joining in surveillance.

"Speaking of which." Jessie grabs Hugo's arm, yanking him up. "Come with me, I need to show you something very important."

"Which is?" Hugo asks, amused.

"There's a guy with the biggest knob I've ever seen. His Speedos are about to explode! You need to tell me if you've ever seen anything this big!" And with that, she drags him off, leaving me completely alone with Reece.

Hugo and my eyes meet for a millisecond as he is whipped out of sight, my expression reading both "Don't leave me," and "Fuck you for leaving me," combined into one glance.

I freeze.

Fuck.

This is my nightmare.

I glance at Reece out of the corner of my eye. He's stupidly beautiful, sculpted, flawless, the human embodiment of a perfectly curated Instagram feed. But there's zero warmth to him, like he's been carved from marble.

Desperately trying to be casual, I take a little sip from my drink like I'm some delicate bird, which only makes me look weirder.

Reece doesn't acknowledge me. At all.

He's still watching the crowd, eyes narrowed behind his sunglasses like he's hunting prey, or maybe just silently judging every single person here.

I clear my throat. "Looking for someone?"

He doesn't move. Doesn't even pretend to care that I'm speaking. "No."

Cool. Fantastic start.

Why I'm even trying to make conversation with this man is beyond me, especially since Luca's pre-hanging recommendation of these boys was so sub-par. A normal person would just decide to not get involved with a guy like this, write him off as rude, full of himself.

I *could* just leave, go off on my own Indiana Jones style hunt for the biggest Speedo package at the party, but no, my social anxiety decides *now* is the time to keep trying.

"So," I say, shifting awkwardly. "Having fun?"

Reece exhales through his nose, which I think is his version of a laugh, and slowly turns his head toward me. Finally, acknowledgment.

"Are you?" he asks, his voice deceptively polite, but with the same tone a cat gives a bird right before it pounces and rips off its head.

I open my mouth, but what do I even say? *Yes, Reece, I'm having an amazing time watching you look beautiful and untouchable, eyeing me up and down like trash, while I sit here like a damp napkin.*

Instead, I just say, "Sure."

Reece tilts his head, studying me in that way that makes me feel like I'm under a microscope.

Silence.

I sip my drink again for something to do, realising I am out of words, completely, utterly out of words.

Why am I like this? Why is he like that?

I feel like a potato in human form, sitting next to this impeccably put-together Greek statue of a man. My self-esteem is currently curled up in the gutter, rocking back and forth and whispering affirmations it doesn't believe.

Finally, after what feels like ten years, Reece just stands up without a word and walks off.

That's it. No goodbye. No excuse. Just leaves.

I sit there, blinking, questioning every decision I've ever made in life, and ultimately hating myself.

And then I chug the rest of my drink.

"Hello, you," a soft voice says from behind me.

Spinning around, a vaguely familiar handsome face is smiling at me.

"Hi," I say, caught off guard somewhat.

"It's Jimmy. You were in Rita's last night," he explains, pointing a finger to himself. "I served you there."

"Of course, yes, hi!" I say overcompensating with excessive enthusiasm for not immediately recognising him.

Jimmy is dressed in a black shorts and polo combo, with a collection of glasses on a tray. "Just working here today," he says, waving the glasses.

"Oh okay," I say. I'm still recovering from the ego obliteration that was my interaction with Reece, but this is a pleasant reprieve.

Jimmy's dark hair is slightly ruffled, grey just starting to creep in at the sides, and his face has that permanent warm, easy-going expression. He grins, setting down his tray for a second. "Didn't expect to see you here."

"Yeah, well, I go wherever my bad decisions take me," I joke, motioning to my drink.

Jimmy laughs, shaking his head. "Having a good time?"

I shrug. "Surviving."

His eyes flick toward where Reece just disappeared to. "Friend of yours?"

I snort. "No. Just… an acquaintance. We're staying at the same hotel. Friend of a friend of a friend, who has no interest in anything that I offer to him."

Jimmy nods. "Ah, I know the type well."

There's a moment of connection between us through a shared warm smile.

"So," he says, lowering his voice slightly, "how'd the date go?"

It takes me a second to process what he means.

And then—Luca.

God. Of course, he was there all evening.

Part of me feels devastated that Jimmy must have served us drinks all night while we were shamelessly sucking each other's faces off throughout. That said, he's surely seen it all before in a place like this.

I exhale. "It was… good. At first." I hesitate, not sure how much I should say. I have no idea whether Jimmy knew Luca or knew that he was dead. He must have heard on the jungle drums by now though surely. That said, something about Jimmy makes him easy to talk to, like a confessional with really good hair.

"He got really drunk by the end," I continue, "started saying some weird things."

Jimmy raises an eyebrow. "Weird how?"

I shift in my seat. "Like there was some bad blood between him and these guys," I nod to where Reece had sat. "But they say they don't know him."

Jimmy scratches his chin. "Huh. Can't say I recognise them, but… I kind of knew of Luca. Just vaguely." This doesn't come as a surprise.

"So, you know what happened to him last night?"

"Yeah, really sad, unexpected," Jimmy says, genuinely. "Didn't really know him, but you get to recognise the locals if they're in the bar a lot."

"It must have come as a shock?"

"Yeah, it definitely did."

I hesitate. "Do you know the name Benny?" I ask, although I'm not sure why.

There's a beat of silence. Jimmy's brows knit together slightly, but he just shrugs. "Doesn't ring a bell."

I nod, even though something about his expression seems off—not like he's lying, but like he's mentally sifting through old memories, trying to place something.

"Why, who is he?" Jimmy asks.

"Oh, just a name I keep hearing," I admit. "I think he was staying here a few years back."

"I see. There's lots of characters around here though." Jimmy nods back towards Reece, who's now talking to some young twink, who doesn't seem like his type at all.

"You know him?" I ask about the twink.

"Yeah, his name is Josh. Now, *he* knows everyone. He's a drag queen at Rocky's. Goes by Miss Candy Chokem."

"Classy," I laugh.

"Yeah, he knows everyone's secrets," Jimmy says, mysteriously.

"Oh really?"

"Yeah, but I'm sure he's got more than enough of his own."

Someone shouts Jimmy's name from the bar. "Gotta run," he says with a smile. "Hopefully catch you soon."

"You too." I watch him slip away into the crowd.

As I sit back down on my lounger, my gaze drifts back to Reece and Josh, caught in an intense conversation.

What are they up to? I think.

And then I see it.

Standing stiffly, arms crossed, Reece's posture is icy as ever, but Josh is grinning like a sleazy car salesman, talking way too animatedly.

Then, in one of the most painfully obvious moves I've ever witnessed, Reece pulls a folded-up wad of cash from his swim shorts—because of course, he carries cash like a mafia boss—and hands it to Josh in a gesture that has all the grace and subtlety of a hostage exchange.

Josh, without even attempting to be slick, palms him something in return—a tiny plastic baggie, which Reece immediately shoves into the waistband of his shorts like a teenager buying weed behind a Tesco Express.

The least subtle drug deal in history.

I blink.

I steal another glance at Reece. He's already walking away, adjusting his sunglasses, expression unreadable. Like he didn't just conduct the shadiest transaction of the century in broad daylight at a pool party.

Chapter 21

MARTIN

Ms. Fanny Liquor—*Martin* when the wig comes off—steps off the poolside stage, having just finished his searing rendition of Lady Gaga's Bad Romance to the vibrant crowd.

"Alright you hungover trollops," he says, his accent thick from the North. "I'm taking a break now to towel my minge off, but I'll be back to carry this on very soon."

The crowd of Speedo-clad gays scream as he leaves the stage. Pressing a napkin to his sweaty brow, his sequined kaftan shimmers under the midday sun like a walking disco ball. He's 55 now, but still got it, thank you very much. A queen of resilience, a veteran of late nights and bad decisions, he's seen more in his three decades in Gran Canaria than most could stomach in a lifetime.

He'll be here all day, running his mouth and keeping this thirst-trap convention entertained, but his real shift? That's later. Rocky's Bar, 9pm till whenever the tourists finally stagger off to the cruising spots or their tragic little holiday romances. And when he's finally free, when the heels come off, the lashes are peeled away, and his voice is shredded from yelling at men in short shorts, he won't go home. Not yet.

Post his shift at Rocky's, his brain is wired, on a high from all the screaming and laughter.

So, like he does most nights, he'll take his walk on the beach.

The tourists are all tucked up by then, save for the odd straggler—some messy leftover from a club, usually shoeless, sometimes crying, always drunk. The dunes are quiet, the ocean stretches out like a dark, endless void, and for a moment, he gets to breathe. The noise of the island fades. The drag, the bartending, the endless, exhausting dance of entertaining other people—none of it matters when he's out there, feet sinking into the cold, damp sand.

That walk saves him. Resets him. It reminds him why he's still here, after all these years.

But not every night has been peaceful.

The things he's seen out there. Things that remind him that this island isn't just an endless carnival of cheap cocktails and pretty boys. The ocean holds secrets. So does the land. And Martin's seen enough to know some of them don't stay buried.

Still, it's home.

Thirty years ago, Blackpool had felt like a death sentence. He got out as soon as he could. Well, forced out, truth be told, leaving behind the small minds and even smaller futures, landing here at twenty-four and never looking back. Well, not really, there are certain parts of his life back there that he still pines for. He's built himself here, brick by sequin-covered brick, from one dodgy cabaret bar to the next.

And look at him now—parading around a pool party, microphone in hand, fully in his element, roasting men who paid too much for swimwear and flirting shamelessly with anyone who'll bite.

It's taken him a lifetime to be this free.

And if he has to take a walk in the dark now and then to remember why he's still here—so be it.

Taking a sip from a bottle of water, Martin looks around the countless men nearby. He has always had a talent for remembering faces. Even after all these years, after all the cocktails and cigarette breaks, after the endless parade of men passing through this island like seagulls on a chip, he can still spot a familiar face in an instant.

Hair grows, beards come and go, new clothes, new muscles, sometimes even a new name—but the eyes stay the same. The eyes always give them away.

And as he scans the pool party, taking in the crowd of half-naked, overly-moisturised bodies, he sees them—so many returning faces. Some from just last season, some from years ago, some he's watched burn bright and disappear, others who never really left, even when they should have.

Then, his gaze lands on Josh.

Miss Candy Chokem when she's on stage, a pain in the arse at all other times. Despite their thirty-year age gap, they bonded immediately, two Northerners escaping the grey misery of their hometowns, finding something bigger, brighter, louder. Drag was their thing, their escape, their power.

And yet, Josh always has a way of getting himself into trouble.

As the mature father figure of the two, who's been there, done that many times over, Martin's always tried to look out for him, offering a guiding hand where he could, trying to steer him away from the worst of it.

But Josh? Josh can't help himself. He's got that restless, reckless energy, the kind that draws him into things he shouldn't be near, the kind that makes people notice him for all the wrong reasons. Josh thinks he's untouchable, but these things always have a way of coming back. He's seen it time and time again.

And here he is now, lurking in plain sight, doing business with a guy who he recognises from a couple of years back.

Never forgets a face.

Remembers this one well.

He sees them exchanging goods in the most unsubtle transaction Martin has ever seen. He exhales through his nose, shaking his head.

Bloody idiot.

He's warned him before. About getting too comfortable with the wrong people, about thinking he's untouchable just because he knows where the bodies are buried, so to speak.

But Josh has never been one to listen.

And Martin knows—some lessons, you only learn the hard way.

Chapter 22

REECE

Reece walks away from Josh, slipping the tiny bag of coke into the waistband of his shorts like it's just another accessory, as effortless as his designer sunglasses. Handy, knowing someone like Josh on the island. No waiting, no awkward bartering with strangers, no risk of dealing with someone who doesn't understand discretion.

Not that Josh is particularly subtle. The idiot was practically waving the cash around like he was paying for a mojito, but whatever. That's Josh's problem.

Weaving through the crowd with his usual detached ease, Reece keeps moving, scanning the sea of men, all glistening in the sun.

Eyes are on him.

They always are.

Powerful. Invincible. Preying eyes feed his self-worth. Normally. But on this holiday, it had started to make him feel tired.

He looks impeccable, of course—because he always does. He's worked too fucking hard for this. His skin, flawless. His body, lean, defined, every muscle just sharp enough. The kind of beauty that makes people assume he has everything together.

But the longer he walks through the party, the more he notices the way people look at him—not just with admiration, but with expectation.

That's the thing about beauty in the gay world. It's a currency. A weapon. A privilege.

He knows the rules. He's benefited from them. He's had the jobs, invitations, free drinks, attention—everything is easier when you look like this. And yet, he's been on the other side of it too. The silent judgment, the way men scan your body, assessing you.

Having policed his body like a tyrant for years, he knows how quickly admiration turns into rejection.

And the hunger—the actual, physical hunger—is still with him, even now.

It started when he was younger, when he first realised how much his looks could protect him, could elevate him. How lean was synonymous with desirable. How sculpted bodies opened doors that would otherwise stay locked. He got addicted to that kind of control, to the numbers on the scale going down, to the way people noticed him more, wanted him more.

But then there were the days where the hunger gnawed at him, dug its claws into his stomach, and he'd ignore it until he felt lightheaded. Until it felt good.

And there were the days he overdid it. Where he slipped, where he ate too much—and then spent hours punishing himself at the gym, restricting harder the next day.

Even now, surrounded by men who'd kill to look like him, he still feels like he's faking it. Still not enough. Because that's the trap.

There's always someone younger. Tighter. Sharper.

Someone who hasn't started losing sleep over fine lines, who doesn't study himself in the mirror under brutal bathroom lighting, cataloguing every imperfection.

Adjusting his posture, he straightens his shoulders, pulls his stomach in slightly—tiny, automatic corrections, ones he barely notices anymore.

With no intention of returning to his group for the rest of the party, he saunters alongside the pool. Not that he knows where they are. There must be more exciting, useful people at this party that he needs to explore.

And then—Tommy approaches.

Reece sees it in his face immediately. Tommy rubs a hand over his face, his expression somewhere between tired and annoyed. “So, what Dan said earlier-”

Reece tenses. “Don’t.”

Tommy sighs, voice low. “I’m just saying—”

Reece turns to him, steely, ice-cold. “*Shut up.*”

Tommy freezes.

For a second, they just stare at each other, the air between them thick, charged.

Reece can see it—the flicker of irritation in Tommy’s face, but more than that, the fear.

Tommy fears him, not in the obvious, cowering way—but in the way that someone who knows exactly what he’s capable of does.

And that’s how it should be.

Reece can’t stand weakness. At school, he was a target before he even knew why—too quiet, too awkward, too something they could smell on him. The other boys picked up on it fast. They shoved him into lockers, tripped him in the corridors, called him things he barely understood but somehow knew were meant to shame him. Teachers turned a blind eye. His parents said nothing. "Just toughen up," his dad had muttered once, barely looking up from the television. Toughen up, like it was that easy.

So he did.

The first time he fought back, it wasn’t calculated. It wasn’t clean. It was rage—raw, wild, and terrifying. A broken nose. Blood on his knuckles. Silence in the hallways afterward, the kind of silence he could live with. It taught him something that day: weakness was dangerous. Mockery was lethal. Power was survival. And if someone tried to take that away—if anyone ever tried to humiliate him again—he wouldn’t hesitate. He’d learned what fists could fix when words never would.

It’s a side of him he usually keeps buried, but every so often, it surfaces. Tommy’s seen it. Mason too—more than once, usually after a few drinks and the wrong word at the wrong time, not directed at them of course, but at some unsuspecting idiot, normally some drunk straight guy, underestimating who he’s “bantering” with. Those triggers—being mocked, dismissed, made to feel weak, especially in public—can light the fuse. And when it goes, it goes fast.

Reece leans in slightly, voice like steel. "I mean it, Tommy. We are *not* talking about this. And neither is that Dan."

Tommy nods.

And Reece just walks off.

Benny.

Reece hadn't expected to hear that name. He hadn't thought about him for a very long time. It caught him off guard, twisted something deep in his gut before he had time to mask it.

Of course he remembers Benny.

They all do.

They remember that night, what happened, the choices they made, the roles they played.

But Reece isn't the type to dwell on the past. The past is dead weight, something to bury, to outrun, to leave behind and never fucking look back. Reece lives in the future—always planning the next move, the next upgrade, the next step up. He doesn't have time for nostalgia, for guilt, for sentimentality.

But now, here it is. Benny. Resurrected in conversation by a man who doesn't know when to keep his mouth shut.

Dan. Who the fuck is he, and why is he suddenly everywhere I turn? Reece thinks to himself. Bringing up Benny like that, in front of everyone. And linking it to Luca's death too. That's dangerous.

Reece clenches his jaw, rolling his shoulders back, heartbeat hammering in his chest, but his expression remains unreadable.

Cold. Controlled.

Dan running his mouth is a problem, he thinks.

And if he keeps digging where he shouldn't, if he keeps dragging up the past, pulling at threads that should stay buried...

Reece will have to silence him.

One way or another.

Chapter 23

DAN

I lie back on the questionable hotel bedspread, phone pressed to my ear, staring at the ceiling.

"Okay, so let me get this straight," Alex says, his voice already dripping with judgment, the kind only best friends can perfect. "You went on *one* date, and now you're embroiled in a full-blown murder mystery?"

"I mean… I wouldn't say *embroiled*—"

"Dan." His tone is firm.

"And it's also not a murder mystery. He hung himself. It's awful."

"It *is* awful." There is a pause as we both sidestep the obvious correlation between what happened between us back home last year and this tragic death.

"But," Alex continues, "a man you were literally *kissing* was found hanging, you're throwing around cryptic names like you're Agatha Christie, and now you think you've *uncovered something sinister*—all while on holiday."

I sigh dramatically. "Okay, well, when you put it like that..."

"It's ridiculous."

I prop myself up on one elbow, rubbing my temples. "Okay, but listen. Luca was acting weird before it happened. Like, properly off. And then he just *mentions* this name—Benny—out of nowhere. And *then* I find out that my lovely hotel acquaintances, who already give off deeply shady energy, may or may not have known him."

Alex makes a kind of "ugh" sound down the phone. He's my best friend from back home. We've known each other for years. He is the calming, rational side, to my erratic, over-thinking brain. We've been through a lot together, share history and secrets, and especially after the events of last year, we're closer than we've ever been.

But he's always one to bring me back down to earth.

"Right," Alex says. "And instead of leaving this nonsense alone and, I don't know, enjoying your holiday, you're now… what? Investigating?"

I pause. "Investigating is a strong word. Let's go with... heightened awareness."

Alex groans again so loudly I have to pull the phone away from my ear.

"Dan, my dear." His voice is slow and deliberate now, like he's explaining basic safety to a toddler near an open flame. "You are *not* Miss Marple. And you are *absolutely* not competent enough to be meddling in something that could, very *realistically*, get you into serious trouble."

I sit up, pouting even though he can't see me. "I just know something's going on. I *feel* it."

"You *feel* it," Alex repeats flatly.

"And my feelings have been right in the past," I point out.

"Yeah, and look how that ended up." I can feel Alex's eye roll down the phone.

I groan, flopping back onto the bed in defeat. "So, you're telling me to just… do nothing?"

"I'm telling you," Alex says, slow and firm, "to drink a cocktail, sit by the pool, and *stop poking at things that do not concern you*. You are *on holiday*, Dan. Stop trying to be the tragic lead in a Netflix thriller and just *enjoy yourself*."

I exhale heavily. "Fine."

"Say it like you *mean* it."

I stare at the ceiling. "I *will* enjoy my holiday and *not* get involved in anything shady."

Alex pauses. "Wow. That was literally the least convincing thing I've ever heard."

"Yeah, well. I tried."

Alex sighs again, fully resigned to the fact that I will, absolutely, not be letting this go. "For the love of God, just don't get yourself murdered."

"No promises."

Alex groans one last time before hanging up.

I toss the phone onto the bed and exhale, letting the ceiling take the brunt of my internal meltdown.

I *should* listen to him.

I *should* drop it.

But as much as I try to push it out of my head, one thing won't leave me.

Benny.

I *know* there's something there.

And whether Alex likes it or not, I'm not done with this story.

Chapter 24

JOSH

Backstage at Rocky’s, Josh is perched in front of the mirror, perfecting his eyeliner with the precision of a surgeon, the drag persona of Miss Candy Chokem slowly emerging from the chaos of makeup palettes, wigs, and cheap sequins. The room smells like hairspray and stale vodka, but that’s just standard for a dressing room in this town.

It’s just gone 10.30pm and Josh is due on stage any minute, with Martin currently on stage warming up the crowd as Ms Fanny Liquor.

As he sets down his eyeliner, Greg walks in.

"Josh," Greg greets him, leaning against the doorframe with the casual ease of a man who knows he runs this town. "You ready to go out there and make my customers buy more overpriced cocktails?"

Josh grins, smoothing out his wig. "You know me, darling, always working hard to keep the men thirsty.”

Greg chuckles, eyes cool, calculating, always looking two steps ahead of everyone else.

He’s the kind of man who commands attention, just by showing up. Early 50s, silver fox, effortlessly handsome in that rugged, *seen-it-all, done-it-all* kind of way. His features are sharp, defined, a strong jawline, a few well-earned creases at the corners of his piercing blue eyes, the kind that size you up in an instant and decide whether you're worth his time.

Even here, in the chaos of Rocky's, surrounded by cheap cocktails and drunk holidaymakers, Greg somehow still looks expensive. He's dressed down—a fitted, crisp black T-shirt and dark jeans—but mixed with the Rolex and the attitude, he knows what he's doing.

"You coming to my place tomorrow?"

Josh perks up. Greg's parties are legendary. Not the kind of parties where people get drunk and dance—the kind where all kinds of shit goes down. Where guys let loose, boundaries are pushed and fantasies fulfilled.

"Wouldn't miss it," Josh says, adjusting the strap of his dress.

"Good," Greg nods, then gives him a knowing look. "Bring some nice boys along." He places a selection of €50 bills on the table next to him.

Josh knows exactly what that means.

Greg's parties aren't just about socialising. They're about access. The right people, the right entertainment, the right kind of fun. And Josh is useful in that regard. He knows people. Knows how to get what Greg needs—and, more importantly, knows how to keep his mouth shut.

"Consider it done," Josh says smoothly, because of course, it is.

Greg smirks, gives him one last once-over, then disappears back out toward the bar.

Just as Josh adjusts his wig one last time, making sure Miss Candy Chokem is looking flawless, he hears the unmistakable voice of Miss Fanny Liquor behind him.

"Everything okay?" Martin asks.

Josh turns to Martin. "Not listening in again, were you?"

"I saw you at the pool party earlier," Martin says, ignoring the question, wiping sweat from his face with a towel.

Josh rolls his eyes, not even bothering to turn around as he adjusts his dress straps in the mirror. "What, and you didn't come over to say hello?"

Martin snorts, arms crossed. "Didn't want to interrupt your little business dealings."

Josh doesn't react, before turning to give Martin a lazy smirk. "Oh?"

Martin raises an unimpressed brow. "You were about as subtle as a hen do in a leather bar."

Josh waves a dismissive hand. "Please. I know what I'm doing."

Martin steps closer, lowering his voice. "Do you? Because I've been around long enough to know how these things go when people start thinking they're untouchable."

Josh leans against the dressing table, tilting his head, eyes full of mischief. "Martin, darling, I'm always careful."

Martin scoffs, but there's genuine concern behind the sarcasm. "Careful people don't get themselves caught up in things."

Josh grins, flashing his most charming, most infuriating wink. "Oh, but where's the fun in that?"

Martin shakes his head, muttering under his breath, before turning to leave.

They have a kind of nagging mother-daughter relationship. Josh knows it's driven out of love and care, but there's always something triggering about it, a refusal to listen to authority figures, to rebel.

Before coming to Gran Canaria, at home, authority was the sound of his dad yelling through walls. Josh grew up in a house where you kept your head down and your mouth shut. His father was the kind of man who called emotion "weakness" and being different a "disease." Especially if you were a boy.

Josh learned early how to hide himself. Every day was a negotiation: what to say, how to move, how to survive without setting him off. Sometimes he was successful, sometimes it was just his mother who was subjected to the violence, but Josh couldn't always escape the fist of his father

By the time he was sixteen, he knew the only way out was to *leave*—not just the house, but everything. His hometown. His name. His past.

He scraped together cash working shit jobs, lying about his age—doing whatever it took. By eighteen, he had a one-way flight and a promise to himself: *start over somewhere no one knows your name.*

Gran Canaria sounded like freedom. Sun, sea, queers in daylight. A place where people like him weren't beaten down or told to change. He thought if he could just get far enough away, he'd finally be safe.

He was wrong, of course. About safety. About men. About what people will take from you when they see you've already lost so much.

But he understands now why Greg's smile worked on him. Why the praise felt like oxygen. When you've spent your whole life being told you're nothing, it only takes one person treating you like something special to make you forget the price you're paying for it.

Even now, when he thinks about home—what little of it he lets himself remember—he feels that same cold shame crawl up his spine. Not for leaving, but for how long it took him to do it. And for how desperately he wanted someone—*anyone*—to love him the moment he got out.

And, as such, deep down, he appreciates Martin's paternal love. It's the closest thing to fatherly love he's ever experienced.

Josh takes one final look in the mirror.

Miss Candy Chokem is ready.

She struts toward the stage, the bass from the speakers vibrating through the floor, the cheers of a rowdy, sunburnt, and over-served crowd already ringing out beyond the curtain.

Josh takes a breath, plasters on a smirk, and steps out.

The show must go on.

Chapter 25

DAN

I take a long sip of my mojito, the ice rattling as I swirl it around, before finally saying it.

“I saw Reece buying drugs today.”

Hugo pauses mid-sip, blinking at me over the rim of his glass. He sets his drink down and gasps, clutching his chest like a Victorian widow hearing outrageous gossip at afternoon tea.

"No!" he says, eyes wide with faux horror. "A homosexual. With illegal drugs at a Gran Canarian pool party. I cannot believe this scandal!”

I narrow my eyes. "Are you done?"

He waves a hand, composing himself. "Sorry, sorry, please continue. What did our sweet, wholesome Reece do?"

I ignore his sarcasm. "He was talking to some twink, and then *in the least subtle move ever*, I saw him literally hand him cash and get a baggie in return—like some sort of dodgy transaction outside Greggs.”

Hugo snorts, nearly choking on his drink. “Oh, babe. That’s just *a Tuesday* for people like him.”

I give him a look. “Why do I feel like you know more about this than I do?”

Hugo grins, swirling his drink. "Because, my innocent baby deer, I have been to more parties than you’ve had Grindr hookups, and I have seen *plenty* of things."

I sigh. "I *know* people take drugs, I'm not a *complete* idiot. But I guess seeing it that obviously just felt... I don't know, weird?"

Hugo tilts his head. "Dan. You know where we are, right? The entire economy here is built on cocktails and men making poor life choices."

I sigh, rubbing my temples. "It just weirds me out, alright?"

Hugo laughs, patting my hand like a concerned parent indulging their naive child. "Oh, you precious, law-abiding citizen. I can't believe I'm on holiday with someone who still finds casual drug use shocking. Next, you'll be telling me you think people come here for the architecture."

I roll my eyes. "I've always just been more of an old-school alcoholic than a drug user, that's all."

"Well, that's fair enough."

"Speaking of which," I say as Jimmy approaches with our drinks, looking infuriatingly fresh for someone who has been working in this heat, in this chaos, serving this many messy gays all day.

"Here you go, ladies. Two mojitos," he says, sliding them onto the table with the kind of ease that suggests he's done this a million times.

"Thanks, Jimmy," I say, flashing him a grateful smile. "You've been working all day; you must be shattered?"

Jimmy shrugs, wiping his hands on a bar towel. "I'm used to it here; gotta pay for the rent and the Botox somehow." He rests a hand on my shoulder, then heads back toward the bar, effortlessly slipping back into the crowd.

I chuckle, taking a sip of my drink, but my eyes linger on him a little too long as he moves away.

"Ohhhh, someone's in love," Hugo says, poking me in the shoulder like a schoolboy trying to annoy his crush.

"Uh, I'm definitely not in love."

"Lust, then?"

"Well, I dunno, maybe a little crush," I admit, stirring my drink to avoid his smug face.

Hugo claps his hands together like he's just been given a mission. "Well, then you should ask him out for a drink."

I scoff. "That feels a bit soon."

Hugo arches an eyebrow, deadpan. "Is that because your last boyfriend only hung himself a night ago?"

I nearly choke on my mojito. "Hugo!"

He winces. "Sorry, I recognise that was quite soon to be making light of it."

I just stare at him, disbelieving, mojito halfway to my lips.

"That said, he did see me here all last night with Luca," I say.

"Eating his face off too, you hussy."

"Well exactly. No one likes sloppy seconds."

Hugo waves his hands around. "Look at where we are. This is the epicentre of sloppy seconds."

"True," I concede.

"But," he continues, completely unfazed, "my point is valid. You're only here for a week, so get in there."

I groan, shaking my head. "You're actually the worst person I know."

Hugo lifts his glass. "And yet, twenty years on, here we are, drinking together."

*

Half an hour later we've moved on from Rita's to Rocky's, the local drag joint. Rocky's is exactly what you would expect—a chaotic, open-air fever dream of wigs, sequins, and ultra strong drinks and yet somehow, it still manages to feel more intense than I was emotionally prepared for.

Hugo and I manage to grab seats relatively close to the front, which is his idea, not mine, because apparently, he wants to "be part of the action." I, however, would rather be as far from "the action" as humanly possible.

The place itself is small but buzzing, tucked into a corner of the Yumbo like a glitter-filled secret that everyone knows about. A mishmash of plastic chairs and wobbly tables are crammed into the space, the kind of setup where someone like Hugo immediately becomes best friends the strangers next to him.

Our drinks turn up. Mine, a simple rum and Coke, in a thin tall glass, which is 70% full of spirits already.

The crowd is mainly a collection of sunburnt gays, a selection of jolly pensioners and a handful of locals. A drunk couple sits at the front, heckling throughout, while the three young children are perched alongside them, which is just painfully awkward for everyone.

"Why would you bring your kids here?" I say, oozing with parental judgement.

"It's educational for them," Hugo says.

"Mentally scarring more like."

Ms. Fanny Liquor takes centre stage, towering in heels that defy the laws of physics, her sequined dress catching every single light in the bar, making her look like a sentient disco ball with attitude.

"Alright, you boozy slags," she bellows into the microphone, "she's had her test results back today, and they were definitely not clear. It's our very own Miss Candy Chokem!"

The crowd erupts in cheers, and I take a nervous sip of my drink, because I know what's coming.

The queens aren't just performing—they're hunting. They're running up and down the tables, yanking people from their seats, dragging them onto the stage for public humiliation, and the mere thought of this happening to me is enough to send me into cardiac arrest.

I grip my glass like it's a life raft and turn to Hugo. "I swear to God, if they pull me up there, I'm leaving this island and never coming back."

Hugo just laughs, sipping his flaming drink like the psychopath he is. "Oh, relax. It's all in good fun."

"It's fun for *you* because you actually *like* attention."

He shrugs. "True. But still—if you do get pulled up, please be assured, I will absolutely record it for Instagram."

I glare at him. "You're a terrible person."

Hugo raises his drink. "Guilty!"

Meanwhile, on stage, a poor man from Sheffield is currently being forced to do the Macarena while wearing a feather boa, as Candy Chokem simulates a blow job on him and I know, deep in my soul, that I may not survive this night unscathed.

"Please can we sit a little further back?" I beg, clutching Hugo's arm like a hostage negotiating for his life.

Hugo twists around dramatically, scanning the available seats. Just as I start to feel the smallest glimmer of hope, he suddenly gasps like he's just spotted a celebrity.

"Oh my God, look who's here!" he screams, as if he's just been reunited with a long-lost sibling on a daytime talk show.

I whip my head around, expecting to see someone actually interesting, but no—it's Jessie, waving like she's trying to land a plane. And next to her? Dito, Mason, Reece, and Tommy.

A walking Abercrombie & Fitch ad with mild to severe personality disorders.

Hugo is already beaming. "There're spare seats with them!"

I turn back to him, dead behind the eyes. "Of course there are."

So now, this is my choice: sit front and centre, where I am at high risk of being dragged onto the stage to perform a humiliating dance routine in front of a crowd of sweaty, drunk strangers. Or spend the entire night wedged between a group of beautiful yet emotionally unavailable men, overanalysing everything I say, while I sweat through my shirt in sheer discomfort.

Truly, a Sophie's Choice for the modern homosexual.

"Fine," I groan.

Moving back fairly swiftly to avoid being targeted by a rampant drag queen, we take our seats, and before I can even fully lower myself onto the plastic chair, Hugo and Jessie are already deep in conversation, talking a mile a minute like two chihuahuas on espresso shots.

Which leaves me to navigate my own personal social nightmare.

I glance at where I've ended up: between Dito and Mason. Could be worse. Could be sat next to Reece.

Reece, who looks like he's one exhalation away from exploding, his jaw so tight, it could shatter glass.

Across from us, Tommy looks like he's on another planet, his head lolling from one side to the next while he sips on a cocktail. I've not known Tommy for long, but I'm sure I've only ever seen him in hangover or drunk mode. But he's also glaring at Reece, like he's got something to say.

I sip my drink, pretending to be deeply interested in Miss Candy Chokem's latest number, but the tension between those two is so thick you could cut it with a complimentary cocktail straw.

Reece mutters something to Tommy.

Tommy mutters something to Reece.

There's just a lot of muttering happening, which leads my overly anxious, self-conscious, over-thinking body to irrationally assume they must be talking about me.

Then, Reece abruptly stands up, his chair scraping loudly against the floor. Without a word, he storms off.

Tommy mutters "fuck sake" under his breath, then, after heaving his drunken body up, follows him outside, tripping over a chair on the way out.

I blink. "So that was normal."

Dito chuckles, leaning back in his chair, effortlessly relaxed as ever. "Oh yeah. Totally casual. Happens all the time. It's their love language."

I raise an eyebrow. "Love? Really?"

He shrugs. "Well, maybe love isn't the right word. There's definitely some intense feelings there."

"On who's part?" I can't imagine Reece has strong feelings for anyone except for his reflection.

I glance over at Jessie and Hugo, who are now howling with laughter over something, Jessie gesturing wildly, probably telling some ridiculous story from her dating disasters.

I turn back to Dito. "So… this group. It's, uh. A lot."

Dito grins. "You've *noticed*?"

I huff a laugh, shaking my head. "How do you even keep up with it?"

Dito sips his drink, thinking for a moment. "I don't. I just sit back, watch the drama, and enjoy the free entertainment."

I exhale, running a hand through my hair. "And to think, I was worried about getting dragged on stage by a drag queen tonight."

Dito smirks. "Oh, don't worry. That still might happen."

I groan, dropping my head onto the table. "Kill me now."

Chapter 26

MARTIN

Backstage, Martin adjusts the wig one last time, tilting his head from side to side, making sure it's sitting just right, before pressing his lips together to smooth out the final layer of lipstick. A deep red—classic, bold, and unforgiving.

Out on stage, Josh is wrapping up his number, dragging the last of the poor sods he'd plucked from the crowd back to their seats. The energy in the bar is buzzing, Martin can feel it tonight. He takes a slow breath, letting the atmosphere sink into him, the way it always does before a show. That little moment where he goes from Martin to Ms. Fanny Liquor—a shift, a sharpening, a transformation that he's perfected over decades.

And then—Greg appears.

Martin doesn't turn straight away, but he knows he's there, lingering just inside the dressing room, the air shifting with the weight of his presence.

"Busy night," Greg says, his tone casual, unreadable.

Martin finally looks over, his expression blank but his eyes sharp. "Always is."

Things between them have been frosty for a while, though Martin would argue they've never been warm.

He doesn't trust Greg. Never has.

He knows what he's like—the way he operates, the kind of power he holds over this island, the kind of things he gets involved in. Greg owns Rocky's, plus half a dozen other bars across the island.

But, he's not just a businessman; he's a presence, woven into the fabric of Gran Canaria's nightlife, the kind of man you don't cross because there's nowhere to hide from him here.

Everyone respects Greg—not just because of his money or influence, but because to survive here, you have to. Greg doesn't run bars, he runs people. And the difference between those two things is everything.

Martin turns back to his mirror, adjusting an earring, voice casual but deliberate. "Heard about your party."

Greg nods, but it doesn't quite reach his eyes. "Okay?"

Martin hums. "Not that I'd be invited, of course. Not my scene."

They both know why.

At Martin's age, you only get an invite to one of Greg's parties if you have money or have influence. Preferably both.

Martin has neither of those things.

He's just been around long enough to know how the game is played.

Greg leans against the doorframe, looking far too relaxed for Martin's liking. "Figured you weren't interested in that kind of thing."

Martin finally turns, eyes locking onto Greg's with quiet intensity. "I'm interested in knowing what happens on this island. That's a different thing entirely."

A pause. A flicker of something in Greg's expression.

Martin doesn't outright threaten him—that's not his style. But he doesn't let things slide either. He leans back, voice low but pointed. "Be careful with Josh."

Greg tilts his head, feigning confusion. "Josh can handle himself."

Martin lets out a slow breath, studying him. "Maybe. But you know as well as I do—this island has a way of chewing up boys like him and spitting them back out."

Greg holds his gaze for a beat longer, then smirks—but there's something unreadable behind it.

"Enjoy your show, Martin."

And with that, he's gone.

Martin watches the doorway for a moment, jaw tight, fingers pressing against the edge of the dressing table.

Then he exhales, shakes it off, and stands.

It's showtime.

*

Ten minutes later, Ms. Fanny Liquor is deep into her set, lip-syncing to Holding Out for a Hero. The music blasts through the speakers, the synth-heavy 80s anthem reverberating through the small, open-air bar, the crowd already whooping and clapping in anticipation. This is his moment, his stage. The heat of the lights, the pulse of the music, the laughter, the alcohol, the energy of the room—this is what he lives for.

Ms. Fanny Liquor is in full command, strutting across the makeshift runway, peeling away layers of her costume as the song builds, each reveal getting a bigger reaction than the last. A sequined robe—gone. A metallic bodysuit—ripped open to reveal something even more outrageous underneath.

The crowd is loving it.

Martin is loving it.

And then—something shifts.

Something, *someone* catches his eye.

A face.

No.

Not possible.

For a moment, he thinks he's imagined it. The lights, the adrenaline, the sheer overload of the moment playing tricks on him. But no—he looks again, and the face is still there, staring right at him.

Not just staring—boring into him.

The eyes. It's the eyes.

He knows those eyes.

He hasn't seen them in a very, very long time.

His body keeps moving, the routine carrying on as if nothing is wrong—the polished, rehearsed motions ingrained into his muscles after years of performing—but his mind? His mind is stuck, locked in place, decades behind, trying to process what the hell he's seeing.

It's impossible.

It's him.

And he is staring Martin down like a ghost back from the dead.

Chapter 27

DAN

Ms. Fanny Liquor is still commanding the stage, strutting up and down the tables, the crowd cheering her on as she belts out the last few dramatic lines of her 80s anthem. I should be watching, enjoying the spectacle, but the atmosphere at our table has shifted.

Tommy and Reece have returned from whatever brooding tension-filled confrontation they just had, and it's awkward.

Tommy, to absolutely no one's surprise, is wasted.

He flops down onto his chair, knocking into the table, causing my mojito to slosh dangerously close to my lap. "Fine, yeah, whatever," he says, half words, half drunken nonsense, which makes no sense without any context. His eyes have glazed over, his body slouching like a puppet with half its strings cut.

Across the table, Jessie and Hugo are still in their own world, chatting away, oblivious to the mess unfolding next to them.

Jessie suddenly huffs dramatically, pulling her vape from her bag and shaking it furiously.

"Oh, for fuck's sake," she moans. "It's dead. I need my spare. It's back at the hotel. Can we go back?" She looks at Hugo, like she's a lost puppy.

"Sure, I'll come with you," Hugo volunteers immediately, already standing up.

I glare at him. "If you don't mind?" Hugo adds, looking at me.

Of course I mind being left here all alone with these four beautiful psychopaths.

"No, not at all," I say instead with a smile.

Jessie beams at him, linking her arm through his as they head off, leaving me alone in the depths of this mess.

Mason and Dito seem unbothered. Mason is silently watching, while Dito is actually enjoying the show, laughing and clapping along as Ms. Fanny parades past.

And then a guy appears.

A handsome chap, in his early fifties maybe, dressed well, in casual but high-end clothing. He slides up to the table, his watch glinting in the neon lights, his presence commanding without even trying.

"Gentlemen," he says smoothly, flashing a grin. "I trust you're having a fun night?"

Dito and Tommy look up to him, while Reece and Mason don't acknowledge his presence.

"Yeah, it's alright," Tommy says.

"Excellent," he says. "I'm Greg, I own this bar. Just wanted to make sure any handsome men like you are enjoying the show." His eyes flick across the table, evidently more interested in the four guys than in me—which is exactly what I expected but still somehow makes me feel small and utterly invisible.

Like an On button has been switched, Reece perks up. "Oh, you own this place?"

"Yes, I own quite a few bars around here, a few restaurants, a few other businesses."

Reece leans in. "Nice, so you're quite the kingpin around here," he says, almost flirtatiously.

"You could say that," Greg laughs. "I've been on this island a long time."

"I bet you've seen it all," Reece says.

"I definitely have."

This is the most I've seen Reece engaged in anything in the short time I've known him. He's either horny for a Daddy type, which we could comfortably box Greg into, or he's horny for the money, power and influence that Greg appears to have. Something tells me it's the latter and I start to understand what makes Reece tick a bit more.

"Do you live nearby?" Reece asks, his right nipple peeking out of his vest.

"My home is a drive away. I have a beach front villa, plenty of room, but out of the way so I get my privacy. Views are sensational."

"Sounds idyllic," Reece coos.

"It really is. You lot should come to my party tomorrow night," Greg says, lounging against the chair like he owns the place. Which, technically, he does. "You'll love it. Stunning place, great crowd, plenty of drinks, everything you could possibly want."

His tone is flirtatious, teasing, with that undeniable smugness of a man who knows he's selling something people want.

I wait for someone to ask what kind of party, but no one does.

Instead, Tommy—who, of course, is still absolutely wrecked—lets out a sharp, derisive laugh. "Oh, I know exactly what goes down at your parties."

Greg, to his credit, doesn't seem phased. He just tilts his head, smirking. "Oh really?"

"Yeah, I do. You don't remember us lot then?"

Greg calmly nods. "Ah, of course," he says, although I'm not convinced he has any recollection of these boys. "You were here last year?"

"Year before that. I remember your place. And I remember exactly what went on last time," Tommy slurs.

"All good fun," Greg says, with a light smile. He seems to be tiring of Tommy's attitude but keeping it casual.

Tommy leans forward, his voice a little too loud, a little more slurred. "Yeah? Well, tell that to Benny."

The air changes.

I feel like I've been punched in the stomach.

Everything freezes for a second, the music, the laughter, the show still going on, but none of it registers anymore.

Greg's face barely flickers, but there's something—a momentary pause, a slight tightening of his jaw.

No one speaks.

And I know, in that awful, heavy silence, that I'm not the only one who understands the weight of that name.

Chapter 28

MASON

Mason sees it coming before it even happens.

The moment Tommy lets Benny's name slip, the air at the table changes instantly—sharp, electric, dangerous.

Reece, who had been half-lounging, half-sucking off Greg, suddenly goes rigid, his entire body snapping to attention.

"Shut the fuck up, Tommy."

His voice is low, clipped, but deadly serious.

Tommy, drunk beyond reason, just laughs, shaking his head like Reece is the one being ridiculous. "Oh, what, we can't say what we're all thinking?"

"Tommy, you're being a dick, quieten down," Reece hisses, like an embarrassed parent telling off his child.

"Fuck you, Reece. You're the one being a fucking dick, as normal, like you fucking own us all."

Mason feels it before it happens. That shift, that moment where Tommy forgets himself, forgets that Reece isn't someone you push too far.

"Tommy…" Mason says, trying to pacify him.

Ignoring Mason, Tommy continues. "What? You're going to put me in my place, silence me too," Tommy slurs, his eyes rolling.

Then, like a gunshot, Reece lunges.

Chairs scrape violently against the floor, metal legs screeching across the tiles as bodies jolt backward. Glasses topple, splashing liquor across the table, ice scattering like shattered debris.

Everything happens too fast.

One second, Reece is across the table, a picture of controlled fury, all clenched jaw and barely restrained tension. The next, he's on Tommy, shoving forward with full force, his fist cocked back like a loaded weapon.

Tommy doesn't flinch. He's too drunk, too far gone, too ready to fight back.

Mason reacts instinctively, his body moving before his brain can catch up.

His hands collide with Reece's chest, pressing hard, fingers digging into overheated, sweat-slicked skin, forcing resistance against muscle and adrenaline-fueled rage.

Dito is on the other side, hooking an arm around Tommy's shoulders, yanking him back as he kicks out clumsily, his voice a messy, slurred mix of insults and laughter.

"Fucking stop!" Mason grits out, shoving his arm between them.

Reece's breath is hot and ragged, his body coiled tight like a spring ready to snap again.

Dito is swearing under his breath, fighting to keep Tommy upright, who's still struggling, still goading, still a fucking idiot.

Meanwhile, Dan just sits there awkwardly, clutching his drink like a child watching divorced parents argue at Christmas.

Once the action gets pulled out of the bar area, onto the street of the Yumbo Centre, Greg takes a step back. He waves to Martin on stage as if to say, "Keep the show going, keep the punters distracted." A few people have turned to stare, but the loud music has diverted many from the altercation

Mason is right in the thick of it. He grabs Reece by the shoulders, spinning him around. "Get the fuck off me!" Reece screams at Mason, who lets him go instantly.

With his chest heaving, Reece's fists are clenched, knuckles bone-white, but after a few agonising seconds, he storms off, shoving bodies, disappearing into the crowd.

For a second, Mason thinks it's over.

Then Tommy, in his drunken brilliance, stumbles after him. "Reece, you're not walking away from me, you prick!"

"Tommy!" Dito calls after him, starting to move in his direction.

"Just leave them," Mason says, exasperated by it all. "Let them fight it out."

And just like that, they're both gone, leaving Mason and Dito standing there, breathless, surrounded by spilled drinks and scattered chairs.

Dito exhales heavily, rubbing his face. "Fucking hell."

Mason says nothing. He should care about what just happened. He should care about whatever mess Reece and Tommy have caused.

But he doesn't.

He turns back to the stage, towards Ms Fanny Liquor. From the platform, bathed in neon pink lights, she keeps performing, keeps moving, keeps lip-syncing—but their eyes lock, just for a second.

And Mason knows.

It's finally clicked.

Ms Fanny Liquor, Martin, has recognised him.

Chapter 29

DAN

The second Reece storms off, Tommy stumbles after him, like a drunken penguin in a nature documentary.

I'm still sitting at the table, drink clasped in my hand, feeling like a spare part, with Mason and Dito, neither of whom seem particularly bothered by what just happened.

Dito stretches, unfazed, like breaking up fights is just a casual part of his evening routine. "Right, well, that was exhausting. Let's go to another bar."

Mason grunts in agreement, rubbing a hand over his beard, seemingly still half engrossed in Ms Fanny Liquor's performance—probably setting up his next mistake of the evening.

I blink. Another bar? With just them?

Don't get me wrong, Dito seems friendly enough, and Mason… well, Mason has a beard, which I respect, but after witnessing that absolute homoerotic WWE match, I have zero desire to continue tonight's social engagement. I have other plans.

I suddenly wonder where the hell Hugo is, having missed all this drama when he wandered back to the hotel with Jessie.

I grab my phone and text him.

Where are you? You've missed a fight between Tommy and Reece…

No response.

I stare at my screen for a moment, willing Hugo to materialise like some kind of extroverted guardian angel, but nothing. Just the pitiful read receipt of abandonment.

Mason finally looks up from his phone. "You coming, or what?"

I panic. I need an exit strategy, fast.

I clear my throat, trying to sound casual. "Ahh, you know what? I think I'm gonna call it a night."

Dito raises an eyebrow. "You're going to bed?"

I nod enthusiastically, committing to the lie with the confidence of a man who absolutely does not intend to go to bed.

"Yep! Big day tomorrow," I say, as if I have any actual plans besides drinking, reading and avoiding social interaction. Maybe contemplating my life choices.

Mason just shrugs. Dito gives me a knowing smirk, like he already knows I'm lying but is choosing not to call me out.

"Alright," Dito says, standing. "Well, try not to lose sleep over the thrilling fight analysis."

"Oh yeah," I say, standing up, backing away slowly like I'm escaping a hostage situation. "Really gonna be thinking about that one all night."

Mason waves me off without looking away from the stage, and I make my grand exit.

I have no intention of going to the hotel.

As soon as Dito and Mason are out of view, I do the exact opposite of what I just said I'd do and immediately pivot on my heel to follow Tommy and Reece.

Because let's be real—Tommy clearly mentioned Benny's name for a reason, and Reece flew off the handle like a chihuahua spotting a postman.

These things are linked.

I don't know how, I don't know why, but I know that something is going on, and my nosy little brain refuses to let it go.

So instead of heading back to the hotel like a sensible person, I turn and head in the direction of their drama, weaving through the chaotic sea of gays in short shorts.

At first, I can't see them.

Just crowds everywhere, the usual Yumbo madness—people drinking on the streets, laughing, stumbling, dancing, their voices blurring into one big, boozy hum. A shirtless guy in a harness winks at me, and I instinctively look away, because I was not built for that level of confidence.

Some guy in nothing but a jockstrap and glitter boots stumbles past me, giggling, followed closely by his friend, who is wearing a crop top with “Daddy’s Boy” written in rhinestones.

Standard.

Then—finally—I spot them.

A glimpse of Reece’s broad shoulders, his ridiculous, perfect silhouette, moving up the steps to the street level, away from the Yumbo.

Tommy’s lagging behind, still talking, probably slurring something antagonistic, but Reece isn’t slowing down.

And just like that, I know I’m going after them.

This might be the worst decision I’ve made all holiday.

And that’s really saying something.

I keep my distance, weaving through the crowds, pretending to be just another aimless tourist wandering the Yumbo, but really, I’m laser-focused on the two figures ahead of me.

Reece is marching up the steps, his whole body coiled with rage, while Tommy staggers behind him, his movements clumsy, drunk, but still determined.

The higher they go, the fewer people there are. The vibrant glow of the Yumbo fades as they reach the top level, where the air is thicker, quieter, more dangerous.

Then, Reece stops.

And spins around.

I freeze. Shit.

I do the only thing my cowardly instincts tell me to do—I dive behind a nearby low wall, pressing myself flat against it, heart pounding in my chest like I’m in a bad spy movie.

From my very unsubtle hiding place, I can hear snippets of their argument, their voices rising, sharp, filled with heat.

Tommy’s voice: “I’m not scared of you, you know.”

There’s a scuffle, the sound of feet shuffling aggressively on the pavement.

Reece is shouting back at him, but I can’t hear it completely.

Then Tommy again, louder, slurring slightly: "Your temper again, always takes over..."

I hold my breath, straining to hear.

“...fucks everything up...”

Reece says something like, “You haven’t a fucking clue!”

"…paying the price of your tantrums…" Tommy spits, his voice mocking, bitter, venomous.

I peek around the edge of the wall—Reece’s fists are clenched, his jaw tight, his entire body tense like he’s about to snap.

There’s more talk, I can’t quite hear it.

And then—Tommy screams it.

"BUT YOU KILLED HIM!"

My stomach drops.

The words slice through the air, through me, through whatever thin illusion of normality I had been clinging to this entire trip.

I can’t move.

Can’t breathe.

Can’t process the fact that those words just left Tommy’s mouth.

And from my hiding place, I hear Reece’s response.

“I don’t give a fuck that I killed him!” he screams. “He was a fucking idiot, dangerous, absolute fucking scum. He deserved to die!” Reece’s words hiss through the night air.

“He got what was coming to him! And the sooner you accept that the better!”

There’s silence. I can’t hear Tommy’s response. Maybe because he’s lost for words.

I know the feeling.

Chapter 30

TOMMY

“I don’t give a fuck that I killed him!” Reece’s voice pierces through the air, like he doesn’t care they’re in public. “He was a fucking idiot, dangerous, absolute fucking scum. He deserved to die!”

Reece glares at Tommy, his eyes bulging, his face red with anger. “He got what was coming to him! And the sooner you accept that, the better!”

Tommy pauses. For a moment they just stare at each other, processing the conversation. Still so drunk, it’s almost as if Tommy momentarily sobers up as he says, “I just think what we did was wrong.”

Reece shakes his head in disagreement. “Then I don’t know what to say to you,” he responds calmly.

Reece turns and walks away. “Leave me the fuck alone.” His voice is sharp, final, cutting through Tommy like a knife.

And just like that, he’s gone.

This time, Tommy doesn’t feel the need to follow him. Instead, he just stands there, swaying slightly, the alcohol back taking a grip of his body.

With his vision blurred, he wanders around the top level of the Yumbo Centre, the lights below blending into a disorienting swirl of pinks and blues.

It's quiet up here, no one's around. His head feels thick, heavy, drowning in the weight of the alcohol, but the sick feeling in his stomach has nothing to do with the drink.

Tommy stands there, rooted to the spot, breathing hard. His heart pounds against his ribs, and his fingers twitch at his sides, itching for something—a cigarette, another drink, anything to steady him.

But nothing will.

Because he can't stop thinking about it.

He will never stop thinking about it.

That night.

The body.

The blood.

So much blood, pooling around them, slick and dark under the streetlights, the smell thick in the air, metallic and rancid. He remembers the way it clung to Reece's hands, his face, his clothes, a stark contrast against his perfect, flawless skin.

Tommy hadn't been able to move. His limbs had locked up, his stomach twisted in knots. He'd swallowed hard, his mouth filling with bile, forcing himself not to vomit then and there. The taste of sick had burned the back of his throat.

And then there had been silence. The kind of silence that swallows everything.

Tommy had stood there, staring down at the mess, breath coming fast and shallow, mind racing but also completely blank.

Then came the words.

"We don't talk about this. Not ever."

Reece's voice, low, controlled, like it was just another inconvenience to be dealt with.

Tommy had nodded. Because what the fuck else could he do?

They had walked away. Left it behind.

Or at least, Reece had.

Tommy never did.

It followed him. Haunted him. Every fucking day, every night, every quiet moment where his brain wasn't clouded with drink or drugs or sex.

The image of that mashed-up face was always waiting for him.

In his dreams, it twisted and morphed, the details shifting, sometimes more grotesque than he remembered, sometimes exactly the same. But always there.

And so he drank. Took whatever he could get his hands on. Fucked whoever was available. Tried to bury it.

Because what else was he supposed to do? Live with it?

Reece did.

He carried on like nothing had ever happened. Like it was a bad memory he could just lock away, throw into some dark corner of his mind, and pretend didn't exist.

Tommy envied him for that.

And he hated him for it, too.

Because Tommy couldn't forget.

It made him resent himself, resent Reece, resent the whole fucked-up situation that had led to that night.

And now, after all these years, after everything, Reece was still putting him back in his place. Still telling him to shut up, to forget, to move on—like it was that easy. Like Tommy was just weak for not being able to.

When he heard the name Benny, it was another trigger, another reminder of the awful things he has seen in Reece's company. The horrific things he's witnessed and buried deep, time and time again. That weakness, that inaction.

He clenches his fists, jaw tight, grinding his teeth together, his breath coming in quick bursts. He wants to scream. Wants to fucking hit something.

But instead, he just stands there, fists tightening and releasing, stuck in this endless fucking cycle of rage and guilt and self-destruction.

Because what is he, without it?

What is he, without the drinking, the drugs, the sex, the constant need to drown out the past?

Just a man who can't even stand himself.

Tommy wipes his eyes, his fingertips coming away damp, and for a second, he stares at them in confusion. He hadn't even realised he was crying. Not that it matters. No one's here to see it.

He lets out a shaky breath, sniffing hard, straightening his shoulders as if that will somehow put all the pieces back in place.

He turns back toward the steps, ready to descend into the chaos of the Yumbo once more, ready to drink until the memories blur, until he forgets his own name if he has to.

But he never makes it.

Something hard and heavy slams into the back of his head.

A blinding flash of pain explodes through his skull, and before he can even react—before he can even register what's happening—his vision fractures, spins, then fades completely.

Everything goes black.

*

Tommy wakes up in stages, like his brain is playing catch-up with reality.

First, there's the throbbing pain in the back of his skull, radiating down his neck like someone's taken a sledgehammer to his senses. Then, there's the overwhelming nausea, his stomach rolling unsteadily as his vision flickers in and out of focus.

And then, finally, the world sharpens.

He's staring up at a neon-lit monstrosity, a massive, garish sign looming above him, glowing against the dark sky.

YUMBO CENTRUM.

And next to it—

A fucking dinosaur.

Tommy blinks. Then blinks again.

What the actual fuck?

His head is pounding, his body aching, and none of this makes sense.

As the cloud in his brain starts to shift, he recognises his location. He's underneath the entrance sign to the Yumbo Centre.

He turns his head slightly, the rough texture of concrete scraping against his bare skin—

Wait.

Bare skin?

Panic kicks in all at once.

He glances down.

His body is naked, completely exposed, the warm night air hitting every part of him, and—

His feet. His fucking feet are tied.

And his hands too, tied across his bare chest.

Thick rope digs into his ankles, pulled tight, restricting any movement, leaving him completely helpless.

His breath catches, pulse thundering, and before he can process it, before he can even try to move—

The rope pulls tight.

And suddenly, he's yanked upwards, dragged feet-first into the air, his entire world flipping upside down in an instant.

The flipping motion as his feet go up causes his head to slam down against the concrete pavement. "Ow fuck!" Tommy screams.

The blood rushes straight to his head, his ears ringing, his vision blurring with the sudden shift in gravity.

He dangles there, disoriented, heart pounding against his ribs, every muscle in his body tensed, waiting, screaming, trying to make sense of what the fuck is happening.

But there are no answers.

Only the blinding lights of the Yumbo sign, the ridiculous fucking dinosaur grinning down at him, and the suffocating terror of not knowing what happens next.

"Hey, help!" he screams, to whom he doesn't know. Because up here, at this time of night, it's quiet. No one around. He can still hear the buzz of the night from within the Yumbo Centre, but that seems miles away from where he is now.

"HELP!!" Tommy screams again, his voice hoarse and desperate, echoing through the empty space beneath the garish neon glow of the Yumbo sign.

But this time, he doesn't even get the chance to finish.

A hand—thick, strong, and covered in a leather glove—clamps over his mouth, muffling the sound, silencing him instantly. The grip is tight, fingers pressing hard against his jaw, the sharp bite of leather against his skin.

His entire body thrashes, the rope burning against his ankles as he kicks wildly, but it's useless. He's completely trapped, hanging helplessly upside down, disoriented, unable to fight back, unable to do anything but choke on his own fear.

And then—he sees it.

A flash of metal, glinting in the artificial light.

The knife moves fast, slicing up toward him, and before he can even process what's happening—

The first slash.

A searing, white-hot pain rips across his neck, and suddenly, there's warmth everywhere.

A wet, thick gush of blood spills down his face, pouring into his mouth, his nose, his eyes, blinding him, suffocating him. He splutters, trying to cough, trying to scream, but all he does is choke—the metallic taste filling his throat, drowning in it, drowning in himself.

Then—another slash.

Deeper this time.

His body jerks, pain radiating through every nerve as more blood floods out, rushing like an open faucet, pooling, dripping, splattering.

His vision blurs, the lights of the Yumbo turning into nothing but a distorted, swirling mess, his ears ringing, the sound of his own heartbeat hammering violently against his skull.

Another slash.

The pain is everywhere. But also, nowhere.

His limbs are numb, his mind fuzzy, slipping, drifting, falling into the blackness waiting for him.

At some point—he doesn't know when—his head falls free, severed from his body.

And then, before it reaches the ground, everything goes dark.

Chapter 31

DAN

The second Reece turns in my direction, I do what any sensible, self-preserving person would do in my situation—I sprint back down the steps like my life depends on it.

Because honestly? It probably does.

I don't stop until I'm safely back in the crowds of the Yumbo, the lights blurring past me, the familiar pulse of bad Europop pounding from every direction. My heart is hammering against my ribs, my breath shallow, and I probably look like I've just escaped an attempted mugging or an unfortunate Grindr hookup gone wrong.

I yank out my phone, fingers fumbling as I type.

Where are you?

It takes Hugo about three seconds to reply.

Just walking back to the Yumbo. Where are you?

I glance around, trying to find some sort of landmark, but of course, in my panicked escape, I've ended up outside Corruption, the Yumbo's biggest Cruising club.

Standing outside Corruption

Hugo's reply is almost instantaneous.

Of course you are. Stay there, I'm on my way.

So now I'm just stood outside a literal sex club, casually loitering like a confused, lost tourist who accidentally stumbled into a very different kind of sightseeing tour.

Every now and then, a group of men walk past me, giving me a once-over, some with amused smirks, others with an assessing curiosity that makes me want to evaporate into the pavement.

How did I get here?

I mean, I *know* how. I was chasing after a murderous jock and his alcoholic sidekick, but still—this wasn't exactly how I pictured my Gran Canaria holiday panning out.

I sigh and lean against the wall, going back over what I just heard.

Tommy and Reece's argument plays on repeat in my head, every word lodging itself deeper into my brain.

"But you killed him!"

Reece admitted it. Out loud. To Tommy.

Not even a denial, not even a moment of hesitation. Just raw, simmering anger.

And the only name that keeps circling in my head is Benny.

Was it Benny he was talking about?

That's the only thing that makes sense—or rather, the only thing that almost makes sense, because I still don't get it.

What the hell happened last time they were here?

Reece had said Benny was awful, that he deserved it.

But why?

What did Benny do?

Hugo fell for him. And Hugo has good judgement. Better than mine, usually. I can't picture Hugo falling for someone terrible. He's had bad relationships, sure—but not evil ones. Not the kind where someone ends up dead.

I stare at my phone, my thumb hovering over the keyboard.

I should tell him everything I just heard. Should I?

But before I can make a decision, I spot Hugo weaving through the crowd, heading straight for me, his face lit up with amusement, like he's expecting to find me in some ridiculous, accidental misadventure—which, to be fair, isn't wrong.

I hesitate for a second.

Then, as he gets closer, I shove my phone back into my pocket.

I'm not telling him.

"So, I hear there's been gay drama," Hugo announces as he bounds up to me.

"Oh, word travels fast around here," I say.

"Yeah, well Dito messaged Jessie to give her the heads up before we got back."

"Ah, I see. Well, yes, they caused a right raucous over at Rocky's, screaming and throwing punches like a couple of hysterical chavs."

"Sounds sensational."

"Mortifying more like. So, what's the plan?"

Hugo gives me three options, none of them particularly appealing:

1. Meet back up with Jessie and the boys. Not happening.
2. Go back to the hotel and call it a night. Tempting, but I'd just lie in bed overthinking everything.
3. Go into Corruption.

I stare at him, waiting for a fourth option, but it doesn't come.

Before I can even pretend to deliberate, Hugo grabs my arm and steers me towards the door of the club.

"You need to relax and have some fun," he says, grinning like he's dragging me into a karaoke bar rather than a full-blown sex club.

I want to argue—list a dozen reasons why this is a bad idea, why I am absolutely not the kind of person who should be here—but the next thing I know, we're inside, and a bored-looking bouncer is handing us a key to a locker.

"Don't pretend like you've never been in a place like this before," Hugo says to me, raising his eyebrows.

And of course he's right. I have been to places like this, on holidays like this, many a time. But that overwhelming sense of anxiety, expectation and terror never feels any easier.

As we enter, I can feel the air is thicker in here, the lighting low, save for the occasional flicker of red neon illuminating the space.

I can already hear the bass of the music vibrating through the walls, but more than that, I hear movement—the shuffle of clothes being removed, whispers, low laughter.

Men.

Everywhere.

Some already naked, some still peeling off their shirts, some in harnesses, jockstraps, underwear, boots— a full buffet of exposed flesh.

Hugo whips off his t-shirt and pops it in the locker. "Come on, chop chop," he says, pulling his shorts off, leaving his underwear on with his shoes.

Not wanting to be the odd one out, I oblige, while sucking in my stomach.

We move out of the locker area into the main bar. So, there are some absolute Greek gods wandering around, the kind of men who clearly have personal trainers, meal plans, and an unhealthy relationship with creatine.

But, there's also a healthy population of 5s and 6s, men with softer stomachs, patchy chest hair, and bodies that haven't been carved by the gods but rather gently moulded by life's pleasures—beer, carbs, and a deep commitment to sitting down.

And this is comforting.

Because as much as I'd love to pretend I don't compare myself to everyone around me, I of course do. And standing among a combo of guys who look like they're also happy to eat an entire frozen pizza at 11pm just because it was there, makes me feel slightly less bad for not doing the three months pre-holiday starvation plan I'd intended.

Hugo, of course, is completely unbothered, scanning the room like he's assessing a buffet. "See?" Hugo nudges me, grinning. "Not so scary."

"Debatable."

He just laughs, like this is just another Tuesday night for him, while I feel like a lost backpacker who accidentally wandered into an underground fight club but is too British to leave out of politeness.

We weave through the men lounging near the entrance, brushing past naked backs, broad shoulders, clusters of men whispering and drinking and watching.

Some are brazenly confident, striding through the space like they own it, while others linger in the shadows, waiting.

I keep my head down, determined to avoid unnecessary eye contact, but it's hard not to look.

I catch glimpses of a few guys leaning against the wall, hands exploring each other lazily, another adjusting his harness, chatting like he's just catching up with a mate over coffee.

And then there's the bar.

Two absurdly handsome bartenders stand behind it, looking too clean, too composed, like they've seen every type of customer walk in here. Behind them, two TV screens play high quality gay porn.

I hear low murmurs of conversation, the clinking of glasses, but mostly, it's the thudding bass of the music—so loud it's pointless trying to talk over it.

Probably by design.

Hugo leans against the bar effortlessly, while I try to position myself like a normal human being who is totally fine and not at all overstimulated by the naked men surrounding me.

The bartender comes over, raising an eyebrow, waiting for an order.

I clear my throat. "Uh, two gin and tonics, please."

He barely measures the gin, pouring it straight into the glass like he's doing us a favour, or trying to incapacitate us.

I take my drink and immediately take a massive gulp, needing the alcohol in my system, fast.

Hugo grins at me as he takes a sip. "So? What do you think?"

"I think I need about four more of these before I answer that question."

He laughs, nudging me. "Calm down, Mary Whitehouse. It's fun."

I stare at him. "We've literally just got here. And I don't know who Mary Whitehouse is."

I glance around, assessing, then take another gulp of my drink, feeling the gin warm my chest.

Hugo grins over the rim of his glass. "We can just have a look."

That's what I tell myself too. Just a look. A quick tour.

Not a full descent into madness—just a curious stroll through the abyss.

We down the rest of our drinks, and without giving myself a chance to overthink it, I follow Hugo down the steps, into the heart of the club below.

As we descend further, the air thickens more—hot, humid, and questionable, like someone tried to bottle the essence of testosterone and regret. It's sweaty, the kind of sticky heat that makes you wonder if you accidentally walked into a sauna, or if this is just what happens when you trap a hundred horny men in an enclosed space.

The corridor stretches out ahead, dimly lit, lined with men leaning against the walls, side-eyeing each other like they're in some deeply erotic Western standoff.

To the right, two separate doors lead into dark rooms, and let's just say—they're not exactly reading nooks.

Low, guttural moans seep out from behind the doors, a symphony of filth, making it impossible not to imagine what's happening inside.

But it's what's straight ahead that truly cements my decision to never touch a surface in this place.

The bathroom.

A long industrial sink stretches along the wall, illuminated by a single flickering fluorescent light, and standing at it—like it's the most normal thing in the world—are three guys, casually washing their post-sex dicks, like mechanics scrubbing grease off their hands after a long shift.

Behind them, two more men wait patiently for their turn, like they're in line at a particularly cursed Pret A Manger.

"Come on," Hugo nods to me to follow him down the corridor as we approach another section of the club.

Ahead, there's a curtained-off area, mysterious and ominous, which, at this point, could contain literally anything, and to our left, another doorway.

We both glance inside.

There, lying in a sling, is a man, legs hoisted into the air, spread like a Christmas turkey waiting to be basted.

He looks very patient.

Very hopeful.

Very much like a man who has committed to the bit and is now simply waiting for the universe to do its part.

I grimace.

"Should we talk to him?" I whisper to Hugo.

Hugo stares at me, horrified. "What?"

"I don't know," I shrug. "Just to make sure he's not lonely?"

Hugo rubs his temples like I've just personally caused him physical pain.

"Dan. This is not a speed-dating event. He is fine."

I glance back at the young man in the sling, who is still just lying there, waiting, painting a sad figure.

I make eye contact for a fraction too long, panic, and spin back around to Hugo.

"Let's go."

Hugo nods, relieved, then turns to me, suddenly serious. "Alright, so let's go our separate ways. No funny business will be had if you're standing next to me."

"Okay, fine," I concede.

"So, ground rules. If we walk into a room and see each other doing anything in here, we immediately leave said room and pretend it never happened."

I nod aggressively. "Agreed."

Hugo claps me on the back like a dad sending his kid off to summer camp. "Alright, babe. Enjoy yourself."

With that, he turns back towards the way we came, disappearing into the darkness.

I take a deep breath, stare at the curtain in front of me, and, against my better judgment, step through it.

Chapter 32

MARTIN

The lights at Rocky's are still fading when the crowd begins to dissolve. Sequins catch on the edges of mirrors, lipstick prints stain abandoned shot glasses, and the last of the queens wobble past in heels too high for this hour. Martin lingers behind the curtain, half-shadowed, letting the buzz of the bar wash over him like surf he no longer dares to swim in.

At first, Martin thought it was a trick of the light—an echo of the past, conjured by the drag high of being on stage. It happens sometimes. Familiar faces where there should be none. A trick his mind plays when it's tired or guilty or both.

But this isn't one of those moments.

Because he's real.

Tall. Upright posture. A thick beard now, cloaking a face that's grown older, leaner. Time has passed, yes—but not enough. Not nearly enough to erase *those eyes*. Cold and fire at once. Martin would know them anywhere.

Mason.

He watches him from the shadows, pulse rising like a warning siren in his ears.

He *must* have seen me, Martin thinks. Their eyes had locked during the show—just for a second. But there'd been a flicker. A twitch of the jaw. A recognition, however fleeting.

A slap across the face, that moment. Brutal. Blinding.

Martin stands frozen for what feels like hours, the weight of memory pinning him where he is. He watches Mason walk away, blending into the tide of bodies, before stopping at a bar on the far side of the square.

Only then does Martin move, ducking backstage, suddenly breathless.

The wig comes off first, flung onto a stand with none of the usual care. The dress follows, peeled from his sweat-slicked skin and discarded like evidence. The mirror glares back at him as he scrubs at his face with rough wipes, as if he can erase what just happened.

Josh is gone, of course. Miss Candy Chokem's wig already hung, her lashes resting like corpses on the dressing table. Josh is probably halfway to Corruption by now. But Martin can't think about him tonight.

Not with Mason so close.

He waits. Long enough to breathe, finishing his drink in one pull, hands shaking, then heads back out into the night.

Mason is still at the bar, exactly where he'd last seen him. Drink in one hand. That same friend beside him, broad and built, the kind of man who looks like he could break Martin in two. The two of them are talking, laughing—though Mason keeps glancing around, eyes restless.

Martin watches from across the square, just close enough to be sure. Just close enough to let the full weight of it sink in.

What are you doing here?

There's only one reason Mason would come to a place like this. To find him. It can't be coincidence. It's too specific.

His face haunts Martin more than any ghost. Not because of what he remembers—but because of what he *doesn't.*

Over the years, Martin had kept tabs on Mason and the others. Quietly. Carefully. Just enough to know he's alive. Just enough to make sure no one else from back then ever found him. But he kept his distance. It was better that way. Safer. Until now.

Now Mason's here. In *his* place.

Martin thought he'd buried that life. That it had rotted away beneath new routines, old drag and quiet mornings where the air smelt of sea salt instead of fear.

But the past doesn't stay buried.

It digs. It claws. And eventually, it finds you.

There was a time Martin didn't think he'd survive it. Not the threats. Not the chase. Not the guilt. Leaving everything. His name. His city. His family. He escaped with his life, but he didn't come out whole.

No one ever does.

Is my life still in danger?

He loses track of time. Eventually, Mason finishes his drink, nods at the friend, and they start walking. Out of the Yumbo. South, toward the quieter roads, away from the drag lights and noise. Instinct kicks in. Martin follows.

He stays a couple of turns back, his feet moving before he tells them to.

The streets down here are still and quiet, the air warmer now that the wind has dropped. The buildings cast long shadows. One or two late-night taxis hum past, indifferent.

Martin keeps them in sight. Watches the way Mason walks—shoulders tight, head lowered slightly.

Who's the guy with him? A friend? A protector? A threat? Martin doesn't like the look of him. The way he glances back every so often. He looks like he could break Martin in half if need be.

Ten minutes later, they've reached their destination as they both enter the Maspalomas Oasis.

Martin exhales sharply, a breath he didn't realise he was holding. It's only momentary relief, though. Now he knows where Mason's staying. But this isn't over. It's only just beginning.

Because Mason didn't come here for sun and sangria. He came here with purpose. And Martin knows, in his bones, that whatever's been dormant all these years is about to rise.

The past never stays quiet.

And some reckonings won't be outrun.

Not forever.

Chapter 33

DAN

I step through the doorway, and it's like walking into another world entirely.

The room is dimly lit, shadows stretching across the walls, but even in the darkness, I can make out the scene unfolding before me.

A massive bed—the size of two king-sized beds pushed together—dominates the centre of the room. On it, seven or eight couples are tangled together, bodies moving in fast, primal rhythm, hands gripping, mouths open, hard grunts and moans filling the air like some kind of unholy choir. That unmistakable sound of skin slapping against skin.

I scan the room, trying to take it all in, but it's a lot.

Along the edges, men are lined up, watching. Some standing, some leaning casually against the walls, most touching themselves as they observe the writhing mass on the bed.

My heart pounds against my ribs.

I feel hot, overwhelmed, overstimulated—but also, strangely drawn to it.

I don't know what I feel.

Am I aroused?

Probably.

It's hard to tell, because there's just so much happening at once. The sounds, the bodies, the movement—it's like stepping into a movie I didn't realise I had tickets for.

I've always been quite comfortable with casual sex. That kind where you just go over to their place and chat for a bit, then that leads to a fumble around and then swiftly moves on to you being pounded over the sofa. We've all been there.

But there's something about walking into this kind of environment, which is just next-level.

I shift my weight from one foot to the other, debating whether I should stay or turn around, when a man steps into my space.

Tall, Latin-looking, handsome. Probably a local.

He's around my age, I think, though in this lighting, it's hard to tell.

He meets my gaze, holds it for a beat too long, then offers a small, confident smile. "Hello," he murmurs, voice deep, smooth, effortless.

"Hey," I manage, my voice thicker than I expected.

He steps closer. Not pushy, not aggressive—just enough to test the space between us.

And without really thinking about it, we start to kiss.

It's intense. Immediate.

The kind of kiss that takes over, that doesn't require thought, just feeling.

His hands slide to my waist, firm but not demanding, his lips moving with purpose, confidence.

I let myself sink into it.

It feels good.

Grounding, even. A distraction from everything else in this room, everything else in my head.

We take a natural break, and as he pulls back, just slightly, he offers me a bottle of water, tilting it towards me.

I'm thirsty. I really fucking am.

My mouth is dry, my throat parched from the heat, the sweat, the overwhelming atmosphere pressing in from all sides.

So I take it.

I twist the cap open and take a sip, swallowing deep.

It tastes a bit off. A little stale, slightly bitter almost, but I'm so thirsty I drink more.

It helps.

Quenches my thirst.

I wipe my mouth with the back of my hand, offering him a small, grateful nod.

He kisses me again, as deep and intense as the previous. As our mouths separate, he smiles at me. But before I can say anything else, he walks away, disappearing into the shadows.

I stare after him for a moment, but then, my attention is pulled back to the room in front of me.

I take another step deeper into the space, gaze sweeping across the bed, the men, the sheer mismatch of it all.

I see a young, absurdly attractive guy—model-hot, chiselled to perfection, a guy who, outside this room, would probably be the type to have "No old, no fats, no fems" on his Grindr profile. He's in front of me, on all fours, being roughly taken from behind by a guy about 40 years older than him. And not some hot sexy daddy type. Just some random old guy who looks like a maths teacher nearing retirement.

What is it about this place? It's like some alternative dimension where standards are out the window. Or is it the environment that takes over? Or the horn? The desire to just go with anyone because of what's unfolding in front of you.

I wonder how many of these men, in the daylight, would even look twice at each other.

Yet here they are, hands on each other's bodies, lost in it, giving into something bigger than preference or type.

I blink, swaying slightly.

My head feels… strange.

A little light, a little fuzzy.

I try to focus, to push past it, but something isn't right.

The music throbs louder in my ears.

The shadows seem darker.

Something feels wrong.

Pressing a hand to the wall to ground myself, the rough wall feels ice cold on my burning palm.

I blink, trying to steady myself, but the room keeps tilting, like I'm on a boat in slow motion. The men around me blur into one another—sweat-slicked skin, hungry eyes, mouths that smirk and don't speak.

A hand grabs mine.

I can't really see by who, but I'm led away into the shadows.

Chapter 34

REECE

Reece steps into the depths of Corruption like he owns the place—because in a way, he does. Not literally, but in the way men look at him, like he's some sort of deity descended from Mount Instagram. The lighting hits his body just right, glistening skin stretched over lean, honed muscle. He's shirtless, obviously, wearing just a pair of gratuitously expensive black briefs. His torso is a masterpiece of obsession and control: not a single ounce of fat, just taut lines and tension, the visible evidence of starvation dressed up as discipline.

Every man looks. Some glance and quickly look away, trying not to be obvious. Others stare shamelessly, drinking him in. Reece knows. He always knows. He doesn't even have to try anymore. He walks through the club like a blade through smoke, eyes sweeping the room, untouchable, immaculate.

But inside? Inside, he's still boiling.

His jaw clenches as he thinks of Tommy.

Fucking Tommy.

Overly emotional, reckless Tommy, who can't hold his drink or his tongue. Who made a scene—again. Who nearly let the entire truth spill out like it was nothing, like it wasn't loaded with consequences.

Reece exhales sharply, moving deeper into the club, pushing past a group of guys huddled to one side. Someone touches his chest, another runs a hand down his back. He shrugs them off without a word. Another goes directly for his package. He swats the hand away like it's an irritating fly. No. Not good enough.

He deserves the best.

Always has.

That argument with Tommy still clings to him like sweat. The raised voices. The accusation.

Yes, it happened. Yes, someone died. Blood was spilled. Reece saw the life drain from their eyes and didn't feel a single tremor of guilt. Not then. Not now.

They deserved it. People like that always do.

Tommy knew it too. He was there. He agreed—or at least, he pretended to. He promised to stay quiet. To bury it deep like Reece did. But he was unravelling, and Reece won't let him take them both down with him.

Tommy's been put in his place now. But the frustration around it is still swirling around his mind. A frustration he needs to release tonight in this club.

He keeps walking. The thump of the music is deafening now, vibrating in his ribs. The club opens up into a larger space. Bodies writhe, pulse, sweat. Reece is above it all. He refuses to settle. Hands keep reaching for him, grazing his hips, his stomach. He bats them away again and again. Attractive men, yes, but not good enough. Never good enough.

Then he sees him.

Tall. Dark. Beautiful. A face so symmetrical it almost annoys him. The most attractive man in the room—apart from Reece, obviously. This is the man he wants.

He approaches with a smirk, confidence sharpened like a knife. He places his hand onto the man's tattooed bicep. "Hey."

The man glances at him, expression unreadable, then shakes his head.

And walks away.

It's like being slapped.

Reece momentarily pauses, like his body has stopped functioning, as he processes the interaction.

He stands there, stunned, heat rising in his chest. Embarrassment. Anger. Confusion. It's all there, simmering beneath his perfect skin.

No. That's not how this works.

He moves after the man, tries again, bringing his palm up to the man's face, turning his head toward him, almost forcing it, in Reece's direction.

"I said, I'm not interested," he says firmly.

The man pushes him back. Physically.

Reece stumbles, just a step, but it's enough to light a fire behind his eyes. His fists clench. His face tightens. He wants to scream. Punch. Anything.

Instead, he spins away, face blank.

He tries to latch onto a handsome couple kissing against a wall. He moves in, hand on one of their backs.

They don't even acknowledge him.

He stands frozen for a beat too long, and then he walks off, pushing blindly through the crowd.

Everything in him starts to spiral. The cracks beneath the polish begin to show.

It hits him like a punch to the gut. Not even a dramatic one—just sharp, silent, humiliating. The kind that doesn't leave a bruise, but lodges itself somewhere deep in his chest.

He's been dismissed. Rejected. Ignored.

He stands there for a moment, blinking, trying to process the man's cold "I'm not interested" as if it must be a mistake.

His stomach turns, his jaw tightens. He forces a swallow.

He can feel it happening again.

That slow, sickening churn that starts in the pit of his gut, then spreads like acid. That thing inside him that always simmers just under the surface—the thing he keeps polished and hidden behind Botoxed calm and sculpted cheekbones.

Rage.

He clenches his fists and shakes it off. Or tries to.

He keeps walking, eyes scanning the crowd with renewed hunger now—not just for sex, but for validation. Something to erase what just happened, something to remind him that he's still desired. Untouchable. Worth it.

They don't want you.

You're getting old.

Your face isn't enough anymore.

Maybe they know. Maybe they can tell.

Maybe they see it—what you really are.

The club starts to feel hotter, louder, smaller. The air is thick with sweat and pheromones and rejection.

Instead, he just stands there, alone in the middle of it all—beautiful, furious, and hollow.

And underneath the anger is that old familiar thing:

Self-hatred.

The thing he never really got rid of. The thing he just learned to dress better.

That fire—it's still there. That old, familiar rage bubbling in his chest like acid. Normally, by now, it would have erupted. A shove. A fist. Something to release the pressure. But tonight, it just simmers. Tight and restless beneath his ribs. Maybe it's the shock. Maybe it's the heat pressing in on him, or the sweat slicking his skin like glue. Maybe he's still processing the humiliation. But for once, the rage doesn't detonate. It coils instead.

A man approaches him. Late fifties, sixties maybe. Just an average guy, who looks like he's an accountant, with a family and a Volvo. Trying his luck. He runs his hand across Reece's firm chest.

Reece just stares at him, as his hand moves lower.

The burn of rejection is louder than the disgust.

Chapter 35

DAN

Everything is starting to feel soft around the edges. Not in a nice, romantic way—more like I've had one too many drinks on a boat.

The man whose hand I've taken leads me away. I don't know where I am exactly—we've drifted into some dark side corner. It's still out in the hustle of the club, but away from the central activity, allowing us a modicum of privacy.

I lean against the wall for a moment, just to steady myself. He's a handsome man, another local, he must be. Latin features, strong beard, thick black hair. Slightly shorter than me.

He doesn't say anything. Just steps in close, hand brushing mine, then gently gripping my waist.

I feel warm. Floaty. Like I've had just the right amount of gin, even though I'm pretty sure I haven't.

He leans in and kisses me, and again, it's intense.

Everything sharpens for a second—the heat of his mouth, the pressure of his hand on the back of my neck, the way his body presses against mine.

I melt into it, my arms wrapping around him as if we've done this before. As if this is natural, even though nothing about this room or this moment is.

The music is thumping in the background like a heartbeat that doesn't belong to me, and I can still hear distant moans, the slap of flesh, all blending into this weird, pulsing fog.

Everything feels dreamlike. Wet. Heavy.

He kisses down my neck, and I tilt my head automatically, my brain half a step behind every sensation.

My skin buzzes, like I've been dipped in static.

His hands are roaming now, firm and deliberate, and mine do the same—not out of confidence but out of muscle memory, like my body's moving on instinct while my mind floats somewhere three feet above my head, watching.

"Passivo?" he says to me.

I nod.

He turns me around and I feel like I've slipped sideways into another version of myself.

One who belongs in this place.

One who doesn't overthink everything.

One who just feels.

I see him pump some lube from the dispenser attached to the wall, which a sober me would appreciate in the moment as a practical facility.

After teasing me for a few moments with the lube and prepping himself, he enters me, slowly at first, allowing me time to adapt to his size. But I feel relaxed, I'm in a fantastic daze. One arm up against the wall, my forehead resting on it like a cushion, I can feel his chest hair brush against my back.

After a few slow movements in and out of me, I'm ready, backing into him to signal I want more. As his rhythm builds up pace, his heavy breathing down my neck, one arm is wrapped around my waist, his other across my chest. I twist my spare hand around his back, pulling him in closer. His skin's warm, wet with sweat.

There's another man now standing next to me, same height, a beard, that's all I can really make out.

I would never like an audience. But in this moment, when it feels so good like this, I don't care.

The rhythm is faster now, rougher.

Another man appears from my other side. I don't really see his face before he is kissing me, he's stroking my cock, which is completely solid.

I feel more eyes on me, bodies near me, hands are touching me, like I'm cocooned in a mass of heaving testosterone.

The room is whirly, I'm feeling hazy.

But this still feels good. I think, anyway.

Another man is kissing me, others still touching me.

A man is on his knees now sucking me off.

What time is it?

I'm being pounded now, the slap of skin on skin still loud above the thumping dance music.

I break away from the man kissing me. It's the guy who I thought was fucking me.

Wait, what?

I turn to see who's inside me but can't twist around enough.

More people around me.

Benny.

The name pops into my head.

Or does someone say it.

The sex gets rougher as it feels like my partner climaxes.

But then it's starting again.

Feels different.

Benny.

I hear it again. Is someone saying it to me?

Is someone else inside me?

The music thumps, I'm feeling woozy.

"Benny."

No, I heard it that time.

"No, stop," I say.

No one listens to my command. Hands still all over me. Someone still inside me, their hands gripping my shoulders.

My head is burning up, pounding to the rhythm of the dance beat.

The heat.

The intense feeling.

Too much.

Overwhelming

Can't breathe.

"Stop. Stop!" I shout.

I push the men away from me and turn to get out of this wall of men I'm trapped inside.

The guy who was inside me, steps back, looking confused. I don't recognise his face.

I need air.

I need water.

I need to not be here.

Pushing myself away from the wall, I pull my underwear up, still feeling dizzy and not quite in control of my legs, like I'm wading through treacle wearing roller skates. My skin is hot, slick with sweat, and my head is pounding to the same tempo as the bassline, every beat thudding like a drum behind my eyes.

I know I need to go. Get out of here. Breathe. Water. Bed. Something, not this.

I make for the stairs—my personal yellow brick road to freedom and electrolytes—when something catches my eye in the shadows.

At first, I think I'm hallucinating again, that maybe the wooziness is morphing reality into some Freudian fever dream, but… no. I squint. Focus.

And it's definitely him.

Reece.

Bent over a table.

Getting railed by an old man.

Like, properly old. Silver-haired, pot-bellied, looks-like-he-owns-a-carpet-shop kind of old.

It's him. Immaculate, impossibly poised Reece, briefs around his ankles, moaning softly with his hands braced on the edge of the table as Old Father Time does his thing.

I blink once. Twice. Is this real?

It is. It really is.

And then something shifts.

Suddenly, Reece turns, pulling himself off the guy mid-thrust with a look of utter fury and horror on his face. Like the realisation of what he's doing has suddenly hit him.

"Get the fuck off me!" he yells.

The man stumbles back and falls—literally falls—onto the floor with a yelp, a kind of sad naked thud. Reece rounds on him, his fist curling, like he's about to punch him out right then and there, eyes wild, chest heaving.

For a second, I think he's going to do it.

But then—he stops.

His hand drops.

And without another word, pulling his briefs back around him, he bolts.

I stand there, blinking again.

Did that just happen?

My stomach turns. My mouth is dry. My head spins.

And somewhere in the background, the man still lies there on the floor, dazed and naked, looking around like someone who just got ghosted mid-sentence.

I take a deep breath.

Time to go.

Chapter 36

JOSH

Josh lies suspended in the sling, the leather straps cradling his body in a familiar embrace. The dim, pulsating lights of the club cast fleeting shadows across his skin, creating an interplay of light and darkness that mirrors the turmoil within him. The distant thump of bass reverberates through the walls, a constant reminder of the world outside this secluded corner.

He's lost track of how long he's been set up here, his legs in the air. Maybe an hour or so. But it has been a fairly quiet night. He's taken a couple of loads from a few guys, but not as many as normal.

Following his performances at Rocky's, the adrenaline still coursing through his veins, Josh often finds himself here. To the patrons, he is Miss Candy Chokem—a vivacious drag queen who commands the stage with charisma and flair. The transformation is his armour, allowing him to become someone else, if only for a few hours. But here, in the clandestine corners of Corruption, he sheds that persona, becoming just Josh—a man seeking connection in the most primal of ways.

Few recognise him out of drag, and he prefers it that way. The anonymity grants him freedom, a chance to escape the expectations and judgments that accompany his alter ego.

In this space, he isn't a performer; he is a participant, yearning for the touch of strangers to fill the void that applause and accolades can't reach.

Each encounter is a fleeting attempt to stave off the gnawing emptiness that has been his companion since childhood. Memories of neglect and abandonment have carved deep chasms in his psyche, leaving him to seek solace in the arms of anyone willing to offer it. The physicality of these encounters ground him, providing a temporary reprieve from the incessant whispers of unworthiness that echo in his mind.

He often wonders if he deserves more—if there is a possibility of genuine emotional attachment beyond these ephemeral liaisons. But the scars of his past run deep, and vulnerability is a luxury he can't afford. It's easier to surrender his body than to bare his soul.

A couple of dark shadows appear at the front of the doorway where his sling is perched. He can't make out their faces, he never can. This anonymity is customary; faces blurred into obscurity; identities reduced to mere physicality. Who they are never really matters.

After a few seconds, they turn and walk away.

Josh sighs and leans his head back, looking at the ceiling.

The thought of Greg's upcoming party stirs a flicker of excitement within him. Greg's gatherings are legendary, a nexus where pleasure and business intertwine seamlessly.

As a supplier, Greg provides him with the means to numb his pain and the commodities to peddle, ensuring a steady flow of income.

The parties are lucrative, offering a parade of potential clients eager to indulge in the night's hedonistic offerings.

This hadn't always been the nature of their relationship.

Josh used to look at Greg like he was the sun.

Back then—fresh off the plane, still carrying more hope than shame—Josh thought Gran Canaria was paradise, thought Greg was a god. Everyone did. He ran the parties, controlled the scene, had beautiful boys orbiting him like he'd been born with gravity. Greg saw Josh at a bar, bought him a drink, and by the end of the week, he was in Greg's bed, high for the first time, convinced he'd found something close to love.

But it wasn't love. It never had been.

It was grooming, only dressed up in glitter and compliments. Greg had a gift for making broken boys feel lucky to be chosen. He called Josh beautiful when he cried. Told him he had potential, called him "wild" like it was a good thing. Introduced him to men twice his age and passed him around like a party favour. Coke, G, pills—Josh didn't even know half the things Greg fed him back then. Just that it made him feel like something else. Something invincible. For a while.

Then, following the night of his overdose, waking up in a hotel room with a private doctor leaning over him, Greg was nowhere to be found. No calls. No messages. Just a crumpled €50 note on the bedside.

That was the end of *them*.

But not the end of everything.

Over the years, the nature of their relationship shifted. Josh stopped being a boy Greg wanted to touch—and became a man Greg realised he needed. A provider. A connector. Josh's natural talent for connecting with people meant he had contacts, clients, quiet influence. He knew who was cheating, who was spiralling, who to approach and who to avoid. And he never forgot anything.

Their arrangement now is practical. Transactional. Greg throws him a party invite or a name. Josh delivers product and discretion. Neither of them pretends it's anything more.

But beyond the transactions, there is a thrill in the chaos—a semblance of control in orchestrating others' highs, even when he struggles to manage his own lows. The anticipation of the party is a beacon, a distraction from the monotony of his nightly routines.

Lost in his thoughts, Josh almost doesn't notice the figure approaching him. The club's dim lighting obscures the stranger's features, rendering him a silhouette against the backdrop of flashing lights.

The stranger's movements are deliberate, exuding a confidence that borders on predatory, as he circles the sling. A rush of excitement surges through Josh, as he lays back and closes his eyes, feeling the man move around him.

Without a word, the stranger moves behind him, his presence a looming shadow.

Strong hands grasp either side of Josh's head.

So he wants me to suck him, Josh thinks. A little more work than just lying there, but it has been a slow night, so Josh is happy to oblige. He's learned to adapt, to surrender control as a means of finding it.

Josh tilts his head back, his mouth open, lips ready for service.

But that doesn't happen.

The grip around his head is firm and unyielding. Uncomfortable.

A flicker of confusion crosses Josh's mind, a realisation that something was amiss.

This is not playing out as expected.

But there is no time to process this.

Before he can react, a sharp, violent twist to the right, snaps his neck downward.

Darkness envelops him instantly, a final escape from the void he could never quite fill.

In the dimly lit club, amidst the pulsing lights and oblivious patrons, Josh's body hangs limp in the sling, body facing up, head facing down—a tragic testament to a life spent searching for connection in the shadows.

Chapter 37

DAN

I wake up feeling like someone's been using my skull as a maraca. My head is pounding, my mouth tastes like the inside of a festival portaloo, and my tongue is stuck to the roof like it's been stapled there.

For a few glorious seconds, I don't remember anything.

And then it all comes flooding back.

Well, bits of it, anyway.

The club. The men. The room. The crowd. The sex. The hands. Jesus.

And then Reece. Bent over a table. That bit hits me like a slap with a wet towel.

I groan and pull the sheet over my face. Maybe if I hide under here long enough, I'll stop being the main character in a cautionary tale.

My phone buzzes loudly on the bedside table, making me jolt like I've been tasered. I blindly slap around until I find it.

Alex.

Of course.

I answer, my voice hoarse and cracked. "Morning…"

"Oh, so you're still alive?" Alex chirps down the line, his tone far too perky for this hour or for my level of near-death.

"Just," I groan back. Holding the phone to my ear becomes the greatest struggle of my life, so I put the phone on speaker and rest it on my chest.

"I thought I'd check in, make sure you haven't joined a cult or got married to a Spanish twink."

"I mean… not married," I mumble, flopping back onto the pillow. "But I'm definitely questioning all my life choices."

Alex laughs. "So, a standard holiday then."

"Pretty much. Although this one includes being potentially drugged and gang groped by an army of horny men."

"Ah, a night in Corruption." This is a statement rather than a question. Alex knows me all too well.

"Indeed."

"Potentially drugged?"

"Oh, I don't know, I took some water from some handsome stranger and then just went a bit wibbly."

"Ah, I remember the days of being wibbly."

"Did it result in you being hammered against a wall by a group of men?"

"No, not my style. I hope you enjoyed it?"

"Yeah, maybe." I don't know the answer to that question.

"Remember, consent is sexy."

"Yeah, not everyone got the memo on that over here."

"Okay, and do we need to talk some more about this?"

"No, no God no, I'll save that for therapy when I get home."

Alex sighs. "Okay, so, any more mystery suicides you're planning on solving instead?"

"Well fortunately, everyone is very much alive as far as I know, but these lads are definitely hiding something." I start to perk up.

"Oh, why is this?" I sense Alex leaning into the telephone to get the tea.

"Reece and Tommy had a full-on fight at Rocky's last night, proper handbags at dawn style."

"No idea who either of these guys are but do tell me more."

"Reece is the one who looks at me like he wants me dead."

"Okay, and Tommy?"

"He's like this pretty boy mess. Looks perfect but is in a permanent cycle of being drunk and hungover."

"Which you can't judge him for?"

"No, I relate to his apparent alcoholism."

"And what was this argument about?"

"Tommy mentioned the name Benny."

"Oh, like your last man?"

"Yes! Then Reece went berserk and they had a fight."

"Gay drama," Alex adds.

"Indeed," I say. "But then I followed them—"

"Dan!" Alex interrupts, exasperated by me.

"Yes, but I had to!"

"What did I tell you about following people!?"

"I just wanted to know what was going on!"

I hear Alex sigh down the phone. "And what did you discover?"

"Well, they were still arguing and then Tommy shouted, 'But you killed him!'" I say, twinged with drama.

"Fuck off," Alex says, not believing me.

"I swear!"

"Was this before or after you were drugged? It sounds like after."

"Alex, this happened, I promise. I'm sure something went down here with Benny and they're all covering it up."

"So, Reece killed Benny. Then a couple of years later returned to the scene of the crime and started shouting about it publicly in the street with his friend. This all sounds very probable."

Alex's sarcasm makes me feel stupid. "Well, you had to be there. And then on top of that, I saw Reece, perfect, stuck-up, arrogant Reece, being railroaded over a table by a ninety-year-old in Corruption last night!"

"A ninety-year-old?"

"Well, he may as well have been. Why would he do that? He's full of guilt and self-hatred."

"Maybe he's into ninety-year-olds."

"*Or* maybe he's just punishing himself, like a form of self-harm."

"For murdering Benny?"

"Yes! I knew you'd come around."

Alex sighs again. "And what does Hugo say about this alleged murder of his ex-boyfriend?"

"I've not told him yet."

"Okay well maybe you should do?"

"Should I?"

"Well maybe don't open with the murder bit. Try and be sensitive."

"Okay," I rub my temples and let out a sigh.

"And murder plot aside, you're having fun?"

"Yeah, I think. It's all a bit... blurry. But I remember enough to know I need an exorcism and probably a therapist."

"And a course of Doxycycline."

"Oh yes, that too. Plus a Berocca," I groan again. "My liver hates me."

"Join the club. Now get up, hydrate, and whatever you do-"

"Yeah?"

"Do *not* open Grindr until you've had coffee."

He's right. God, he's right.

I hang up and lie there for a moment, trying to piece myself back together.

*

An hour later, hangover in full flow, I'm sensitively telling Hugo that I think his holiday romance from two years ago was murdered and covered up by Reece.

Hugo just blinks at me a lot.

"I'm sorry, what?" he says, after a moment of processing.

"I think that maybe Reece murdered Benny," I say with conviction.

"Um, that's a little bit of a stretch," Hugo replies, not buying my theory.

"But it all did turn nasty at Rocky's, once Tommy mentioned Benny's name."

"Okay...?"

"And remember they all denied knowing Benny and now..." I look at Hugo to endorse my hypothesis.

"Okay...?" is again all he can say.

"Come on, Hugo, there is definitely something going on here."

"I mean, maybe they do remember him. Maybe. But covering up a murder, come on now." Hugo raises his bushy eyebrows as he talks.

"But he just completely disappeared!"

"Or he just ghosted me."

"They must have known him," I insist.

"Look, I spent about seven days with Benny here, and I never saw him with them once."

I frown.

"And to be fair, as beautiful as I thought Benny was, he was scrawny and lanky with a big lovable nose and a pot belly, which doesn't seem like a classic acquaintance of someone like Reece. Not exactly Insta friendly."

"Well, tell that to Grandad who was pounding him in Corruption last night," I say, feeling like I'm playing my trump card.

"Which you saw while you think you were high on drugs?"

"I saw it!" I insist.

Hugo sighs, a similar tone to Alex. "Okay, okay. If you want to pursue this, then fine, but I'm not getting involved. Just be careful, sounds like Reece has a temper."

"He does."

"I don't want him to murder you," Hugo says with faux seriousness.

I roll my eyes.

"Right, drink your coffee," Hugo says. "We're meeting Jessie and the rest of the Manson family in twenty minutes to go to the beach.

"Urgh," I say. "I hate the beach."

"How can you hate the beach?"

"Just all that sand—gets everywhere."

"Well, we'll be going via the Dunes, so that should perk you up," Hugo says with a wink.

"I don't know," I say, shaking my head. "Think I've been involved in enough gangbangs in the last twenty-four hours, don't want to get caught up in another."

"Come on!" Hugo cries. "It'll be fun!"

And with no other apparent choice, I'm off to the Dunes.

Chapter 38

DAN

It’s midday, and the sun is already angry. Not warm and gentle like it was when we first arrived—this is hostile sunshine, the kind that fries the top of your scalp through your receding hair.

Hugo and I meet Jessie, Dito, Mason and—to my surprise—Reece outside the hotel entrance. Jessie is, of course, bouncing off the walls already, sunglasses pushed up into her hair like she’s filming a travel vlog.

“Boys! You made it! Let’s go, I’m sweating my tits off here, I want to jump in the sea!” she announces, adjusting her kaftan, which today is flamingo-themed and clashing violently with the beach towel draped over her shoulder.

Dito and Mason say hi, and Reece kind of nods. We have some sweaty hugs with Jessie and start to move.

There’s no sign of Tommy.

“Where’s Disasterpants?” Hugo asks, scanning the group.

Jessie waves her hand. “Oh, he’s gone full ghost mode, which usually means he’s either passed out in a stranger’s bed, or lying in a gutter somewhere trying to piece together his name. Standard Tommy behaviour. He’ll turn up eventually.”

It's a ten-minute walk or so from our hotel before we reach the start of the dunes. As we enter, I can already feel the heat bouncing back at me from the sand, like we’re entering some post-apocalyptic gay Mad Max landscape.

“So, I had to slap this German guy yesterday!” Jessie announces.

“Oh, any reason?” Hugo asks.

"Well, we were chatting for ages, he bought me a bunch of cocktails, I was all ready to take him back to my hotel room and give him the best tit wank of his life."

"As you would," Mason adds.

Everyone nods.

"But then he had the nerve to call me sturdy."

"Oh," is all Hugo can say.

I stay quiet.

"Don't get me wrong, I'm a sturdy bitch. I used to play scrum half at the Widnes Ladies Rugby Club," Jessie declares. "But that's not the words I want to hear to give me wide-on."

I briefly process the concept of a wide-on in my head, before deciding this is not for me.

"Oh, so no tit wank for him then?" Dito asks.

"No, but he did slip a cheeky finger in up my skirt while we were chatting at one point. That was before the sturdy comments though."

"Ah, I see," Hugo nods.

The walk through the dunes continues, and I can't help but feel slightly disappointed. I expected more.

I don't know—maybe I've just spent too long hearing mythologised versions of this place. Every gay man I've ever met who's been to Gran Canaria talks about the dunes like they're some mythical queer pilgrimage site. Like the sand is paved with glitter and foreplay.

But walking through them in the middle of the day? It's just quiet.

No crowds. No harnessed Adonises swinging from palm trees. No orgies behind every bush. Just endless golden sand, occasional gusts of hot wind, and the gentle wheeze of Jessie complaining about her thighs chafing.

The dunes stretch out in every direction like a massive, sun-bleached duvet someone forgot to make. The heat rises off the ground in visible shimmers, and every step is a calf workout I did not consent to.

It's beautiful, don't get me wrong—breathtaking, even. We barely pass a soul. No cruisers. No naked wanderers. Just footprints in the sand, slowly filling in with windblown dust.

I thought it would be like walking into some hyper-sexual gay mirage, but instead it feels like a quiet moment in the desert where the only thing making noise is your own thoughts and Jessie's flip-flops.

As we walk, I become conscious that Dito is slowing down, staring at his phone.

His expression shifts.

"Wait…" he says, eyes scanning the screen. "Two people died last night. At the Yumbo."

We all stop and turn to him.

Jessie leans over. "What?"

"Look—" He holds his phone up so we can see the headline: "Two Dead in Overnight Incident at Yumbo Centre."

Dito gives us the breakdown as he scans the article. "No names. No details. Just vague statements about 'a tragic incident' and that Corruption has been shut down pending investigation. Police presence heavy."

"Dan and I were in Corruption last night!" Hugo announces.

Everyone stares at me for some reason with eyes of judgement. And my heart takes a road trip up into my mouth. "Well, I didn't see anything," I say, and my eyes can't help but look at Reece who is keeping his eyes to the floor.

"No, me neither, it was fairly quiet last night. My God, I wonder what happened?" Hugo says.

Jessie frowns. "I mean… I know it's Gran Canaria, but two deaths in one night?

"And that guy who hung himself last week," Dito adds, looking at me.

"My God, what the hell happened?"

Dito exhales, still reading. "No names yet. But it says there were witnesses at the club who are being interviewed."

"Must be drugs right?" Reece says. "Someone's taken something dodgy."

"Yeah, maybe," Mason says.

We stand there awkwardly in the shifting sand, the mood completely flattened. Even Jessie's bouncing stops.

"Do you think Tommy…?" Hugo asks quietly, but Jessie waves him off.

"Nah. Like I said, he'll be spooning someone who still lives with their parents. He's fine. I mean—he's feral, but he's fine."

Hugo nods.

"But I'll text him again just in case," Jessie says, whipping her phone out.

*

About twenty minutes later, we've finally made it to the beach.

And by "made it," I mean survived the 30-minute hike through the Sahara in flip-flops, battling dunes, sunstroke, and Jessie's non-stop narration about how she once "nearly died" on a hen do in Marbella.

Now we're spread out like a mismatched Pride-themed picnic, towels overlapping, bags bursting with SPF, snacks and currently-cold-but-won't-be-for-long beers.

Hugo and Jessie are already in full-on banter mode, screech-laughing about something I didn't hear, and now it's too late to ask. Jessie's lying on her side like a glamour model from a plus-size Lambrini commercial, Hugo propped up on his elbows, both of them shouting over each other in chaotic harmony.

Reece is stretched out a few feet away, sunbathing silently, one knee slightly bent, arms behind his head like he's posing for an ad campaign. The body of an Adonis and the soul of a closed wardrobe.

Splashing around in the sea already, Dito appears to be having a whale of a time on his own, waist-deep and grinning, splashing water on his chest to cool down.

And Mason is off to the side, sat upright on his towel, staring at his phone like it's personally offended him. No expression. Just aloof, vaguely haunted energy, like he's either deep in thought or texting Satan.

I lie back, dig into my bag, and casually open Grindr—as one does when surrounded by the genetically blessed and desperate for any external validation.

A bunch of messages await me. Most I ignore, but one immediately catches my eye.

Jimmy! The bartender from Rita's, that I potentially may have a bit of a crush on.

Hey, handsome ☺

I sit up a bit straighter like my phone can see me. Heart doing a small, excited flutter. I glance around, like I'm committing a crime.

Hey! Fancy seeing you on here. Thought you might be too classy for this mess.

Please. I work at the Yumbo Centre and live off mojito tips. Classy left me in 2009. You on the beach today?

Yeah, just got here. You spying on me?

Only a little. Saw you as I was going to work. You looked cute walking towards the dunes.

My whole face goes hot. Is this flirting? This feels like flirting.

Flattery will get you absolutely everywhere.

Good. Maybe it'll get me a drink later. Or something slightly filthier. Depending on your mood. ☺

Okay, yes. Definitely flirting.

I'm always in a filthy mood ☺

Glad to hear it. Just got to work, will text in a bit.

I bite the inside of my cheek to stop myself from grinning like a teenage girl in a coming-of-age movie. I shut down Grindr before my grin gives the game away.

It's fine. Just a message. Just Jimmy. A mildly flirty exchange and I'm acting like I've just been proposed to.

Calm down, Dan. It's not a rom-com.

Before I can sink too far into a mental spiral about whether or not a winky smiley actually means anything these days, Hugo and Jessie stand up in unison, brushing sand off themselves with the kind of aggressive flair usually reserved for interpretive dance.

"We're going for a little wander," Jessie declares. "I want to get a pic of that rock shaped like a willy."

"Yeah, and I need to walk off that packet of crisps I inhaled," Hugo adds.

They head off, chattering loudly, leaving behind Reece, who is fully horizontal and in a deep, model-like coma, and Mason, still perched on his towel, scrolling on his phone with all the joy of someone checking their bank balance after a trip to Zara.

I glance around. It's just us.

Brilliant.

As part of my self-growth, every now and then I force myself to indulge in some awkward small talk with someone who has no interest in talking to me. Partly to get me more used to the discomfort that rocks through my body during it. Partly to prove that it matters not one bit whether the other person is interested in talking to me or not as I am worthy enough as an individual. This is all helpful advice from ChatGPT as I can't afford a therapist to tell me these things without giving up luxuries like Jessica Fletcher inspired cruising holidays to Gran Canaria.

Anyway, I decide Mason is an opportune victim to try this self-harming ritual on. I hesitate for a beat, then awkwardly clear my throat.

I take a breath.

"Nice out here, isn't it? Peaceful."

Mason looks up, surprised that I've started a conversation. "Uh yeah, I suppose," he vaguely agrees.

I nod.

There's a pause as I plan my next attempt to interact. "Not a beach person?"

He shakes his head. "Nah, not really."

"*Too much sand*," we both say in unison, which makes Mason smile and laugh.

"Yeah, exactly," Mason agrees.

"It just gets everywhere."

"Everywhere!" he says, suddenly animated. "And not just here, when it follows you back to the hotel."

"Yes. And somehow four days later you can still feel it in your underwear."

"How does it do that?"

"No idea." I smile.

He gives a little shrug. “And too many beautiful people pretending not to know they’re beautiful.”

I huff a laugh, noting the irony of Mason judging the beautiful people. But I’ve seen an opening, so I’ll go with it. “Yeah. I’ve already body-shamed myself four times and I’ve only been sat down twenty minutes.”

Mason looks around at the flux of gays in speedos that surround us. "People don’t see it, but half of these guys are just as messed up as anyone else. They're just better at hiding it."

"Yeah, well... I’m more of a ‘let the internal spiral show on the outside’ type."

“Oh well, that’s the best way to be.”

“Honestly, I only came on this holiday because I hear drinking everyday somewhere sunny is more socially acceptable.”

“Which it is. And replace ‘drinking’ with ‘complete emotional breakdown’ and same.”

“Ah, okay, good to know. So, this holiday is about getting some self-care?”

Mason tilts his head. “My version of self care is pretending I’m fine until someone cries or is arrested.”

I know he’s joking, but behind the lightness, I can tell there is something more to this story. But I carry on as it’s nice to feel a small connection with him. “Yeah, I should be indulging in some self-care myself rather than drinking my way through the day and thinking about not practicing mindfulness ever.”

“I drink to forget that I drink too much.”

“Sounds like a fun cycle.”

“It is. You don’t seem that broken though. Bit quiet, but not broken.”

“Oh, I’m very much broken, don’t you worry,” I say, flicking a bit of sand off my knee. “Like most of the gays in my era. All a bit fucked up. Raised on shame and internalised homophobia. The Daily Mail hanging around the house, Section 28, those fucking horrific AIDS adverts. No wonder we’re all screwed up.”

Mason snorts, then nods, slowly. “Christ. That’s bleak. But accurate, I suppose.”

“We’re the generation of trauma response dressed as personality.”

He gives me a look—somewhere between amusement and recognition. "Yeah. That feels familiar. I suppose we've all had fucked up childhoods."

"Presented as perfect childhoods," I add.

"Oh, well speak for yourself, mine wasn't perfect at all," Mason confesses.

"Oh, sorry to hear that."

"It's fine, just classic broken family, Mum trying to make ends meet living in a rough part of Manchester. Homophobia was just a sport for most back then."

"Sounds tough," I say genuinely.

"Yeah, well it is what it is," he says, shrugging.

And just as I'm enjoying the small connection Mason and I have shared, Jessie comes bounding back to us at full speed, her tiny bikini clinging on to her volatile breasts for dear life.

"One of the guys who died at the Yumbo last night! Only got his fucking head chopped off!" she screams.

Chapter 39

JESSIE

Jessie doesn't bother to wait for dramatic effect—she blurts it out the second she's in earshot. Everyone turns to stare like they've all been bitch-slapped.

The words hit like a gust of cold wind in the middle of the scorching dunes. Dan sits up straighter, his sunglasses slipping slightly down his nose. Mason's head snaps up. Reece, of course, says nothing—but his jaw tightens.

"Wait, what?" Mason asks, blinking. "Like murdered?"

"That's what they're saying," Jessie confirms, her voice hushed now. "We overheard two guys talking and I asked them about it. Police everywhere. Proper crime scene."

"Shit, both of them?" Reece says, firmly out of his nap coma.

"Sounds like it," Jessie confirms.

"Well, we don't know that they both lost their heads, but it seems like they were no accident!" Hugo declares.

"So that's three guys dead after your mate killed himself," Reece says, glaring at me like I sent him over the edge.

I don't respond.

"Jeez, what a week," Hugo says.

"Maybe the Yumbo's been cursed," Jessie says, apparently seriously. "Because of all the debauchery that's happened over the years."

"That's probably not happened," Mason rolls his eyes.

"But three deaths in a week is insane," Dito says.

"Actually, it's four," Dan says. Everyone turns to him. "I read about it at the hotel yesterday. A guy fell off the roof at the Yumbo or something."

"No way," Hugo says. "Who?"

"I don't know. Some local businessman I remember it saying."

Silence falls. The kind of silence that only exists when something suddenly feels real.

But inside Jessie's head, the noise is deafening.

She tries to shake it off, the way she always does. But there's a sick feeling starting to rise in her stomach, and this time it's not from one too many cheap rosés the night before.

It's Tommy.

Where *was* he?

He'd been missing since early morning—standard Tommy behaviour, sure. Disappearing after a heavy night was as much a part of him as that stupid dolphin tattoo wearing sunglasses on his leg and his flirtatious smirk. But something about today felt different.

"I know I'm being ridiculous, but there's something in my tits that's making me worry about Tommy."

"I'm sure he's fine," Hugo says gently, picking up on her expression.

"Oh, he texted me earlier. Said he met some guy and was crashing at his," Mason casually drops into the conversation.

"Oh," is all Jessie can say at first. "He didn't message me."

Mason just shrugs.

"Well at least you know he's okay," Hugo adds, clearly trying to pacify the situation.

Jessie nods slowly, her face betraying nothing, but inside, her heart does a small drop. Of course. Some guy. That's always the story. That's always the excuse.

It's not the first time Tommy's wandered off mid-holiday, mid-conversation, mid-*her*. And every time, she tells herself it's fine. That this is just who he is. That he's spontaneous. Free-spirited. A mess in human form.

But beneath all that, what she never says out loud is that it hurts. Every time.

Because she always ends up being the one left on the beach towel, watching the tide roll in and pretending she doesn't care.

She had hoped this trip would be different. That maybe it would bring them closer again. But once again, she's just being treated as someone insignificant in his life. And she hates herself for how desperate that makes her feel.

Now, with murder in the mix, the whole island feels heavier.

"Did he say who the guy was?" she asks Mason, casually.

Mason shrugs. "No. Just said he was alive and getting laid. His words, not mine."

She lets out a soft, breathy laugh, the kind people mistake for amusement but is really just her trying to breathe past the lump in her throat.

So, Tommy really was fine—safe, hungover, probably naked in someone else's bed. But the problem wasn't where he was. It was why he didn't tell her.

Why he never told her anything anymore.

She's tired of being the one chasing after him. Of being the friend who *cares too much* and gets nothing back.

"Right," she says, shaking herself off then plonking herself down onto her towel. "Well. I'm not letting a murder ruin my tan."

Everyone chuckles, but no one really laughs.

Jessie puts on her sunglasses and leans back, pretending to sunbathe. But under the surface, she's not thinking about tans or cocktails or cute boys anymore.

She's thinking about Tommy.

And she's angry. Very angry.

Chapter 40

DAN

The sun is scorching today. Not in a dreamy, holiday brochure sort of way—more like I'm being lightly seared alive in a human-sized air fryer. I shift uncomfortably on my towel, which is now approximately the temperature of a stovetop.

It's quiet. Hot. Tense.

No one is speaking at this point. Even Jessie is uncharacteristically quiet. Everyone is on their phones, playing detective, trying to gather more information about what happened at the Yumbo last night.

Then Dito returns from the sea, water still dripping down his chest. He glances at us all, registering the mood instantly.

"Okay, what's going on?" he asks, brows raised.

Hugo looks up. "We just heard some news. About the people that died last night?"

Dito shakes his head, grabbing his bottle of water. "Heard what?"

Mason just casually adds, "They were murdered."

Dito freezes. "Wait—both of them?"

Jessie nods, looking up from her phone. "Yeah. One inside Corruption—I'm just reading now, a guy had his neck snapped."

I wince. "Jesus…"

Mason continues, "And another one found this morning. Hung upside down. Head cut clean off." He squints at his phone as he reads. "Naked, so they haven't ID'd him yet."

There's a silence that follows that kind of statement. Not just awkward—*heavy*. Like the kind of pause where everyone suddenly becomes very aware of their own heartbeat.

"Fuck," Dito mutters, finally sitting. "That's… that's insane."

Hugo shakes his head. "They must be connected, surely? I mean, that's not random club drama. That's… serial killer energy."

"Why would anyone do anything so horrific?" Jessie says, shaking her head.

"I wonder," I say, maybe too quietly, because everyone turns to look at me.

"What do you mean?" Hugo asks.

Jessie tilts her head. "You think someone had it out for them?"

I shrug, not really sure why I've opened my mouth but unable to stop now. "I just mean… you don't hang someone upside down and decapitate them unless you're really angry with them. Someone must've had a reason."

"Is there any reason that's worth decapitating someone?" Dito asks.

"Well, no, but surely in their head they must have thought they deserved it." Everyone's eyes are laser focused on me, which makes my heart beat out of my chest. But I have to continue. "I mean, I'm not an expert in plotting the perfect murder, but if you just want someone dead, surely there are many more simple, cleaner ways of doing it."

"I mean, hanging someone upside down and decapitating them is the more excessive way," Dito agrees.

"From the Yumbo Centre sign too," Mason adds, nodding as he reads the information from his phone.

"Fuck my fanny," Jessie says in disbelief.

"Exactly," I continue. "It's so high risk. Only rage would make you do something so gruesome."

"Well," Reece says suddenly, voice cool and detached, "maybe they were just bad people."

It lands with a dull thud in the middle of the group.

I glance over at him. Still flat on his back, sunglasses on, like he's commenting on the price of petrol.

Jessie shifts onto her side. "Bit harsh, don't you think?"

Reece shrugs. "Just saying. People do shitty things all the time. Sometimes, the world catches up."

"Still," Hugo adds carefully, "being a shitty person doesn't exactly warrant being murdered in a dark room."

Reece finally sits up a little, resting on one elbow. "Depends what they did, doesn't it?"

Jessie blinks. "Sorry, are you actually saying they deserved it?"

"I'm saying," Reece replies, voice low and measured, "that some people are just bad through and through. Maybe they got what's coming to them."

I stare at him. The sun suddenly feels colder, or maybe I'm just registering the goosebumps on my arms. It's not just what he said—it's how casually he said it. Like he's not just speculating.

He lies back again, as if that settles the matter. The conversation fizzles out with it, everyone unsure what to say next.

I glance at Jessie. Her mouth is tight, like she's chewing on the silence. Dito says he's going back to paddle in the sea. Mason's back on his phone. Hugo offers me a crisp, which I decline, because I'm feeling queasy.

That comment wasn't normal.

It also didn't sound hypothetical.

I'm watching Reece out of the corner of my eye. Watching the way he exhales. The way his hands are still. The slow rise and fall of his chest.

A few minutes pass before he sits up again and grabs his towel. Without a word, he stands, brushes himself off, and starts walking down the beach toward the dunes. I see him texting on his phone as he walks away.

Jessie watches him go. "What's his problem?"

Nobody answers.

I sit there a moment longer, then slowly get to my feet.

"I'm gonna cool down in the sea," I lie.

No one stops me or notices as I walk in the opposite direction from the ocean.

Instead, I follow Reece.

Chapter 41

DITO

Dito walks slowly toward the sea, the sand warm between his toes, the crash of the waves a steady hum in the background. Behind him, the others continue to lounge—sunbathing, chatting, probably dissecting the strange turn the trip has taken.

He doesn't blame them. Four deaths in less than a week tend to shift the holiday vibe.

He reaches the water and lets it lap at his ankles, cool and calming. He closes his eyes for a moment, breathing in the salty air. This is where he feels most grounded—water, wind, no one performing or posturing.

Maybe they were just bad people.

Reece's words linger in his mind like the final line of a play. Brutal. Blunt. But Reece always speaks in absolutes—like he's allergic to nuance.

Still… sometimes the bluntest people speak the hardest truths.

Not that anyone in this group knows what truth looks like anymore. They're all pretending, in some way. Reinventing. Dodging the mirror. Creating versions of themselves that suit the setting.

And Dito's no better.

He's the master of self-presentation—whatever the crowd needs, that's who he becomes. Quiet and brooding around the intense ones. Bubbly with the extroverts. A little mysterious when it suits. It's not dishonest exactly—it's... adaptive. It keeps things light. Easy. Surface-level.

He was raised to be like this.

His mum—Portuguese, graceful, always five steps ahead of everyone in the room—is a body language analyst by profession. Not some TikTok psychic or fluffy life coach. A real expert. She consults on criminal investigations, corporate lie detection, jury assessments. Dito grew up around conversations about micro-expressions, eye-line deviations, hand tension, vocal pitch changes. She once told him she could tell when his dad was lying by the way his nostrils flared.

His dad, meanwhile, is a high-flying British entrepreneur—charming, old-school, the kind of man who orders claret at lunch and closes million-pound deals over dessert. From him, Dito learned the art of conversation, the importance of thank-you notes, and that networking is just making people like you enough to owe you something.

Between the two of them, he's been raised with manners, charm, and emotional intelligence that could cut glass.

But sometimes he wonders what it's all for.

In fairness, he's not always displayed this level of maturity and confidence, but over the last couple of years, he's felt it develop, coming to the surface stronger than ever.

For all his social dexterity, Dito still finds himself surrounded by people who are spinning out of control. Jessie, hiding her loneliness behind eyeliner and big laughs. Mason, simmering with unspoken rage. Tommy, chaotic and crumbling. Reece, cold and calculating.

And Dan, granted he's known him all of five minutes, sweet but clearly drowning under the weight of his own insecurities.

Stepping deeper into the water, he lets it wash over his shins. He turns to look back at the group.

They're all lying to themselves, just trying to stay afloat, he thinks.

Just as Dito's about to wade in deeper, something catches his eye—movement at the edge of the beach, near the start of the dunes.

It's Reece, pulling on his vest and walking off into the dunes. A few seconds later, Dan appears, hesitating, glancing back toward the group, then trailing after him at a distance, awkward and obvious.

Dito narrows his eyes.

He stands there a moment longer, the sea swirling around his ankles, watching them disappear into the golden haze.

What is going on? he wonders.

Chapter 42

DAN

The Dunes are quieter than they should be. No breeze, no distant beach chatter. Just me and the soft crunch of sand under my feet as I follow Reece's trail, keeping far enough back to avoid detection—close enough that I might catch something.

He's on the phone now. I can't hear much, he's talking fluidly, but I just can't make out clearly anything that he's saying. I need to get closer.

I duck behind one of the bigger ridges, crouching like a child playing spy. This isn't the first time I've followed someone, if I'm honest. Eavesdropping is sort of my special skill. Not in a creepy way—okay, slightly creepy—but more in a *high-functioning anxiety mixed with nosy gay Sherlock Holmes* sort of way. People think silence means safety, but I've always found that quiet is where the good stuff leaks out. Most people confess to the air when they think no one's listening.

I lean forward just enough to make out a few stray phrases.

"Just call me back, when you get this, for fuck's sake," I do catch him say.

Damn, he's just leaving a voicemail and seems like I've missed it all.

I pause for a second, debating whether following Reece any further serves any purpose at all, and just as I make the conscious decision that I should head back, he stops walking. His head turns.

I duck—too late. He's already stopped walking. Silence stretches for a beat. Two. I peer up, and there he is—arms crossed, body angled like a man mid-ambush, sunglasses pushed up onto his head.

"You following me?" he calls out, loud enough to echo.

Shit.

I step out, brushing sand off my knees, trying to look more casual than I feel. "Uhhh, no. I wasn't following you. I was just… walking."

"In a straight line behind me, into the dunes?"

"Well, not like deliberately," I say defensively while knowing I was definitely deliberately following him.

Reece's mouth twitches, somewhere between amusement and irritation. "Why?"

I pause.

"Were you trying to listen in to my conversation?" he asks, his expression blank, giving nothing away.

Damn, he is good.

"No, of course not." More denial. He's seeing right through me.

He walks towards me slowly, his eyes narrowing, like a cat about to launch at an unsuspecting robin.

I think I make an audible gulp. But also, my brain has decided to stop working as the situation intensifies.

Conflict has never been my strong suit. The moment voices get raised or tension thickens in the air, my brain folds in on itself like a badly pitched tent. Words disappear, reason evaporates, and I'm left blinking like a stunned rabbit, desperate to retreat into the nearest hedge. I've always envied those people who can stay cool under pressure, who can deliver razor-sharp comebacks or stand their ground. Me? I just sweat and mentally black out, occasionally muttering something vague like "okay" or "that's fair" while my internal organs attempt to evacuate my body.

Reece glares at me, the same death stare I've seen before. "Then stay away from me," he says, before turning and walking away.

And this is good advice. I should just stay away from this, but, in that moment, something in my brain flips and I have to ask.

"Who's Benny to you?" I blurt out.

Reece's head flicks back. "What?"

"Benny. You know that name, right? I can tell, the way you react when you hear it."

"Dan, what the fuck are you talking about?"

"Benny. You and Tommy had a fight over it when he mentioned his name at Rocky's."

Reece doesn't respond.

"And Luca mentioned the name too, after he saw you guys. He recognised you."

His face stills. I've never seen Reece truly still before. He's always vibrating just under the surface—coiled, calculated, always half-prepping his next move.

I keep going. "I was behind the steps, after you and Tommy argued. I didn't mean to overhear, but I did. He said you killed someone."

Reece freezes. Something shifts in his eyes. "You heard what?"

"I heard you!" I shout, more certain. "You were arguing with Tommy. He said, *'You killed him!* I know what I heard, Reece. You didn't deny it. And if it wasn't Benny, then who was it?"

Reece laughs. But it's not funny. It's brittle, cracked at the edges.

"You think I killed Benny?" he says, stepping closer. "Is that what you've decided now? Did I kill those guys last night too, then?"

"I don't know what to think!" I shout. "But Benny went missing, everyone keeps being weird when his name is mentioned and you're acting like you've got nothing to hide when it's written all over your face."

"You don't know me," he growls, voice low now, dark. "You've known me five minutes."

"I know enough," I spit, my verbal diarrhoea coming out of the blue, like some rabid animal. "I know something happened last time you were here!"

That's when he punches me.

There's no warning, no cinematic build-up. Just the sharp crack of his fist against my jaw and the sky spinning as I hit the sand.

Pain explodes across my face and I taste blood in my mouth.

"Stay out of it, Dan," he snarls, towering over me, chest heaving. "You have *no idea* what you're talking about."

I push myself up, dazed. "Is this what happened to Benny?"

That sets him off.

One second he's glaring at me, the next he's on me—grabbing me by the collar, slamming me down into the sand so hard it knocks the wind from my chest. I grunt as my back hits the ground, the world lurching sideways. Before I can even react, his hand is at my throat.

It's not a full choke—not yet. But it's firm. Unmistakable. The way his fingers clamp down, thumb digging into the side of my neck, it's controlled.

His knees are straddling my hips, pinning me like I'm prey. His face looms above mine, eyes burning with fury, teeth clenched.

My heart is hammering so hard I can feel it behind my eyes. My limbs are going numb, not from lack of air—yet—but from panic. I want to speak, to de-escalate, but my mouth is dry, my tongue thick, and his hand is pressing down just hard enough to stop me from getting anything out beyond a stuttering gasp.

I bring my hands to his wrist, trying to push him off, but he's solid. Unmoving.

My legs thrash in the sand—pathetic.

I feel the edges of my vision starting to shimmer. My head throbs.

I need to move. Now.

With what little strength I have left, I reach blindly to the side, fingers scrabbling in the hot sand, searching for anything—anything—to grab onto. A stick. A bottle. A miracle.

Then—hard. Solid. Heavy.

My hand closes around a rock.

I don't think.

I just swing.

The thud is horrible—dull and wet, like someone slapping raw meat. Reece grunts as the blow lands just above his ear. He reels sideways with a curse, clutching his head as he falls off me. Sand flies in every direction as I roll away, coughing, spluttering, chest heaving like I've just broken the surface after drowning.

He stumbles back, one hand still pressed to his head, blood trickling down through his fingers. He's not speaking. Just breathing hard. His face is stunned.

I scramble to my feet, holding the rock between us like a wild-eyed Boy Scout who took self-defence a little too literally.

"Don't," I rasp, my throat raw. "Just—don't."

He doesn't move. He just stands there, staring at me through a haze of blood, sand, and whatever storm is going on behind those eyes.

"Jesus Christ," he says, wiping his face. "You actually hit me with a rock!"

I nod, still holding it. "Well, yeah—you were choking me!"

"I wasn't choking you," he says, still slightly dazed.

"You were fucking choking me!"

"You accused me of murdering Benny!"

"And this is supposed to convince me otherwise!"

And just like that, the temperature shifts. Still hot. Still tense. But something's cracked open between us now. Something sharp and strange and honest.

Reece takes off his vest and presses it against the gash I created on his head. It's like he's just been worn down.

"I didn't kill Benny," he says, calmly, earnestly. "You just triggered me, accusing me of something I didn't do. I've had enough of that in my life."

And for a moment, I see a brief glimpse of humanity behind Reece's beautiful, soulless eyes.

"It wasn't Benny. I didn't even know Benny. Not really. Yeah, I know the name, we met him briefly last year at a party. I don't know what happened to him."

"So, who did you kill?" I ask. I have to.

There's a long pause.

I don't expect Reece to answer, but he looks drained.

He rubs his eyes and to my surprise opens up.

After a big sigh, he starts.

"It was a few years ago," he says. "Tommy and I were walking home in the middle of the night, we'd just left a club back home. Some guys—three of them—decided to follow us, pick a fight. Called us queers, you know standard stuff. Pushed Tommy. One of them punched me."

He closes his eyes.

"Why am I telling you this?" Reece says, shaking his head trying to push himself up.

"What happened?" I ask, softly.

Now upright, Reece just looks at me. "Nothing, just forget I said anything," he says, as he starts to walk off, but is unsteady on his feet.

"So, you fought back? Hit them?"

Reece doesn't answer, holding his palm to his head.

"Yes," he finally admits.

"And someone died?" I ask.

"Look, it just escalated really quickly. I don't remember much after that. I saw Tommy go down, and I saw red. I just didn't stop punching until it was over. The next thing I knew, one of them was on the ground, barely breathing, and my hands were covered in blood."

He looks down at his palms now, covered in his own blood from his head, like it's serving as some kind of flashback.

Another pause.

"And…?"

Reece stares at me, his eyes piercing straight through me.

"And he died that night. We read about it online a few days later. A father of two. An 'unprovoked' attack. No one knew it was us. The other two didn't talk. We didn't either."

The air hangs heavy. Even the wind seems to have gone still.

"I tell myself he deserved it," Reece says. "And maybe he did, I don't know. He started it, right?" He looks at me as if he's looking for an agreement.

I stay blank faced.

Reece continues. "Tommy couldn't get over it, though. He feels a lot of guilt, regret, even though he's not responsible."

I sit in silence, still holding the rock. Not sure what to say. Not sure what this makes him.

Reece sighs, removing the bloodied vest from his head and checks whether the blood is still flowing. "I don't know why I'm telling you this. Maybe you've given me a concussion. Maybe I'm not thinking straight."

"Well, thank you for telling me the truth," is all I can say.

Reece nods, and with his eyes laser-focused on me, he ends with, "Just to be clear, if you tell anyone this, I will kill you."

Chapter 43

REECE

"How's your head?" Dan asks.

Reece presses his vest to the side of his head again where the rock connected—still tender, still bleeding a little. "It's fine," he lies.

"If it was really fine, you'd have said 'I've had no complaints'," Dan quips, which falls flat.

Reece just glares at him. They've broken down some walls, but they're not exactly in jokey fun times territory yet.

"So can I ask what did happen with Benny at the party?"

Reece shakes his head. "Nothing, there was a party at some beach house, Tommy and Mason came along. We met Benny there, he just looked totally out of place. No idea what he was doing there, we felt sorry for him."

"And what happened at the party?" Dan asks, but Reece has had enough now. He's opened up more than enough to Dan today and his head is still throbbing. He just wants to go back to his room.

"Nothing. It was just a party. A bit of fun, guys were there, some drinks, drugs, standard stuff."

"And did Benny get involved in that?"

Reece sighs like he's bored of this conversation already. "I don't know, I think he got something from a dealer there."

"The drag queen?" Dan asks

Reece glares at him, not quite sure how he knows about Miss Candy Chokem's side hustle. "Yeah."

"So, what happened then?"

At this point, Reece has lost complete interest in the topic and starts to walk away. "Oh, I don't know, Benny did some drugs, made a show of himself, who cares. Jesus, Dan, give it a rest. It was a party years ago. Why are you so obsessed with this?"

"He was seeing Hugo that's all," Dan says honestly. "They had a bit of holiday romance and then he just disappeared. I thought it would help him if he knew what happened."

Reece rolls his eyes. "Well, Hugo needs to move on and get over it," he says, checking his vest to see if the bleeding has stopped on his head.

Dan nods and takes it as his cue to leave.

"I'll leave you be then," Dan says.

Reece is unsure whether he's satisfied by his response and doesn't care in this moment. Dan doesn't apologise for hitting him with a rock, so Reece doesn't apologise for throttling him.

Just like that, Dan is gone. Reece watches until he disappears into the heat haze, the last glimpse of his awkward silhouette swallowed by the sand.

He presses his palm to the side of his head again where the rock hit. He deserves that. Not for what just happened. But for everything before it.

His mind drifts—unwillingly, yet inevitably—back to that night back home.

That stupid, terrifying, life-altering night.

The man he killed didn't even have a name to him at the time. Just a face twisted in hate, a voice barking slurs, fists flying without hesitation.

It just started as defence. Punches were thrown at him first. So, he just retaliated as you would. To protect yourself, to protect your friend.

But there was a point where the tables turned. His attackers were no longer fighting back, they couldn't.

And once he started, he couldn't stop.

He remembers the sound of his fists hitting bone. The hot splash of blood. The way Tommy screamed—not at their attacker, but at him.

And the worst part wasn't what happened.

The worst part was that Reece felt powerful doing it.

It was like all the rage he'd ever swallowed—every time he'd bitten his tongue, every time someone told him to tone it down, blend in, act straight, shut up, be grateful—it all erupted in one violent burst.

He never felt more alive than when he took that man apart.

And he's never felt more hollow since.

It wasn't just the attack. It was everything before that.

Growing up working-class, gay, invisible unless he was useful. Watching his mum scrub floors while men treated her like she didn't exist. Learning that in this world, kindness gets you nothing but bruises. That power isn't handed out—you have to *look* like you deserve it. You have to *take* it.

So he reinvented himself. Skin smooth. Body lean. Jaws chiselled. Clothes immaculate. He erased everything soft, everything vulnerable. Even his accent, slowly filed down to something neutral, professional, cosmopolitan.

He became someone people noticed. Someone they listened to.

Someone they feared.

And yet, no matter how sharp he looks or how high he climbs, that night follows him like a shadow stitched to his heels.

Reece doesn't want to be the villain in someone else's story.

He's already the villain in his own.

The woozy feeling in his head is starting to clear. *Shit, what have I done*, he thinks, regretting telling Dan.

He will go tell someone. Probably Hugo. Maybe Jessie. Maybe the police. Reece isn't sure. It's his word against Dan's, though, so he has no fear that it means anything.

But part of him feels a deep sense of relief, telling his side of the story. Letting that built up tension ease out of him.

Reece slowly starts to walk further into the Dunes, heading back towards the hotel.

Thinking about how Dan accused Reece of murdering Benny almost makes him laugh out loud. What planet is Dan on to jump to that conclusion?

What Reece said was true. To a certain extent.

He didn't know Benny before that night. Yes, they went to the same party together. He just looked like such a goon, with his wiry receding hair and scrawny frame. Tommy thought it would be funny to invite him along. Seeing him in that environment, with all the drugs and sex and God knows what else happening around him, looking like a lost puppy, it was all just supposed to be a laugh. Reece didn't really care either way but went along with it.

Benny was an adult, who made his own decisions.

Anything that happened later that night two years ago was nothing to do with Reece.

Benny was responsible for his own fate.

That's what he tells himself anyway, as he continues to walk on.

The sun's lower now, casting long shadows across the dunes, turning the golden sand a deeper, rustier hue. It's quiet. Still. Almost serene. The throb in his head is settling into something manageable and he's feeling calmer.

He doesn't hear the footsteps behind him.

Not until it's too late.

The blow comes sharp and sudden, a dull *thwack* at the base of his skull. His world tips sideways as pain explodes behind his eyes. He crashes to the ground, face-first into the sand, dazed, blinking up at the sky that suddenly looks too bright.

He groans, tries to push himself up with one hand, but a vicious kick lands squarely at the side of his ankle. There's a crunch. He screams—*no,* not screams, wails—and collapses, grabbing his foot.

The pain is blinding. Radiating up his leg like lightning. It's broken. He knows it instantly. The bone, or the joint. Maybe both. He tries to twist, to crawl, but his limbs feel loose, uncoordinated. His vision swims.

Then—another blow. Something heavy. A second *crack* to the side of his head.

This time, he rolls onto his back, barely conscious, sand stuck to the blood on his temple. He blinks up at the sky, then toward the figure now towering above him. Just a silhouette. Blurred by light, by confusion. His eyes won't focus.

He tries to speak. His voice doesn't come. Just a dry gasp.

The figure crouches. Reece thinks maybe they'll say something. Instead, they lift a rock—huge, rough-edged, heavy. The size of Reece's chest. Both hands needed to lift it.

Reece finally manages a whisper. Just one. "…wait…"

But there's no time to beg.

The rock comes down fast, slamming onto his skull with a sickening, wet crunch.

The sound echoes through the dunes.

And then, silence.

Reece doesn't move again.

His perfect face—flawless, sculpted, surgically maintained—is unrecognisable. The man who controlled every part of his image, who hid every crack, every flaw, has been reduced to nothing but blood and ruin.

The figure stands over the body for a moment. Breathing hard. Watching. Then disappears, swallowed back into the dunes as if they were never there.

And Reece—perfect yet flawed, broken and finally vulnerable—becomes another secret the island will try to bury.

Chapter 44

DAN

I'm lying on my bed, one leg hanging off the edge like I've melted there, still in the same swim shorts from earlier that are refusing to dry, the faint sting of sunburn blooming across my shoulders. The ceiling fan is spinning but offering the cooling power of a tired hamster with asthma.

I've got my phone resting on my chest, on speakerphone. Alex's voice crackles in and out, distorted by the questionable Wi-Fi.

"You what?" Alex shrieks through the speaker.

"I hit him with a rock," I mumble.

There's a pause. "Like… properly hit him?

"Yes. Like, connected with his head. There was a proper whack. It was awful."

"And he was trying to strangle you?!"

"Yes, I mean, he was kind of pinning me down by the neck. He just lost it."

"Dan!" he scolds, horrified but clearly thrilled. "Are you okay? Is he okay?"

"I think so. I didn't hit him *that* hard. I mean… I did. There *was* blood. But he seemed to bounce back eventually."

"Wow, you badass," Alex says, sounding impressed. "Who'd have thought you had it in you."

"I know!" I say. "I've never been in a fight before. Not even in Year 9 when Kelsey Dawes stole my gel pens and called me a virgin. I just—he had his hand on my throat, and I couldn't breathe, and the rock was there and—"

"Okay, okay," Alex cuts in, his voice softer now. "So, has it all been put to bed now? He's not going to kill you in your sleep?"

"No, I think we came to some kind of understanding. He walked it off. We talked. Well—he talked. Eventually."

Alex pauses. "So, what triggered him?"

I sit up slowly, the sheets sticky with sweat. The room's too quiet. I can still hear the low thrum of music from the pool bar in the distance, people laughing like nothing terrible's ever happened in the world.

"I accused him of killing Benny," I say.

"Benny? The guy you've never met, who may or may not have gone missing based on the zero evidence you have?"

"Well, you just make me feel silly when you say it like that."

"I think I'd throttle you if you pulled the same stunt with me."

"I mean there was some evidence."

"Oh yes, the mid argument confession with Toby."

"Tommy," I correct him.

"Right," Alex says, not buying my theory.

"So, presumably he denied it."

"Yes, straight away," I explain.

"As you would expect."

"But, post being hit over the head, he seemed to open up to me."

"Did you give him a concussion?"

"That's what he said!"

"So, what did he tell you?"

"Well, he explained to me what really happened."

"Which was …?"

"I promised I wouldn't say."

"You promised the guy who you thought was a murderer and nearly choked you an hour ago."

"Yes, I promised."

There's a pause, Alex with zero respect for my promises.

"Okay, fine, but you can't tell anyone," I give in.

"Just to remind you, I have no idea who any of these people are."

I sit up straight in bed.

"He said he killed someone," I say, quietly now, like someone could be listening. "Not Benny. Someone else. During a homophobic attack. A fight. He was protecting Tommy, and... he went too far."

"Shit," Alex whispers.

"Yeah."

There's a long pause between us. The weight of it all sitting heavy.

"And do you believe him?"

"I mean, he seemed genuine," I continue. "Probably the only time I've been around him where he seemed like a normal vulnerable human."

"Homophobe murdering aside," Alex adds.

"I don't think he was lying. I mean, he wasn't trying to impress me. He looked—ashamed. Not because he did it, but because that's just the person he is."

Alex hums thoughtfully. "That's the thing about trauma. It doesn't always come wrapped in remorse and redemption arcs. Sometimes it just makes people hard."

"Hmmm," is all I can really say to that.

"So, you don't think he killed Benny anymore?"

"No, I don't think so."

"So, are you going to put this whole Benny murder plot to bed?"

"Well, probably, however, just to make things even crazier, four people have died at the Yumbo in the last couple of days, and they think two were murdered."

"Jesus, what the fuck!"

"I know!"

"Okay please tell me this is not inspiring some kind of Miss Marple style investigation."

"No, no," I insist. "Just think it's weird, right? One suicide. One accident. Two murders. In less than a week."

"And who died?"

"Well, the two yesterday, no idea. The police are still trying to identify them. Then there was Luca."

"Post date suicide."

"Not my fault."

"Sure."

"Then there was some local businessman who fell off a roof or something, just an accident apparently. But there's been a lot of death at the Yumbo Centre this week. All seems like too big a coincidence."

"Yeah, strange."

We both ponder this in silence for a moment.

"Right gotta go, got a hookup coming around in ten," Alex informs me.

"Oh, go you," I respond.

"Before I go, standard gentle reminder that you're on holiday and not Nancy Drew."

"Fine, I know."

"Be safe, and no more strangulation fights, please."

"Of course."

I hang up.

Going into autopilot, I flick into Grindr. A collection of messages await, most of which I have no interest in, the standard collection or Hi's and dick pics. The only one I'm interested in is Jimmy's.

Hey, still up for meeting later?

My heart skips a little beat at the thought that he's still wanting to meet me.

Yes definitely! What time? Where do you fancy?

I'm working until 9pm, most of the bars are closing early because of what happened, fancy just coming over to mine at 10pm?

Fuck yes

Yeah that sounds great, I'll message you later

And with a hop, a skip and a jump, I peel my sweaty back off my bed, and dive into the shower to get ready to meet Hugo for dinner. What an evening this is shaping up to be!

Chapter 45

DAN

Hugo stares at me across the table, jaw slack, fork frozen in mid-air like his chicken skewer just personally insulted him.

"Reece *what*?"

"I know," I whisper, even though there's no one around to hear. "I'm still processing it myself."

I glance around the hotel restaurant, as if someone might be eavesdropping. But it's mostly old German couples trying to cut into overcooked lamb.

"I promised I wouldn't say anything to anyone," I tell him, "so, you have to promise me you won't either."

"Dan," he says, leaning in dramatically, "I've told no one about the time you gave Dave Whitby a hand job under the table at his own wedding. Of course I'm not going to tell anyone Reece's murder secret."

"Yeah, Dave Whitby wasn't my finest hour," I say, rolling my eyes at myself.

"No, it wasn't. But the point is my lips are sealed," Hugo assures me. "I mean, I will if I'm ever arrested and need a plea deal—but that's the only scenario."

I nod. "I'm pretty sure me giving a secret hand job to a groom at his wedding isn't plea-bargain material," I mutter, picking at a cold chip.

"Well, there you go then," Hugo says.

And with that I update Hugo on everything that happened with Reece in the dunes earlier.

I feel like I've been dropped into a different reality since this afternoon. Maybe it's the sun or being in my first ever fight. Or just all the talk of murder and suspicious deaths that keep cropping up. I'm tired, wired, and also strangely ravenous. Trauma really is a buffet of contradictions.

Then I see her—Jessie.

She spots us and walks over, all oversized sunglasses and floral wrap dress, but even under the forced pout and big hair, I can tell she's off. There's a *vibe*. She's clutching her phone like it owes her money.

"Evening, boys," she says, dropping into the chair beside me without waiting for an invitation.

"Jess, you look like you've just walked off a reality show mid-season," Hugo says, sipping his wine. "Where's your entourage?"

Jessie sighs. The dramatic, performative kind that suggests she's winding up to a monologue.

"Well," she says, "Tommy's still vanished into the void, surprise surprise. Didn't text me. Didn't say where he was. But—" she holds up a finger, "—he texted *Mason*. Of course. Because when it comes to choosing between his tragic, emotionally supportive best friend and the sexy bearded bad boy… we know how that goes."

"Oof," Hugo winces.

Jessie waves it off, but not convincingly. "I'm fine. It's just—whatever. It's happened before. He always ghosts me after a big night out. Like I'm the comic relief he can discard when the real fun kicks in."

"You're not comic relief," I say quickly.

"I *am*, Dan," she says with a sad little smile. "But tonight, I'm letting Dito play leading man. He's taking me out for dinner. Somewhere with cocktails and flattering lighting. He said he'd cheer me up."

Hugo raises his glass. "Ah well, here's to your lovely date with an unobtainable gay man."

Jessie stands, smoothing down her dress. "You two enjoy your romantic buffet. I'll see you later—unless I get drunk and decide to become a lesbian out of spite."

And with that, she's gone, strutting off into the dusk like a woman walking directly away from all her feelings.

I glance at Hugo. "Do you think she's okay?"

He watches her disappear out of sight, then shrugs. "No. But I think she'll be okay *eventually*. Probably after three mojitos and a dramatic cry in the toilet."

Fair.

I pick up my fork again, but I'm not sure I'm hungry anymore.

The evening continues, but we're in no rush to leave. We talk about the holiday so far, the new friends we've made. I update Hugo that I had some mini-nuance of a connection with Mason at the beach today as he opened up about his upbringing. Plus, the Reece confession too, we of course circle back around to that. These boys maybe aren't as vapid and one-dimensional as I assumed.

We're still at the table long after our plates have been cleared, the wine glasses mostly empty, the buzz of the restaurant fading into background clatter and quiet music. The sky is dusky now, streaked with amber and lavender, and the pool glows faintly in the distance.

"While it's lovely that you care so much about what happened to Benny, throwing out murder accusations, when there's no evidence and not even a body, may be slightly hasty, even for you," Hugo says, staring me down over his wine glass.

"Do you think anything sinister happened to him?" I ask Hugo.

"Oh, I don't know," Hugo shrugs. "Maybe, but probably not. Either way, if I'm honest, part of me doesn't really want to think about it."

"Why not?" I ask.

"I wouldn't want to think about what could have been. I need to just move on."

I'm staring down at the tablecloth, tracing circles with my fingertip.

"Hugo," I say quietly, "can I ask you something?"

He looks up, eyebrows raised, but his expression is soft. "Of course."

"Benny," I say. "That week you had with him. What… what did it mean to you?"

He doesn't answer right away. He leans back slightly, folds his arms across his chest. Not defensively—more as a symbol that he's taking my question seriously.

"It meant everything," he says finally.

I stay quiet.

"I know it was only a week," he continues, his voice steadier than I expect. "And it's so easy just to roll your eyes and laugh about what I'm saying over a week-long holiday romance, but for seven days, I felt like someone really *saw* me. Not just liked me, not just wanted to have sex with me, but… saw me. Every stupid part. Every insecure bit. And didn't flinch."

I nod slowly.

"And that's rare, right?" he says.

Again, I nod in agreement. I know from my own experience, that unlikely feeling is precious.

"Rarer than I ever realised," he says. "I kept thinking it was just a fling. Just a holiday thing. But as the days went on and we would just talk and laugh and talk. And I would tell him everything. Everything that I'd ever felt without any sense of holding back or shame or regret. Stupid little pieces of me and massive, deep parts of my life. And he would tell me the same. It all felt so easy and so natural, the connection, the chemistry, effortless, and I just found myself falling for him so hard."

Hugo looks down at his empty glass, holding the rim by his fingertips.

"When it ended suddenly, and I never heard from him again, it felt like something had been ripped out of me I didn't know was there."

He pauses, watching the candle flicker between us.

"I think—" he starts, then stops. He lets out a breath and looks at me again, eyes shining, but not crying. "Dan, all I've ever wanted is to be loved. Like, really loved. The all-consuming, wreck-me kind of love. The kind that makes you forget what it felt like to ever be alone."

My throat tightens.

"I know I make jokes," Hugo adds, voice softer now. "I know I'm loud and sarcastic and always up for a cocktail and a gossip. But underneath that... I just want someone to look at me like I'm their favourite person in the world."

I swallow hard. "You deserve that."

He shrugs, smiles a little, but it's shaky. "Do I? I'm not sure anymore. I've spent so long trying to *be* the perfect person for someone else, I'm not even sure who I am when I'm alone. I chase the spark, I jump into things, I fall too fast, too hard. And then it never lasts. And I start again."

"Hugo—"

"I would give everything," he says, cutting across gently, "if I could just wake up next to someone who chooses me. Every day. Without question."

There's nothing I can say. So I just reach across the table and place my hand over his.

He squeezes it, and for once, neither of us tries to make it funny.

And in the silence, I realise that maybe all of us—me, him, Jessie, even Reece—we're just trying to be chosen. Just trying to matter to someone.

Chapter 46

MARTIN

Martin stands at the edge of the beach, the tide lapping gently at his bare feet, the salty breeze catching the edges of his kaftan and whipping it around his legs. It's dusk, the sky smeared with purples and bruised pinks.

He hasn't cried in years. Not properly. But tonight, the tears come without asking.

He wipes them away with the back of his hand, stubbornly, angrily, but they keep falling. Josh is dead.

Miss Candy Chokem. So much more than just his work colleague. His close friend, confidant. Josh felt like a son to him; all he ever wanted was to protect him.

He still can't quite believe it. The words don't fit together in his head. The news spread quickly—faster than anything else ever does in Gran Canaria. Greg had told Martin the news, the last person he'd ever want to hear something like that from, but there was no easy way to hear news like that.

In fairness to Greg, by midday, the decision was made to close Rocky's for the night at least, a rare and solemn move. Other bars followed suit, the unspoken agreement rippling through the Yumbo like a shiver. Even now, during the busiest time of the year, the heart of the nightlife is dimmed. Mourning. Suspicious. Quiet in a way it never should be.

Martin stares out at the sea. The horizon blurs where water meets sky.

He always knew Josh would end up in trouble. He saw it in him from the start—that restlessness, that craving for validation, for danger, for more. He saw it and he tried to help. Took him under his wing. Let him borrow wigs. Taught him how to glue a lash on without losing half his eyelid. Stood up for him when others wouldn't.

But it wasn't enough.

And now he's gone.

Martin clenches his fists. His jaw tightens. The guilt sits heavy, like wet sand in his chest.

I should've done more.

He remembers that last chat backstage, Josh rolling his eyes at the warnings, brushing him off with that cocky smile—the one that always covered a thousand cracks.

"I know what I'm doing," he'd said.

He didn't.

None of them ever do.

Martin takes a shaky breath and turns his eyes toward the sea again. It's darker now. Deeper.

The shallow waves hit his feet and the memories return. He can't not think about them after everything that has happened today.

That night.

The waves.

The moonlight.

The body lying in the shallow water.

That feeling of shock, panic.

Two years had passed, but he'll never forget finding the body, right here by the ocean.

The island has brought him joy, sure. But more and more, it's brought him loss. It's a graveyard of secrets and sequins.

His gaze drifts back toward the dunes, the soft curve of sand that hides so much.

And then, of course, Mason.

That sudden reappearance. As if summoned by the past itself. Just when things are spiralling again.

Martin feels a sour twist in his stomach. He hasn't seen Mason in years.

He knows that they need to talk. He went to Maspalomas Oasis today to do just that but couldn't see it through. Just left his number at reception and ran. Maybe tomorrow he'll have the courage to speak to him. Maybe Mason will call him.

Martin lets the breeze dry his face and straightens his shoulders. He hears a noise behind him, a flicker of a shadow. With a jolt, he spins around to see the familiar face in front of him.

But it's not a face that gives him any sense of relief or comfort. His chest tightens as he feels his breath becoming quicker and shallower.

It's rare he's lost for words, but in this moment, they escape him. Finding the right thing to say just seems like an impossible task.

The figure steps forward into the moonlight.

That long beard covering the face he used to know.

Mason, eyes staring intently, his expression intense, focused.

"Alright, Dad?" is all he says.

Chapter 47

MASON

“Mason,” Martin says back, almost gasping for breath as he speaks.

Seemingly calm, his face expressionless, but Mason’s fists are unknowingly clenched as he approaches.

Breathing heavily, Mason has fantasised about this moment for years, decades even. Playing the confrontation between him and his estranged father over and over in his head, when he’s lying in bed, when he’s out shopping, or having a shower. The most mundane moments in his life suddenly get consumed by thoughts of this very moment. He’s written the script from within, edited it innumerable times—memorised it, etched it into his consciousness.

All for this very moment.

But now the day has come, with the blood rushing through his head, adrenaline coursing through his veins, he doesn’t know where to start.

“It’s nice to see you,” Martin says, softly.

Mason feels his shoulders tense up.

There’s a lengthy pause. The only sound, the light waves lapping the sand.

“How did you know I would be here?” Martin asks.

"I followed you, from your apartment," Mason says, breaking his silence.

"You know where I live?"

Mason nods. "I know a lot about you."

There's silence again as Martin considers what this really means.

"It was definitely a surprise seeing you at the show the other night. I didn't recognise you at first with that beard. You've not got it in any of the pictures your mum sent."

"She sends you pictures?" Mason's voice wobbles at the mention of his mum.

Martin nods. "Occasionally, not for years, but every now and then. Older now, but you still have the same eyes, her eyes. I saw them straight away.

Mason has frozen in place, like his brain is buffering, trying to get back on track.

"How did you know I lived here?" Martin asks.

Mason's eyes narrow. "Well, that was just a bit of luck, if you can call it that."

Martin's hands hover in front of him, unsure what to do with them.

"I saw you last time I was here," Mason says, voice flat but shaking at the edges. "Couple of years ago. Walking through the Yumbo. I didn't recognise you at first. It'd been so long since I'd seen you, only really remember you through the old photos that are still around. But it didn't take long to know it was you."

"So, I followed you," Mason goes on. "The fact that you turned out to be a fucking drag queen," he laughs, "well… that was a twist I didn't see coming."

Silence crackles between them.

"Why didn't you say something then?"

"Me?" Mason snaps. "After thirty years, yeah sure, it's up to me to come and talk to you!"

"Mason…" Martin starts to mumble a response.

"I couldn't even look at you back then. I can't even look at you now! You just make me feel so angry," Mason hisses.

Martin's lips part, like he's starting to say something, some kinds of defence, but the words don't come.

Mason shakes his head. "I used to imagine what you were. Dead. Homeless. Some straight guy with a second family. A millionaire. A famous actor. Anything. But this? This was never on my bingo card."

"Mason—" Martin says at last, his voice soft, cracked. "I didn't know you were here. I didn't know—"

"Don't!" Mason snaps. "Don't play dumb. Thirty years it's been. Thirty years!"

Tears start to stream down Martin's face, as his eyes widen.

"You have no idea, how we've struggled, what Mum had to do to make ends meet—put food on the table, the men that came and went. And I was just a kid, I didn't understand why you left us. I still don't! Do you know what that does to a six year old? That kind of rejection?"

He wouldn't expect Martin to know, to understand at all, how his leaving left a deep and tangled scar that shaped almost every part of his life. Even if he didn't understand it at the time, the loss created a void—not just in terms of a parental presence, but in his understanding of self-worth and love.

"No, I don't know, I'm so sorry. So very sorry," Martin pleads. "Not a day goes by when I don't think about what I did, why I left—"

"And why did you leave?" Mason snaps back.

Martin closes his eyes. "I was nineteen when I got your mum pregnant. I was still so young, just trying to figure out who I was. I had all these confusing feelings and then suddenly I was a father. Your mum and I, we tried to make it work, I swear. We lived together, I worked all the hours I could in the factory to provide for you both. But our relationship broke down pretty quickly after you were born. We didn't love each other, not like that."

"So, you just decided to leave because you didn't want to be with mum?" Mason shakes his head, not buying it.

"No, no! Your uncles had it in for me right from the start. You must know what they were like?"

And although it kills him to admit it, Mason does know exactly what it's like. With no father figure, Mason grew up surrounded by his uncles—hyper-masculine, homophobic, aggressive men who ridiculed anything soft, emotional or vulnerable. His idea of what it meant to be a "man" was built on dominance, suppression and violence.

But despite the common understanding, Mason refuses to acknowledge any form of excuse from his father and stays silent.

"They found out I was meeting men. I don't know how, but they did. They beat the living shit out of me. Broke my ribs, fractured my cheekbone, my nose. My leg broken too. I was in hospital for weeks."

Mason was too young to know any of this, but somehow the news doesn't feel like a surprise.

"They said they'd kill me if I ever came back."

"And so, you just *didn't*," Mason growls. "You just ran."

"They were going to kill me, they threatened me."

"They threatened your *ego,*" Mason spits. "You want to talk about fear? You think you were the only one afraid?"

He steps closer now, jabbing a finger in Martin's chest. "I grew up in that same fucking house. With those same uncles. Two raging, homophobic *cunts.* Mum wasn't much better. I love her but you kind of ruined any trust she had in the gays, I see that now. She must have held onto that grudge like it was gold-plated."

Martin flinches, "So, you are…gay, then?"

"Of course I am. What the fuck do you think I was doing here?!"

"Mason, I'm sorry, I had no idea. I didn't even think for a second…" Martin's voice trailing off.

"Imagine being twelve, sitting on the sofa, and hearing your uncle say that if he ever found out his son was a queer, he'd rather drown him in the bath. And your mum doesn't flinch. Doesn't argue. Just nods and keeps peeling potatoes."

Martin's heart aches and he knows all too well how that would feel.

"Or when Uncle Jonny called me a 'fucking nancy' when I was thirteen because I cried during *The Lion King.* He made me scrub the kitchen floor with a toothbrush, telling me it'd 'man me up,' while Aunt Linda told me I wouldn't go to heaven if I 'kept acting soft.'"

Mason then almost hysterically laughs out loud. "And the fucking ridiculous thing is Uncle Jonny's been dead six years," Mason continues. "Heart attack. After years of being a lazy, fat fuck. Terry's thirty stone, can't even walk up the stairs without collapsing. They've not been a threat to you for years. You could've come back anytime. You could've tried. But no—you stayed here. Topping up your tan and singing show tunes."

"It wasn't that simple," Martin mutters.

"No," Mason barks, "it wasn't simple. It would have been the hard uncomfortable choice. But *you* made it simple. You chose the easy option. You dumped your son so you could swan off to some party town in the sun. I bet you've been living the fucking dream for the last thirty years. Cocktails by day, drag queen by night! Aren't you the lucky one?"

Martin shakes his head. "It wasn't like that."

"It's *always* been like that," Mason says. His voice cracks now, finally, after everything. "All I've ever wanted was... support. Some kind of understanding. Someone to look at me and not be disgusted or disappointed."

He swipes at his face. Angry that the tears are coming now. Of course now.

"But I didn't get that. I got *silence*. I got nothing. Do you know what it's like," Mason whispers, "to walk around your whole life thinking you weren't worth staying for?"

Tears stream down Martin's face as he pleads for his son's understanding.

"Mason, please, I'm so sorry. I didn't think you would want me in your life. Yes, I knew what kind of environment you were being brought up in! What they say about people like me. Did I think for a second that you would want *me* to be your father? Gay! A drag queen! I thought I'd just be an embarrassment to you, a complication, nothing you would really want in your life,"

Despite the anger Mason is feeling, he knows that there is some logical sense within that, but right now he's not interested in logic.

Martin steps forward. "Mason—"

"No," Mason says, stepping back. "And that's the point! You made no fucking attempt to find out. Maybe that was exactly what I needed. Someone who really understood me! Where the fuck were you when I came out? When I was bullied at school. Or beaten up outside a club? When I OD'd? When I sat in the back of an ambulance thinking, maybe if I die, someone will finally turn up?"

Martin looks like he's been slapped.

Mason's breathing hard now, fists clenched, chest rising and falling like a wave about to break.

"You're a *coward,*" he growls. "Just a fucking coward!"

And that's when it happens.

Martin doesn't see it coming.

One second, Mason is standing there, red-faced, fists clenched, breath ragged. The next, he lunges. A shove—sudden, brutal—sends Martin stumbling backwards, feet skidding through the wet sand. He crashes into the shallows with a choked cry, water splashing up around him.

Mason is on him before he can get up, hands slamming down against his chest, forcing him back into the surf. The tide rolls in around them—frothy, dark, uncaring.

Martin splutters, trying to rise, but Mason's hands are at his shoulders, pressing him down. His head jerks above the surface for a split second—gasping, coughing—before Mason pushes him back under.

Martin thrashes beneath him, limbs flailing, bubbles breaking the surface, then vanishing.

Mason's heart is pounding. His hands shake as he holds Martin down. The sound of his own breath drowns everything else out. Waves crash against his legs. The sky spins.

He sees his reflection in the water.

His own face. Twisted. Wild. Terrified.

Chapter 48

DAN

"Well, that escalated quickly," I say.

I'm lying on my back on Jimmy's sofa, my heartbeat still racing, my head buzzing from the rush of adrenaline. One leg hooked over his shoulder, the other wrapped around his waist, Jimmy's head is buried into my neck, his chest pressed up against mine, as he tries to catch his breath. My right hand clamped onto his upper back eases off and I feel his sweat against my palm as I move it down to his waist.

Jimmy makes a kind of grunting noise, like he's just run a marathon in treacle but is also really happy that he completed it. I laugh and give him a kiss on the side of his head. I can still feel his heartbeat thumping through my chest.

The sex was initiated unexpectedly early. Or maybe predictably so. After I arrived at Jimmy's apartment, a few moments of small talk about my trip to the beach and an offer of a drink, led to a firm and passionate kiss, which unsurprisingly led to me being pounded into next week on his settee. Without any pre-conversation about roles, the endgame was unknown, but Jimmy's dominance, which was both surprising and remarkable, made it clear who was the top. Rougher than expected, I didn't think Jimmy had it in him, but it was just what I needed after the last couple of days.

With an almighty groan, like he's pushing over a 4x4 with his bare hands, Jimmy hoists himself up off my chest. His dark wavy hair, messy and over his face, is wet from the sweat, which he wipes away with the back of his hand.

"That definitely did escalate quickly," Jimmy says with a laugh, his breath still lightly panting.

"But I'm glad it did," I say with a smile.

"Oh yeah, most definitely." He comes back towards me, and we have a tender kiss, slow but deep, his lips immersed in mine as if they were one. My hand rises to his neck, my thumb resting on his moist cheek. As we break apart, he remains close, a breath away from me as I stare for a moment into his hazel eyes.

"So, I do believe I did offer you a drink at one point this evening?" Jimmy says.

"Yes, now would be a perfect time for that to appear."

Jimmy gives me a quick kiss on the lips, then heaves himself up, wandering naked over to the kitchen unit behind us. "Water, or alcohol?"

"Well, I should be asking for water," I say, wiping more sweat off my brow. "But I'd murder a white wine."

He smiles and heads to the fridge.

Moving seems like such hard work, so I remain horizontal on Jimmy's sofa. His apartment is modern, stylish but with a touch of wear around the edges—like someone who once cared a lot about aesthetics but has let some things slide. The balcony doors are cracked open to let in the sea breeze, making the white curtains ripple softly, which feels heavenly on my warm skin.

"We probably shouldn't be making puns about murder today," Jimmy says, raising his eyebrows.

"Oh shit, no, I suppose you're right."

Jimmy takes two wine glasses out of the cupboard below him and rests them on the worktop, pouring out two generous servings.

"Have you ever known anything like this happen here before?" I ask him.

"God no, this island has its fair share of drama, but murders aren't very common, not that I've known. It's come as a massive shock to everyone."

"I bet," I say, taking the wine glass he offers to me. I take a gulp, the cool liquid soothing my dry throat.

"I've been here nearly fifteen years, never known anything like this."

"Fifteen years? So, no regrets then?"

"I have plenty of regrets," Jimmy says earnestly, sitting back down on the sofa next to me. "But not coming here, no. Life is simple, but it's how I like it."

"And what made you come here?" I'm trying hard not to make this sound like a job interview, but there's so much I don't know about Jimmy.

He talks me through his life before Gran Canaria, growing up on the wrong side of Newcastle, rough around the edges and too cocky for his own good. His mum was a nurse who worked nights and smoked too much; his dad left when he was ten and only reappeared in the occasional angry voicemail or drunk birthday text. Alluding to being involved in the shadier side of life, getting involved in a few things he shouldn't, he escaped here to live a quieter life and never looked back.

"So, you've made many friends here over the years?" I ask.

"Some, yeah. It's a transient place. People come and go. You get to know the other guys who work around the bars. Some here just for a summer, some longer, some stay forever." He points to himself.

"And you never want to go home?"

"God no, there's nothing for me there. Home here's now. I have everything I need."

Jimmy's phone, resting on the coffee table in front of us, buzzes and he picks it up.

"Well, if you're going to retire anywhere it may as well be in the sun," I say slurping back my wine, but Jimmy's face shows that he's distracted.

"Everything okay?" I ask.

"Uh, oh, just a friend of mine, he works at the police station. He's keeping me updated on what's going on," he says, his eyes focused on what he's reading.

"And what's the latest?" I have to ask.

"They found another body," he says.

"What?"

"In the Dunes. Tonight. Face smashed in with a rock."

I feel my stomach twist like it's trying to get away from the rest of me. "Jesus. Who?"

"He doesn't know yet. It's not been confirmed. Had ID on him though, so he'll tell me soon enough. They're trying to contact the family."

I sit forward on the sofa, the cushion puffing back into shape behind me. "Was it… someone you would know?"

Jimmy shrugs, the kind of shrug that said he didn't want to know the answer either. "They think it was a holidaymaker. Not local."

The phone buzzes again. "Hang on. There's more," he says.

I wait.

"Shit. They don't think Luca jumped."

My brain froze. "What?"

"They think it wasn't a suicide."

I just stare at him. For a second, I think I haven't heard him right.

"They got some CCTV footage," Jimmy continues. "Grainy as fuck, taken from some rooftop across the street. But it looks like someone was up there with him. Like he was forced."

I feel cold, suddenly and completely. Like the air conditioning has kicked in full blast, except there isn't any. My mouth is dry, so I take another gulp of wine.

"You're serious?" I ask, my voice barely more than a whisper.

Jimmy nods. "Dead serious."

I lean back, eyes fixed on the ceiling, trying to picture it. Luca, alone on that rooftop. Except he wasn't alone. Someone was up there. Someone pushed him?

"Jesus Christ," I muttered. "Why didn't they say anything before?"

"Because they only just got hold of the footage," Jimmy says. "And it's not even definite yet."

I look at him. "So, this must all be connected right, four guys murdered in a couple of days?

Jimmy hesitates then nods. "Yeah. It must be."

"And that other guy, the businessman at the beginning of the week, that was reported as an accident. But surely after all this…"

"Yeah, it feels like it. His name was Harry Shaw. I know *of* him. He runs a construction company that builds all the new apartments in the area."

"And the others are unknown?"

"So, Luca we know," I nod as Jimmy speaks. "Josh's body was found in Corruption."

"Josh?"

"He was one of the drag queens at Rocky's,"

"Shit, I didn't know."

"Had his neck snapped while he was in a sling," Jimmy says, his voice quivering slightly.

"Jesus," is all I can say.

"The other two, no idea yet. Let me see what else I can find out." He begins to tap away on his phone.

After this, we don't say anything for a long time. Just sit there on the sagging teal sofa, the wind from the balcony brushing against my arm.

And for the first time, I wonder if we are in fact in any danger.

Chapter 49

DAN

It's heading towards midnight as I walk back towards the hotel. I'd left Hugo alone in the hotel bar after dinner so I could meet Jimmy, but conscious that he's not in the best frame of mind tonight. Despite wanting to spend more time with Jimmy, I make my excuses and leave, after making plans to catch up again tomorrow.

As I approach the entrance to the Maspalomas Oasis, I see a familiar face perched on a seat outside. It's still warm out, but the light breeze is cooling.

Mason is sitting, head down, bottle of beer in one hand, piece of paper in another, but he's not focusing on either. His hair looks like he's had a fight with a wind machine.

"Hey," I say, as I approach.

He looks up at me, his eyes are red like he's been crying. "Hey," is all he says, before hanging his head back down.

"Are you okay?" I ask, which seems like a stupid question. He's wearing a hoodie which is half done up, but as I get closer, it looks damp, like he's been swimming in it.

"Uh, yeah," he says, clearly not okay.

I take a seat next to him, noticing the piece of Maspalomas Oasis branded notepaper in his hand, which has a number scrawled on it. Although we had a very brief connection on the beach this afternoon, we're hardly friends, but I feel I should say something.

"For a hot date?" I ask.

He looks at me confused.

"The number." I nod to the paper. "You pulled?"

He pulls the paper into his chest. "Oh, no, nothing like that. It's from my dad; he left me his number at reception earlier. I just found out now." His voice is croaky, raw.

Not what I was expecting. "Oh, your dad's visiting here too."

"Uh, no, he lives out here," is all he says. His voice is slurring — he's clearly been drinking a lot.

"Oh, I didn't know." I want to ask more but based on what he told me earlier today about his family situation, having a dad who lives in GC I'm sure isn't the blessing it sounds like.

There's a long pause, and just as I'm about to make my excuses to leave, Mason continues. "I didn't know he'd reached out to me."

"Ah, I see." I scratch my head, choosing my words carefully. "Have you not seen each other for a while then?"

"You could say that," Mason says, sounding deflated. "I've not seen him for thirty years."

"Jesus, I didn't realise. And now he wants to talk?"

"Yeah, he did," Mason's words sound laboured, worn down by the alcohol and mental exhaustion.

I stay still. Not pushing. Letting him steer this.

"He left when I was six," Mason says. "Just vanished. No warning, no goodbye. One day he was there, the next it was like he never existed. Just gone."

I glance at him. His jaw's tight. Shoulders hunched like he's bracing for something. He takes another big swig of beer from the bottle.

"I grew up with my mum and her brothers. Two of the most homophobic bastards you can imagine. Real tough-love type shit, except without the love."

"I'm sorry," I murmur.

He shrugs. "It is what it is. But I always thought—well, hoped—that my dad didn't know. That maybe he *couldn't* come back. Maybe stuck in prison somewhere, even dead would have made me feel better."

He finally turns to look at me, his neck is loose from the alcohol.

"But then, two years ago, I came to Gran Canaria. And I see him. Just walking through the Yumbo. Living his best life. Gay as they come."

I stare. "You're kidding."

"Nope," he laughs bitterly. "Turns out he didn't die. He just ran. Built a new life. Became a drag queen. A fucking drag queen! Had all the freedom, the fun. And never once came looking for me."

"Jesus," I breathe.

"I always thought he wouldn't understand what it was like to grow up gay in that house. But it turns out, he would. And somehow that makes it a hundred times worse. He *knew* what he was leaving me to."

I don't know what to say. So I don't say anything.

Dropping his bottle to his feet, Mason buries his head in his hands. "I think I've just made a stupid mistake."

"Why, what have you done?"

He doesn't answer.

Instead, he jumps up and screws the paper up and chucks it on the floor. He stumbles slightly, an evening's alcohol rushing through his system.

"Mason?" I call to him as he turns to walk. I grab the mangled paper and hand it back to him. "Maybe put it in your phone, just in case."

"I already have his number," he replies. "Got it from my mum a couple of months ago." He turns and stumbles off up the road.

"Where you going?" I call to him.

He stops and turns to me. "To a party at some beach house we got invited to last night. Tommy texted me about it earlier. He's there so I'm gonna meet him there and get wasted."

"Okay," is all I say as he walks off. I want to say "be careful", which sounds like something my mum would say.

But with everything that's been going on here this week, that's advice we all need.

Chapter 50

DAN

Following on from my brief chat with Mason, I wander through the doors of the Maspalomas Oasis and head to the hotel bar, where I spot Hugo straight away. Sitting with him are Jessie and Dito, back from their dinner date. They've collected an impressive number of cocktail glasses between them. Hugo waves me over like I'm a long-lost relative.

"Well, well, well," Hugo says, shifting to make space. "Look what the slut dragged in."

I sit down heavily. "Hello to you too."

Jessie leans in. "So, I hear you've been out on a romantic date?"

"*Hook-up*," Hugo coughs through his hand.

Dito's smiling, clearly intrigued. I, on the other hand, would like the floor to open up and swallow me whole.

"I—uh—we just had a drink," I mumble.

Hugo laughs. "You had sex," he says bluntly.

While I'm all for giving Hugo every lurid, awkward detail of my sordid sex life, having Dito and Jessie all ears is just making me feel somewhat uncomfortable.

I roll my eyes. "We *may* have had some wine *and* some sex."

"Knew it," Hugo says, looking smug.

"Well, wine can lead to sex," Dito says, knowingly.

"I don't believe for a second you even got to the wine before the sex bit!" Hugo screams.

I just glare at him. Clearly, he knows me all too well.

"Oh, well good for you! I'm still waiting for someone to give my fanny a good stuffing on this holiday," Jessie adds.

"And I'm sure you will get that soon, my dear," Dito says, bringing her in for a side hug.

"Ahh, are you offering?"

"Definitely not," he says, kissing her on the forehead.

"So, you had the sex, and then what?" Hugo says, turning attention back to me.

I laugh, awkwardly. "Uh, we just chatted. He's nice. Funny."

"Ah, that's lovely babe," Jessie says. "What did you chat about?"

"Um, well, mainly just murder," I say.

"Okay, not what I was expecting," Hugo looks confused.

"Well, he knows some people."

Hugo raises a brow. "What, like in the biblical sense?"

"No, in the *police* sense."

That gets their attention.

"What kind of police sense?" Dito asks.

I glance around and lean in a bit. "Well, he knows some people within the local police department. Someone else was found dead this afternoon."

That wipes the smirks off their faces.

Jessie frowns. "Another body?"

"Yeah. In the dunes. Face completely smashed in with a rock."

Hugo flinches. "Bloody hell."

I catch them up on everything Jimmy told me. The death of the drag queen in Corruption, the CCTV suggesting Luca was attacked, that they're investigating the businessman who died earlier in the week.

"The police think it might be connected. Including the body they still haven't identified."

"The headless one?" Dito whispers.

I nod.

Jessie covers her mouth. "That's... that's horrific."

For a second, no one says anything.

"So, you're saying there's a serial killer on the island?"

"I suppose it would be," I agree.

It's bizarre—being in this perfectly normal hotel bar, warm lighting, cheerful music drifting in from the speakers, people laughing and drinking like it's any other night. Meanwhile, we're sat in the middle of some twisted whodunnit with real stakes and actual bodies.

"Well," Hugo says eventually. "So much for a relaxing getaway."

Jessie groans and throws her head back. "We should've gone to Torremolinos."

"Well, he said he's going to keep me posted on anything else he finds out," I add, feeling that I should conclude this topic of conversation, to avoid bringing us any further down. "I saw Mason outside just now," I say, as a redirect.

Jessie perks up. "Yeah?"

"He was upset. Started talking about his dad. He lives here apparently."

Dito raises his eyebrows. "His dad lives *here*?"

"Apparently."

Jessie blinks. "That's *so* Mason. Just casually dropping a huge bombshell like that. He's such a mystery."

"I said something about family and he got cagey. Said his dad's a drag queen now apparently."

Jessie's jaw drops. "What?! I'd love my dad to be a drag queen! My dad was a PE teacher, it's not as interesting."

"Mason said Tommy messaged him," I continue, "and invited him to some beach house party. He's gone to meet him there."

Jessie's face clouds over. "Oh, has he now. He can text *Mason* but not me. I've still not heard from him!"

Hugo offers a small shrug. "He's clearly enjoying himself."

"He always does this," she mutters. "Disappears, then pops back up when he needs someone to bail him out."

I don't really know what to say. I reach for my phone, mostly to check the time, and that's when the notification pops up.

I see the name first—Jimmy. It's just a quick text.

Got the name of the body they found in the Dunes.

I fire a message back.

Who is it?

Can I call you?

"What is it?" Hugo asks, picking up on my expression immediately.

"They've confirmed the ID of the body in the Dunes," I explain.

"Oh, crumbs," Dito adds.

My phone rings and I pick it up immediately. With minimal pleasantries, Jimmy confirms the name of the body found in the dunes earlier.

My heart catapults into my chest.

"What's Reece's surname?" I ask cautiously to the group.

"Why?" Jessie says, although we all know where this is heading.

"It's Walker, Reece Walker," Dito fires back.

"Fuck," I say in disbelief. "It's Reece, the body they found in the dunes. He's dead."

Chapter 51

DAN

Silence. Despite the buzzing of the hotel bar, it's just silence amongst us as we process what we've heard.

Jessie looks like she's been slapped, Dito doesn't look much better.

"Let me call you back," I say to Jimmy, hanging up.

Reece is dead.

"Are we sure it's him?" Hugo asks, breaking the silence.

"I mean, there could be more than one Reece Walker," Dito says, with a twinge of desperation in his voice.

"He was in the dunes earlier, he walked home on his own. Has anyone heard from him since?" Jessie asks.

I feel Hugo's eyes on me, knowing full well he's thinking about the fight Reece and I had earlier in the dunes. I don't say anything, knowing most likely I would have been one of the last people to see him alive.

"I'll call him," Dito announces, tapping on his phone and holding it to his ear. "Voicemail," he responds.

"I need to tell Tommy." Jessie says, voice quiet and cracked.

She's already dialling before anyone can stop her, holding her phone up like she's hoping his face will just magically appear. Straight to voicemail. "Fuck sake Tommy, answer your phone! Call me back as soon as you get this!" she leaves as a message.

She texts him again.

"Try Mason," Dito says. "I'll do the same."

She tries Mason next. Same thing. No answer.

Her lips press together into a tight line. "Why does no one ever bloody answer their phone anymore?!"

"Straight through to voicemail," Dito says.

"Same," Jessie says, shaking her head.

"Let me call Jimmy back, see what else I can find out," I say, already swiping to call him. My fingers feel too big, like I'm wearing gloves. I step away from the group as the phone rings.

He answers on the third ring. "Dan?"

"Yeah. Hi." I exhale. "We know Reece, he's a friend."

There's a pause.

"Yeah, I thought as much. I knew that guy I'd seen with your group was called Reece. I thought it could be the same one. I'm sorry," Jimmy says, and I can tell he means it.

"I mean, I've only known him a couple of days," I say, although that doesn't help ease the shock. "Do the police know anything else?"

"I believe they've contacted his next of kin, who are on their way over. Because of the way he died, they'll need to ID him through his DNA."

"Shit, I can't believe this. Do they have any leads on who did this?"

"Not right now, but they're looking to speak to people who knew him, so I assume they'll be over to your hotel in the morning."

I freeze. "Right."

I'm a suspect.

I was one of the last people to see him alive, so I must be a suspect. The fact that we argued, and I hit him with a rock earlier today doesn't look good. Plus, the fact that I still have Reece shaped hand marks around my neck, also not a blessing. I just hope no one else saw me with him.

"They've still not ID'd the guy who had his head cut off. They're checking a tattoo on his leg. That's their main lead."

I sit upright. "What kind of tattoo?"

"It's like a cartoon dolphin. Wearing sunglasses."

My stomach drops.

I can see it so clearly—Tommy, half-cut, lounging by the pool, that awful tattoo by his calf.

"Shit," I whisper.

"What is it?" Jimmy asks.

"Where on the leg is the tattoo?"

"Not sure, why?"

I walk further away from the group, so they can't hear me.

"Tommy has that tattoo," I say, almost whispering. I don't even care how stupid it sounds. "On his calf. I saw it the other day."

"Tommy?" Jimmy asks.

"He's part of the same group, he's here with Reece."

There's a pause on the line, and for a second, I think Jimmy's dropped out.

"Are you sure?" Jimmy responds.

"Yes, one hundred percent, I remember it vividly. Can you get a photo of it?" I ask. "From your police friend? Just to be sure?"

"I can try," he says.

My brain is whirling at a million miles an hour, I can't keep up with all the thoughts rushing through my head, heart thumping against my ribs like it's trying to escape. But now that I've started thinking, everything's unravelling.

"Look if Tommy's dead and Reece is dead, this isn't a random coincidence. They're connected."

"Yes," Jimmy agrees.

"Reece knew the drag queen-"

"Josh," Jimmy adds in.

"Yes, Josh—we saw them talking at the pool party, they did a ridiculously unsubtle drug deal. Then Luca knew them too, he went so weird when he saw them at the bar. How are they all linked?"

Jimmy pauses, maybe processing what I'm saying.

"Benny," I say.

Jimmy is still not speaking, holding out for my explanation.

"Luca mentioned the name Benny when he was spiralling just before he killed himself, Tommy and Reece knew him from a party they went to a couple of years ago, the night he went missing. Josh was there too! He sold Benny drugs, Reece told me!" I say, internally screaming, but it's coming out more of an aggressive whisper as I'm trying to keep my voice down.

Jimmy still isn't talking.

"Jimmy? Do you know anything about this?" I remember asking Jimmy about Benny at the pool party and him denying it, but he's been around these parts long enough to know what goes on.

Jimmy breaks his silence. "Look, I don't know a lot. There's a guy called Greg, he owns loads of the bars in the area, he has parties at his place every few months."

I remember Greg from Rocky's. "There's one on tonight, he invited the guys. Tommy said they'd already been to one of his parties before. It must be that."

Jimmy pauses again.

"Jimmy, what happened at that party?"

"I don't know, I swear!" Jimmy says. "But I remember talk of something happening that night. There was some trouble with a guy there, maybe he was called Benny, I don't know, but I never found out any detail. I remember asking Greg about it, but he just shrugged it off."

"And the businessman who died?

"Harry Shaw?"

"Yes, was he at this party?"

"I don't know, but he's good friends with Greg, so probably quite likely."

I know deep down it's all connected.

"Has anyone seen Tommy today?"

"No, no one's seen him, but he was texting Mason earlier."

"Oh okay, well that's a good sign."

"Is it?" I wonder. "Not if the killer took his phone. He had nothing on him, right?"

"No, you're right."

"So, Tommy has invited Mason to this party, but he obviously can't do that if he's dead! Mason could be in trouble too, he could be the next target."

"I get it," Jimmy says, suddenly serious. "Okay. So, we need to get Mason away from that party.

"We need to get the police there," I insist.

"Based on what? They've not ID'd Tommy yet. There's no evidence Mason's in any trouble."

"Okay, well, we need to find him. Then we stay together until we know more. Do you know where Greg's place is?"

"I'll send you the address."

My phone buzzes with the location seconds later.

"Dan," he adds. "Be careful."

"I will."

I hang up and go back inside.

They all look up.

I sit back down, heart thudding, head spinning.

"Well?" Jessie asks.

I lie. I can't bring myself to say anything just yet.

"Nothing new yet. But I know the party where Mason's at, I think we should get over there and get him and bring him back so we're all together."

"And Tommy," Jessie says.

I just nod.

"Yeah, that's a good plan," Dito says. "I'll get reception to get us a taxi."

Jessie downs the last of her cocktail, hopping off her bar stool and hurriedly walks with Dito to the front desk.

As they walk off, Hugo pulls me back. "Dan, what's really going on?" he asks, a rare serious tone in his voice.

"I think Tommy is dead. And I think Mason is next." Not quite how I wanted to break the news, but we only have a few moments alone. I explain about the tattoo and what I know so far about the party.

"I think it's all linked to Benny's disappearance," I say.

"Dan—" Hugo's eyes bulge. I can feel his evident discomfort.

"Hugo, I know you don't want to dredge up the past, but I'm sure it's all linked to him."

Hugo nods in agreement as I briefly replay the conversation I had with Jimmy.

"Come on, let's get to the taxi," I say.

Chapter 52

DAN

The taxi slows to a stop, tyres crunching against the gravel driveway, and I instantly feel out of my depth.

Greg's beach house rises in front of us like something out of a glossy lifestyle magazine—white-walled, sleek, all clean architectural lines and dramatic uplighting. It's perched on a cliffside with a view overlooking the black sea that shimmers under a half-moon like molten slate. There's a pool to the side, glowing electric blue under sunken lights, a few men already gathered at its edge—drinks in hand, some in swimwear, some barely in anything at all.

The place is secluded. Too secluded. No neighbours in sight. Just ocean, palms, and stone.

"This place is... a lot," Hugo mutters, stepping out next to me.

Jessie whistles. "Wow. Bit 'Eyes Wide Shut', innit?"

"More like 'Eyes Wide Open and Blasted on GHB,'" Dito adds under his breath.

I feel a twist in my stomach. Reece is dead. Tommy might be. And Mason—well, Mason is somewhere inside this millionaire sex dungeon, and none of us have a clue what we're about to walk into.

"Shit," Hugo says suddenly. "I've left my phone in the hotel room!"

"It's okay," I say, "I'm hoping we'll be out of here in five minutes. I don't want to hang around."

A thud of bass leaks through the walls. The party's already going. Music with no melody, just a heavy, rolling rhythm. Like a heartbeat with a hangover.

We make our way up the stone steps to the main entrance. The door's already ajar.

Inside, it's dim and hot, all mood lighting and modern art that looks expensive but emotionally repressed. I see some abstract human-like statue by the staircase, but it's holding a cock-shaped balloon, which somehow undercuts the gravitas.

The smell hits me instantly: cologne and sweat.

Hugo leans in. "Jessie, maybe you should—"

"I'm coming in," she snaps. "Not standing outside like some discarded handbag. I've seen plenty of cock in my time, nothing in here is going to shock me."

"Fair enough," he shrugs. "Just stick close, yeah?"

We walk in together. The party is in full swing.

The living area opens up before us like something off a Netflix property show. Sleek black furniture, floor-to-ceiling windows framing the sea, a fireplace burning low despite the heat, which just makes no sense. But what really catches my attention are the people.

It's a who's who of gay wealth: older men with manicured hands and expensive smiles, flanked by younger guys—some shirtless, some in harnesses, a few already deep in conversations that definitely aren't about art.

There's laughter, clinking glasses, an actual guy casually being fed strawberries on a leather sofa while someone strokes his thigh.

"I feel like I should be paying an entry fee," I mutter to Hugo.

"Or a therapy bill."

We edge in further. No sign of Mason.

"Let's split," Hugo says. "You and me do downstairs. Jessie, Dito—you go up?"

"Should we really be splitting up?" I ask.

"Yes, yes," Jessie insists. "It'll be quicker this way. Let's get this over with."

"Okay, just be careful," Hugo says.

Jessie nods, clearly a little thrown but hiding it under bravado. "If I get murdered, I'm haunting all of you."

"I welcome the company," I say, and we part ways.

As Hugo and I make our way deeper into the house, the music gets louder and the vibe gets weirder. We pass through a dining room-turned-champagne bar, then into a darker corridor lit with flickering candlelight, where I see a man on his knees unzipping another man's trousers as if it's just part of the evening's canapés.

Hugo taps my shoulder and points toward a double door at the back.

"Reckon that leads somewhere?"

"Only one way to find out."

We push through.

It opens into a poolside lounge—glass walls all around, low white sofas, fairy lights strung lazily across the ceiling. There's a hot tub in the corner. Three men are inside, clearly enjoying themselves. One of them, looking old enough to be the ostracised great uncle of the other two, is smoking a cigar, while I'm pretty sure he's receiving a not-so-casual hand job under the water.

"This is festive," Hugo mutters.

Still no sign of Mason.

I feel a bead of sweat slide down my spine. It's not just the heat. It's the atmosphere. The *wrongness*. Everyone here is smiling too wide or looking too hard. I don't know who anyone is, but I can feel eyes on me. The kind of eyes that undress you, weigh you, and find you wanting.

"Let's try the kitchen," Hugo suggests.

I nod, unable to find my voice.

We head back through the house, checking doorways, glancing over shoulders. Someone is definitely getting a blowjob behind one of the curtains. A man in a mesh tank top stumbles past us, laughing to himself, nose dusted white.

"I hate this," I whisper.

"I know," Hugo replies. "Me too."

But we keep going. Because Mason's here. Because something is happening. And because we might be the only ones sober enough to notice it.

"Do you really think Benny came to a place like this?" I ask.

Hugo shakes his head. "It doesn't really seem like his kind of vibe. But that said, what do I know? I only knew him a week.

Last time we spoke wasn't the greatest, so maybe he did come here."

I stop and turn to Hugo. "What happened that last night, what did you fight about?"

Hugo scrunches up his face, like admitting the truth is causing him pain. "Well," he sighs, "he told me to give him some space."

"Space?" I ask.

"Yes, space." Hugo admits. "As in 'stop being so intense and full on' kind of space."

"Oh," I say.

"I just got caught up in it all, like I was some Disney princess. I was making plans for when we got back. I just wanted to be with him all the time. I had never felt like this before."

I rest my hand on Hugo's arm. "I see."

"I know I was just love-bombing him in hindsight, but it didn't feel like it at the time."

"So, he just needed a break?"

"Yes, it was all very Ross and Rachel."

I nod. "I'm sorry."

Hugo shakes his head. "He said he needed some space, or maybe he said leave me alone, I'm not sure, but either way he walked off. But I never thought that would be the last time I saw him again. I clearly just pushed him away."

I look around at the house. "I'm not so sure that was the case."

"Gentlemen," a voice says from behind us. "I don't believe I've had the pleasure."

We both spin around to find Greg standing in front of us. I recognise him immediately as the owner of Rocky's who introduced himself yesterday. Albeit to Reece and co, and not specifically me. He steps out from the shadows like he's been waiting for this moment, his tall, broad-shouldered frame, with that rugged, silver-fox quality screams *money*. His shirt is half unbuttoned, crisp white linen hanging open just enough to show off a perfectly groomed chest. The sleeves are rolled up, forearms tanned and veiny. He's not dressed for a party, not really—no gimmicks, no glitter—just expensive green snakeskin loafers and a face that says he runs the whole damn island.

And, unlike everyone else here, he looks stone-cold sober.

"Hi, Greg," I say. "Nice to see you again." My immediate tactic being to pretend we were invited.

There's a brief pause as Greg's calmly tries to place my face. Although his piercing blue eyes appear to burn through my very soul as he does this.

"Uh, you introduced yourself last night, at Rocky's. I was there with my friends, Reece and Tommy. You invited us."

Greg nods. "Ah," he says as if to suggest he still has no idea who I am.

"Lovely house you have," Hugo says, holding out his hand. "I'm Hugo, it's a pleasure."

Greg takes his hand. "The pleasure is mine, Hugo and…" he looks to me.

"Dan," I fire back.

"Dan, of course," he smiles, a warm Patrick Bateman-style smile. "Well, welcome. Please make yourself at home."

Hugo and I exchange a quick look.

"We're looking for a friend," I say, trying to sound casual, even though my heart is punching the inside of my ribs.

"Ah," Greg says smoothly. "A lot of people are 'looking for friends' tonight."

"No," Hugo cuts in, stepping forward. "Actually looking. Like, *physically locating* him. His name is Mason."

Greg's face doesn't flicker. Not even a hint of recognition.

"Tall guy, dark beard, resting I-will-fuck-you-up face," Hugo adds helpfully.

Greg gives the most imperceptible shrug I've ever seen. "Doesn't ring a bell."

Of course it doesn't.

"But," Greg continues, "you're welcome to enjoy yourselves. Within reason."

"Oh, we're not here to enjoy," I say, voice tighter than I mean it to be. "We'll be on our way as soon as we find him."

Greg's eyes flick between us—me and Hugo—assessing. Calculating.

"We'll be quick," I say.

Greg nods, slowly. "No rush."

Then he turns. And for a second, that should be it.

But just before he disappears through the corridor, he glances back.

And our eyes lock.

His expression shifts—only slightly—but it's enough. The warm host mask slips for just a second. What's underneath is something colder. Harder. Calculated.

It sends a shiver straight through me, down my spine and into my gut.

And then he's gone.

"Okay," Hugo mutters beside me. "That was... not terrifying at all."

"I feel like I've just had a conversation with a Bond villain."

"Or someone who definitely owns a boat called *The Punisher*."

We keep moving, faster now. Greg's presence lingers behind us like a scent. My palms are sweaty. My mouth is dry. This house is a maze of mirrors and corridors and shadows, and every second Mason is out there with these people feels more and more dangerous.

We need to find him.

Chapter 52

GREG

Greg walks away from the two men—Dan and Hugo, was it?—his polished green snakeskin loafers clicking softly across the marble floor.

He doesn't look back. Not properly, anyway. Just the brief flick of an eye over his shoulder. Enough to let them know he's watching. Always watching.

Something about them doesn't sit right. He doesn't remember inviting them. Not high enough, not disoriented enough to blend in with the crowd. Sober gays at his parties always make him uneasy. They see too much.

Still, he's not worried. Suspicious? Maybe. But worried? No.

He has other things on his mind.

This is his favourite time of night—the party in full swing, bodies moving in a low hum of music, sex, money, and cocktails. The lights are dimmed just enough to flatter but still show off the designer interiors. His house is a masterpiece. A playground. A palace of flesh.

He strolls through the lounge, fingers lightly brushing the edge of a marble-topped sideboard. The scent of expensive aftershave and something less definable—sweat, lust—hangs in the air like incense. There's a boy dancing in the middle of the room, shirtless, high as a kite, twirling for the attention of an older gentleman in Gucci shoes who hasn't blinked in five minutes.

Greg smiles to himself.

This is what he's built. A kingdom of pleasure. Of indulgence. Of control.

Power. That's always been the thing.

He doesn't care much about the boys—not really. Faces come and go. They're decoration. Distractions. And he likes his distractions beautiful, pliable, and preferably too broke to say no.

He's earned this. Every square inch of it.

Years ago, when he first came to this island, he was no one. Just another man with a smile and a suitcase. But he was clever. And patient. He made the right friends. Slept with the right people. Acquired the right businesses—bars, clubs, apartments. Slowly. Strategically.

Now? He's not just someone. He's the one.

Everyone wants to be on his guest list. Everyone wants to be invited back. And that gives him leverage. Influence. The kind that's worth more than money.

Greg finishes his wine and swaps it for a full glass from a tray someone's left unattended. He wanders down the stairs to the basement.

This is his favourite room in the house.

It used to be a wine cellar. Now it's something much more… interesting.

A low thrum of sound pulses through the space—deep, vibrating house beats, steady as a heartbeat. Red lights glow from hidden fixtures, casting everything in shadow. The orgy is in full swing.

There are bodies everywhere. Twisting, writhing, arching. Gasps and moans echo against the walls like a choir of indulgence. One man is tied to a leather bench, another is being ridden on a mattress in the corner. Most of them don't even notice Greg.

That's how he likes it.

He sips his wine and watches in the shadows. Not out of lust, necessarily—though there's always a bit of that—but out of fascination. This is what happens when you give people freedom and anonymity. They show you who they really are. And who they really are, most of the time, is desperate. Desperate to be touched, seen, wanted, devoured.

He gives that to them. For a price.

He's always pushing things to the limit. The parties. The drugs. The favours. But he knows when to stop. That's the difference between him and the others. He knows the line—and how to walk right up to it without tipping over.

Usually.

He finishes his glass and heads back upstairs, past a train of men, one inside the next.

Outside, the air is cooler, cleaner. The ocean churns softly below, moonlight glinting off the waves. The pool is calm now, but he knows it'll be used later. It always is.

He stands near the edge, taking a breath, already mentally planning the next event. The anniversary party next month. A charity theme, maybe. People love to pretend they care while getting their cocks sucked.

He hears a sound behind him. Footsteps. He turns slightly, expecting one of his staff—or maybe some boy looking to impress.

But the world tips sideways.

Pain explodes at the back of his head.

Then blackness.

*

He wakes up cold. Disoriented. Something wet is seeping into the back of his shirt. He's not on the floor, he's upright. On a chair. He's… tied?

His arms are bound behind him, wrists burning. Ankles too. Something shoved into his mouth. Rough and salty—maybe a napkin. Or a sock.

He tries to cry out, but it's muffled. Pointless.

And then he sees the house.

His house.

Lit up in warm yellows and flickering reds. The music still thumping inside, the party continuing.

No one has noticed him.

He's tied to a chair just metres from the back patio, facing the pool, on the edge of the garden. Outside. In the dark.

Helpless.

The irony would be funny if it weren't so horrifying.

Greg tries to wriggle free. Nothing. He kicks his feet. The chair doesn't budge. Whoever did this knew what they were doing.

Panic sets in like a rising tide. This is his house. His domain. How the fuck did this happen?

Who did this?

Maybe someone from the party? Someone he wronged? Someone he forgot?

That list is... long.

He gags around the cloth. No one hears him.

The party continues.

Greg stares at the house, at the life he's built, and for the first time in years, he feels truly powerless.

A figure moves near the window.

Too far away to see him.

Too busy being entertained.

He thrashes again, but it's no use.

He's just a man in a chair now.

And no one's coming to help.

Chapter 53

MASON

Mason sits slouched in a worn leather armchair in one of the quieter side rooms of Greg's beach house, though "quiet" is a generous description. The thump of house music still pulses through the walls, and the muffled chorus of moans and laughter from the other side of the door creates a strange, rhythmic background noise, like a heartbeat with a hangover. The room itself is low-lit and hazy, the overhead bulbs flickering slightly, casting long shadows over the handful of half-dressed guests draped across the furniture like cats in heat.

There's a man on a chaise lounge in front of him, lips locked with another whose hand is buried under the waistband of his swim shorts. Another is lounging on the rug, sipping something neon out of a martini glass, scrolling on his phone like this is all perfectly mundane. To them, it probably is.

Someone—broad, shirtless, and flushed with drink—grins down at Mason and beckons him over with a sloppy flick of the hand. "You just gonna sit there all night, handsome?"

Mason squints through the fog of alcohol clouding his head, gives the man a half-smile that doesn't reach his eyes, and shakes his head. "Not tonight."

The guy shrugs and stumbles back to his friends, attention span shot, and Mason is left alone again. Fine by him.

He tips the half-empty glass in his hand—vodka, something citrus—and downs what's left. The burn doesn't even register. He's past the burning stage. Just numb now. Floaty and slow, like his limbs are underwater.

Where the fuck is Tommy?

He pulls his phone out of his pocket and looks at his messages. There's no signal at the house, so his last few messages to Tommy asking where he is are still unsent.

It's not just the reception that's blocked in this house. It's the air. The atmosphere. It's suffocating in a way only memories can be.

He knows this house well. It wasn't until he walked up to the entrance that it clicked with him. The last time he was here, that awful night.

He doesn't think about it often—not in daylight. But tonight, with the house buzzing like a wasp's nest and the ghosts of that night slipping into the corners of his vision, he can't help it.

He remembers shadows in the hallway. Raised voices. Greg, the party's host smiling too much. The way the music didn't stop, even when things got dark.

And him—Mason—standing back. Watching. Frozen.

He tells himself he didn't know what to do. That he couldn't have stopped it. But that's a lie he's chewed on for years, and it tastes just as bitter every time.

Benny's name flickers across his mind like static. He takes a deep breath and lets it out slowly. No. Not now.

Benny.

A guy he met once, for a few hours, years ago. He should have forgotten all about him, but back here that name is as fresh as the moment they met.

Mason plays back that moment, when their eyes locked, when it was all going on, that look, dazed and confused.

But Mason did do enough, like so many that night.

Like a fever dream, his brain fused by alcohol, thoughts shift to earlier today. The confrontation on the beach. Seeing Martin—his father—for the first time in decades.

The rage he felt, the anger, the violence he couldn't control.

His father's face under water, gasping for breath, pinned to the seabed.

And now the regret of what he did.

The door creaks open, and light spills in from the hallway.

He squints, but then he sees the familiar shapes of Hugo and Dan stepping inside.

"Mason!" Hugo exhales like he's just finished a marathon. "Thank fuck."

Mason pushes himself upright. "Hey," he says, voice low and cracked. "What are you doing here?"

"We've been looking all over," Dan says, stepping closer. "Are you okay?"

Mason shrugs. "Define 'okay.'"

Hugo glances at Dan. "I'll go get the others. Stay with him."

Dan nods, his eyes never leaving Mason's. He sits on the armrest beside him.

"What others? What's going on?"

"Jessie and Dito are here, we were looking for you."

"What, why??"

Dan finally says, "I need to tell you something."

Mason doesn't respond. Just waits.

"It's Reece," Dan says quietly. "He's dead."

Mason blinks. "What?"

"They found his body in the dunes."

Mason stares at him, trying to process the words. It's like someone's pulled a plug in his chest. The air rushes out of him, and everything feels a little dimmer.

"Dead?? How?" he croaks.

"We don't know the details," Dan says. "But I think Tommy's in trouble too. We haven't heard from him. And maybe you, which is why we came here. We need to just get everyone away from here and get everyone safe."

Mason's intoxicated mind is whirling with confusion. "I don't understand. Reece is dead. Why would anyone kill Reece?"

Dan pauses like he's choosing his words carefully. "I think it's all connected to the party, that happened here a couple of years ago."

Mason doesn't respond, like his brain is playing catch-up. There's a sick feeling in the pit of his stomach as he processes Dan's theory.

"Something happened here before, didn't it?" Dan says

Mason's mouth opens, but no words come out. He leans forward, elbows on knees, staring at the floor.

"Benny," Dan says. "You know the name Benny right?"

Mason nods.

"And what happened? What happened that night with Benny?"

"Benny, he…" he says finally. "It was… fucked. All of it. I should've—"

A scream cuts through the night like a razor.

They both freeze.

The scream continues, a horrific, torturous scream coming from outside.

They bolt to the window.

Outside, near the pool, something is burning. Flames rise high, orange against the inky black of the ocean beyond. At first, it's hard to make out what's happening—just the fire and a shape within it.

Then Mason sees it.

The chair.

The body within the flames, thrusting back and forth in desperation, engulfed.

"Oh my God," Dan breathes.

Mason doesn't speak. He can't. His stomach lurches.

He's frozen.

In his almost fugue state, he thinks about Benny. About the man tied to a chair, burning.

History repeating itself.

Once again, he's in this house, watching something unspeakable happen in front of his eyes.

And once again, there's nothing he can do to stop it..

Dan grabs his arm, yanking him out of the trance. "Come on. Now."

Mason doesn't argue.

Chapter 54

DAN

We burst through the French doors and into the thick night air, Mason a half-step ahead of me. The smell hits first—burning hair, fabric, flesh. I gag. The fire is raging now, the shape in the chair fully engulfed, like something out of a horror movie that no one asked to be part of.

Flames dance in the dark, reflected in the glossy surface of the pool. It's like hell has cracked open in the middle of a luxury villa.

Then I hear Dito's voice behind me. "Oh my God—what the fuck?!"

He barrels past us, eyes wide, and without hesitation yanks a heavy blanket off one of the pool loungers. He throws it over the body with a horrifying whoosh and a puff of smoke. The fire crackles angrily as it suffocates beneath the fabric, but the worst of it—the high flames and the screaming—has stopped.

It's too late. Of course it is.

Jessie skids to a halt beside me, barefoot, breathless, holding her wedges in one hand.

"Who is that…?" She clamps her hand over her mouth. "Oh my God."

I see the scorched shoes of the body, what looks like the green snakeskin loafers I saw earlier, and I know immediately who the victim is.

Hugo appears, eyes darting between us and the scorched figure slumped in the chair. "We need to call the police," he says, already pulling out his phone. He taps the screen. "No fucking signal."

"No one has a signal here," Mason mutters. "It's like a dead zone."

"That's appropriate," I whisper before I can stop myself.

The five of us stand there, horrified and helpless, while behind us, the party continues to unravel. People are pouring out of the house now, stumbling into the garden, glassy-eyed and trembling, clutching onto coats and handbags and vapes and lovers.

"What happened?" a man asks.

"Oh my God, what is that?" another shrieks.

And then the panic spreads like wildfire. One guy takes off running, and it's like a signal. Suddenly, everyone's scrambling to leave. Married men with tan lines and secrets; Insta-hunks on vacation trying to forget their real lives; twenty-somethings in tiny shorts still wired from whatever they've shoved up their noses. No one wants to be around when the police arrive.

It's chaos.

Bodies everywhere, shouting, footsteps pounding across the decking. Someone crashes into a table. A glass smashes.

A man screams, "We're all gonna get blamed!"

"They're gonna take our passports!"

"Don't fucking touch me!"

"I'm not getting involved in this shit!"

It's like watching a ship sink in real-time.

There's a collection of expensive cars parked outside and within mere seconds, they are full with party goers diving in the seats, desperate not to be part of the drama unfolding. Those without the access to transport just run off down the drive and head out to the street, miles from anywhere, no clear plan on how to get home.

As we move inside, I turn to Hugo. "I think that was Greg out there."

Hugo nods. "The shoes."

"Yeah, they were the ones he was wearing earlier."

"The green snakeskin ones."

"Yes, another one from that party."

Dito shouts, "I'm going to look for a landline!" And darts off.

Jessie grabs my arm. "Where's Tommy?" she demands. Then turns to Mason. "Mason, where's Tommy? He was supposed to meet you here."

My stomach drops. I look at her—her wide, hopeful eyes—and I hate what I'm about to say.

"Jessie…" I start, but the words stick in my throat.

"What?" she snaps. "Where is he?"

I swallow hard. "I think… I think Tommy might be dead."

Silence.

The chaos around us fades for a moment, like someone's turned down the volume. Jessie stares at me as if I've slapped her.

"What are you talking about?" she whispers. "He's been texting Mason."

"I don't think that was him," I admit. "One of the bodies from the Yumbo Centre, Jimmy told me. There's a tattoo on his leg of a dolphin, like Tommy's..." I trail off.

She stares at me, lips trembling.

I glance at Mason, then back at Jessie. "I think it's him. I think it's Tommy."

"No," she says, shaking her head. "No. No, it's not. He's been texting Mason. You know what he's like—he does this."

Her voice cracks as she bursts into tears.

Hugo puts a hand on her shoulder, but she shrugs it off and takes a step back. "Why didn't anyone tell me?" she demands. "Why didn't you tell me this earlier?!"

"Because we didn't know for sure," Hugo says gently. "We still don't."

"No, we don't know for sure. But it's all connected, it must be," I say. "I think someone was trying to get Mason here using Tommy's phone. And now it seems like we're in danger, I can't not say anything. It has to be. Reece, Tommy, Luca, Josh, Greg. Whatever happened here two years ago."

"What happened here two years ago?" Jessie screams, begging for answers.

I turn to Mason, heart pounding.

"Tell us," I say. "Tell us what happened at the party. The one from before. What did you see?"

Mason doesn't answer at first. He's staring at the smouldering chair through the window, the blackened blanket, the flames still licking at the edges. His face is unreadable—stone-cold and yet clearly breaking apart.

"Mason," I repeat, firmer this time. "You said it was a terrible night. That you should've done something. So tell us. What happened?"

Jessie looks at him, tear-streaked and trembling. "Please."

He looks down at the ground for a long moment, as if hoping it might swallow him whole. Then, finally, he speaks.

"It was just supposed to be a laugh," he says. Although we can tell by the look in his eyes, what transpired was by no means funny.

Chapter 55

BENNY

2 Years earlier

Benny's heart races as he marches away from the bar, out to the street. The Yumbo Centre buzzes around him, but it all blurs into background noise. All he can hear is Hugo's voice echoing in his head, the words too fast, too much, like always.

"Just listen to me!"

Benny had listened. For days. For nights. Through whispered confessions and stolen kisses and sweet promises that felt good—too good—for something born on a sun-drenched holiday.

"Please, Hugo-"

Now Hugo's chasing after him, again. "Benny, come on. Don't just walk away."

Benny stops and spins around to face Hugo.

"Look, Hugo. I can't breathe."

Hugo freezes. That warm face, usually lit with joy, twists into something fragile and breaking.

"I love how romantic and passionate you are, but it just feels very.... intense."

"You said you liked that about me," Hugo says, quietly.

Benny exhales. His fists are clenched. His throat feels tight. "I do. I did. I don't know." He runs a hand through his dark, wiry hair, eyes scanning the sky as if the stars will tell him what to do. "I just need a minute. Some space. Some… time."

A long silence stretches between them.

"Don't you want to see me again?" Hugo asks.

Benny's voice softens. "No, no, this week has just been…a lot. It was supposed to be a relaxed week, but we met on my first night and have spent every moment together since."

There's a pause of silence which hangs uncomfortably between them. Benny adjusts his thick glasses, more as an action to break the tension than anything else. He's a good six inches taller than Hugo, but his skinny frame and hunched posture almost level out against Hugo's domineering personality.

But now Hugo is being uncharacteristically quiet.

He hadn't meant to hurt Hugo. God knows, he never meant that. But this was the right thing to do.

"Look, I'll give you a shout tomorrow," Benny says.

Hugo just nods as he turns and walks away.

Benny exhales and moves in the opposite direction, into the beating heart of the Yumbo.

The week they'd spent together had been, honestly, *magic*. Hugo was all charm and brightness, with a laugh that could bounce off the Yumbo's walls and land directly in Benny's chest. For the first few days, he'd let himself fall into it.

The affection. The flirtation. The way Hugo had looked at him like he was someone worth loving.

And he'd liked it. More than liked it.

He still does.

But sometime after night four—and somewhere between shared tapas plates and slow kisses on dark balconies—Hugo had started talking about *after*. About brunch spots and weekend trips and whose friends they *had* to meet. About being exclusive.

And Benny had started to feel the noose tighten.

And maybe, after a night apart, it won't feel so heavy. Maybe they can have a last night together that feels like the beginning *and* the end. One that doesn't carry pressure or promises.

That's all he wants.

Just… space.

Just a little more time to breathe.

And now he has it, he just wants to let loose, do something wild and crazy, like the free single man he is. He came on this holiday to let his hair down, to experience the fun side of life. Tonight is his night to do that.

As he walks through the Yumbo, the eyes of the patrons are on him, as they are on everyone. Benny's not exactly the type to turn heads and he knows that. He's lanky, in that slightly awkward way—like his limbs never quite caught up with each other. He's skinny, almost scrawny, with a wiry frame that makes clothes hang off him like he borrowed them from someone else.

His features are sharp, a bit angular, giving him a look that's not exactly handsome, but definitely memorable—quirky, maybe even endearing in the right light.

Any eyes on him don't linger, they immediately flip to the next person behind him. Noticing his shoelace is untied, he adjusts his square glasses again and stoops down to tie it up.

As he does, he hears a conversation between four handsome men stood right by him.

"What kind of party?"

"The fun kind."

Benny's ears prick up.

"Come on guys, it'll be fun," a man with an accent says, almost flirtatiously. "The house is incredible, like Beverly Hills mansion kind of shit. Endless drinks, lots of hot guys, some older rich men if you're looking for a sugar daddy," he continues and although I can't see him, I imagine him winking as he speaks.

"I don't know," one of the guys says.

"I can drive you there myself," he says. "And I can take you back after."

"Come on Mason, it'll be fun," says another, looking to the third friend. "Reece?"

"Fine, sure, why not," the third guy presumably called Reece replies. "Will make a change from this dump. And what was your name again?"

"Luca," the man says.

"Well nice to meet you, I'm Tommy. This is Reece and Mason."

"Pleasure to meet you lads. My car is up on the street."

Benny, having finished tying his laces, stands up. He gets out his phone, pretending to check something but really just loitering—doing that casual earwigging thing he's always been weirdly good at. The four men standing together are the type you don't usually see mingling with someone like him: sun-kissed skin, sculpted arms, expensive sunglasses perched in precisely artless ways. One of them—Luca, he thinks—is talking about a party.

Then Luca asks, "I have another space in the car. Any other friends you want to bring?"

It's a casual enough question, but there's a brief silence between the three of them—like they've all just scanned their mental contacts list and found it lacking. Mason grunts. "Nah."

But Tommy turns, eyes locking with Benny.

Benny stiffens.

He wasn't expecting to be noticed, let alone spoken to. He looks up from his phone and forces a smile.

Tommy's got that grin. The kind that's all teeth and just slightly mean. "What about him?" he says, nodding Benny's way. "You coming to the party, mate?"

The one called Reece just glares at him. Mason doesn't even look over.

Benny blinks, surprised. "Me?"

"Yeah, why not?" Tommy says, his voice light, faux-friendly. "You up for a bit of chaos tonight?"

Benny hesitates. Part of him knows it's probably a joke, that he's the punchline to something he hasn't quite heard. But the larger part of him—the one that's spent the past three nights watching other people have fun, the one that's sick of being boring, of being *safe*—jumps at the chance.

He nods, maybe a bit too eagerly. "Sure. Yeah. That sounds… fun."

Tommy claps him on the shoulder, not hard, but enough to make him stumble half a step. "Good man."

Luca glances at him now for the first time—really looks at him. His expression doesn't shift much, but there's a sense of disappointment in his eyes. This wasn't the face he was looking to fill the extra space in his car with.

"Alright then," Luca just says. "Let's go."

And just like that, Benny is climbing into the backseat with three strangers, his heart pounding with a cocktail of excitement and nerves.

He knows he's out of his depth.

But for once, he wants to dive in anyway.

*

Benny has never been to a house like this.

Not just because it's huge—though it is, absurdly so—but because the whole place hums with the kind of energy that makes your skin prickle. The kind of place where things happen. Things you don't talk about the next morning.

The four of them arrive together, stepping out of Luca's car into the golden glow of a villa perched on the edge of the coastline, the sea whispering in the dark beyond. The air is warm and thick with salt, and there's already music pulsing from inside—low, bassy, and ominously slow.

As they approach, a man steps out from the shadows of an archway to greet them.

Tall. Rugged. Maybe in his forties or fifties. Tanned, dressed down in that rich-man-on-holiday way: white linen shirt open to the chest, gold chain, expensive sandals. His face creases into a knowing smile as his eyes scan over the group—Benny swears he lingers for a second too long on him, which makes his stomach twist. He introduces himself as Greg.

"Luca," Greg says, clapping him on the back. "You always deliver."

"No problem, boss," Luca replies with a casual smile, as Benny notices Greg hand a selection of notes to Luca, like payment for a delivery, which he stuffs in his pocket.

They step inside, and instantly the atmosphere swallows him.

It's all happening—everywhere. Dim lights, red-tinted rooms, semi-naked men lounging around like they're in a music video. The low thump of music. Glasses clinking. Moans from behind half-open doors. Two men are openly having sex on a leather chaise in the hallway, barely registering the newcomers as they pass.

Benny tries to hide the shock on his face, but Tommy clocks it.

"Still feeling brave, Professor?" Tommy grins.

"Absolutely," Benny says, forcing a grin. "All good. Totally fine."

Reece raises an eyebrow. "You look like you've just walked into a crime scene."

Benny laughs nervously. "I'm just… taking it all in."

Which is true. He's trying, desperately, to act cool. Like this is just another wild night. Like he's not sweating through his shirt and wishing he'd stuck to the quieter side of the island. But he's here. This is what he said he wanted—something different. Something wild.

Drinks are thrust into his hand before he can think. People come and go, laughter echoes in bursts, and every so often someone brushes too close to him, too familiar, too casual. There's an undercurrent of something he can't quite name—power? indulgence? danger?

They do shots—five in a row. Benny's throat burns. His head's spinning already, glasses sliding down his nose. He wipes the sweat from his palms onto his shorts.

He's completely lost concept of time, when Reece leans in, looking bored. "We need something stronger." He says nodding to a young slim guy in the corner.

There's a familiarity between him and Reece, a shorthand that Benny doesn't understand. Reece calls him Josh. They talk for a minute—low, close—and then Josh dips his hand into a small pouch and pulls out a bag.

White powder.

"Ket?" Josh says, offering it like it's breath mints.

Benny feels his stomach flip. He's never done drugs. Not really. He once took a half-ecstasy pill at uni and ended up crying in a bathtub. He hasn't touched anything since.

Tommy's already pulling him by the wrist. "Come on, live a little, Benny-boy."

Reece nods at him, smiling in that way people do when they're daring you to do something dangerous but framing it like a gift.

"You want to have real fun, don't you?" he says.

"I'm fine with the shots," Benny mutters.

"No one wants to be just fine," Reece replies smoothly. "Just one line. It'll loosen you up."

Tommy screams with laughter.

"A line? Jesus Reece," Mason says.

Benny hesitates. Then looks at Mason, but Tommy pushes him out the way and wraps his arm around Benny's shoulder.

"Come on B-Man, this is what the big boys do," Tommy says.

Benny opens his mouth to protest, to say he's not sure, but suddenly Reece is holding the bag open and Tommy's already chopped out a line on a glass table.

A straw is handed to him.

Benny looks at it. Then at all of them. Then back at the powder.

And he thinks: *Maybe this is what people mean when they say they came out of their shell on holiday.*

He leans down and does the line. It burns. Immediately. His eyes water.

"Another," Reece says.

"What?" Benny's voice cracks.

"Double dose," Reece says, voice silky. "It'll hit better. Trust me."

Tommy is laughing. Josh is already prepping the second line.

"Steady on," Mason says. "He's already wasted."

"Buzzkill," Tommy groans. "Come on, he's a grown man. If he can't handle a bump of K, he shouldn't be at a party like this."

"This is more than a bump," Mason warns.

Benny glances at Mason again, but this time, Mason just shakes his head and looks away.

Benny snorts the second line.

The world begins to tilt.

The edges of everything start to fray.

Benny can't tell if he's standing or floating or falling. The music warps, stretching and twisting like it's underwater. His own breathing is distant—like it belongs to someone else. The room spins sideways. Or maybe the house is tilting.

His feet are gone. No—he's lying down. Was he lying down?

Voices. Laughter. Somewhere far away. The familiar scratch of Tommy's laugh—except now it sounds cruel. Harsh. Like it's bouncing off the walls, too loud, too sharp.

A kiss, he feels a kiss, a smooth warm kiss, tickling his lips, it makes him smile

He blinks, and the ceiling is above him. High and swaying. There's heat. Hands, maybe. Something heavy pressing down on his chest, then nothing at all. His arms won't move, won't respond.

Another kiss, this time smoky breath, different, makes him cough, retch.

He wants to sit up. Ask a question. But his mouth won't cooperate. His tongue is lead. His voice lives behind a locked door.

And he feels like he's naked now, exposed.

More pressure on top of him.

And the pain within.

The lights blur into streaks. Movement. Shadows of bodies. One. Then two. Then more. A mess of skin and shape. Faces melt and reassemble. One of them looks like Greg, right on top of him, smiling like a man who owns everything. Another face flashes—Luca? No, too fast. Gone again.

He hears someone say his name. *"Benny."* Like a whisper, like a command. It might be Reece. It might be no one.

He blinks again. Or thinks he does.

Now it's darker. Hotter. There's laughter again—somewhere above him. He thinks someone's watching him. A group. He thinks someone says something like, *"He'll be fine."*

Time is a swamp. He's sinking. Drowning in velvet fog and static. He tries to raise a hand. Nothing.

Another laugh. Close. Loud. Mocking. A camera click?

Just the pounding of blood in his ears. The slap of skin on skin. His skin. The throb of bass that's started to mimic his heartbeat.

He's on his front now, face pressed down.

Deep breathing against his ears.

That pain from within that he can't fight.

His glasses are gone. He thinks about that, briefly. As if somehow, putting them back on would make this make sense. Make it real, or maybe unreal enough to escape. But his arms don't move. His head doesn't turn.

The faces around him blur—some familiar, some strangers. One of them is Josh, standing off to the side. Watching. Another might be Mason, lingering near the edge of the room like he wants to disappear.

Reece is there. Or maybe it's someone who looks like him. Benny can't tell anymore.

Something cold runs down his cheek. Sweat. Or a tear.

A flicker of himself rises for a second—panic fluttering in his chest—but it's drowned by the weight pressing him back into the mattress. Back into the noise and the blur and the heat.

He wants to scream. But his mouth won't open.

Wants to fight. But his body has forgotten how.
Wants to vanish.
Instead, he floats deeper into the dark.

Chapter 56

MASON

The words are still hanging in the air like smoke.

Everyone is staring at him—Jessie, Hugo, Dito, Dan—eyes wide, jaws slack. Disgust. Horror. Mason can feel every emotion like it's a weight pressing down on his chest.

And all he can feel is shame.

"I didn't do anything," he says, voice brittle. "I swear, I didn't touch him. I didn't hurt him."

"And what about Reece, Tommy?" Dito asks, his eyes narrowed, unreadable.

"No, they didn't do anything either," Mason stammers, too fast, too defensive.

"Except got him drunk and plied him full of ketamine," Hugo says bluntly, tone like ice.

"Yes, yes, I know..." Mason's voice tails off, hoarse and broken.

"And you just let it happen?" Jessie asks, her voice shaking. Her eyes glisten but don't soften. "Fed him to the wolves."

Mason doesn't respond.

"And how many men?" Dito asks quietly, dangerously calm.

"I... I don't know... five, ten maybe... I don't know," Mason's eyes are welling up as he speaks. He's trying to keep it together, but the tears come anyway.

"Ten?" Dito repeats, stunned. "Jesus Christ, Mason."

"And you all just sat back and watched?" Dan says, voice tight.

"I just can't believe anyone would do that. That Tommy would do that!" Jessie cries, "Why didn't you stop it?"

"I don't know. I couldn't. There was so much going on… we all had so much to drink, and coke, and ket… and it just started happening and it was like some fever dream, I just wasn't thinking straight."

"And what happened after? Where did Benny go? What did they do to him?" Hugo asks, his voice rising. There's something deeply personal in his tone—something cracked.

"I don't know!" Mason shouts. "I don't, I swear! They just took him away—"

"Who?" Hugo demands. "Who took him away?"

"I don't know, really. It's all just a blur—"

"Look," Jessie cuts in, trembling, "we can't talk about this anymore right now. Can I remind you all that there's a char-grilled corpse outside and we need to find a phone and call the police?"

Around them, the house is thinning out. The crowd—what's left of it—is fleeing into the night. Rich men and pretty boys, scattering like cockroaches when the lights come on. No one wants to be here anymore. Not after the fire. Not with a dead body. Not with the police bound to come crashing down at any second.

"There has to be a phone in this house," Hugo mutters.

"I had signal out by the road earlier," Mason says, barely above a whisper. He's already moving toward the door.

"Okay. Go check," Jessie says, not looking him in the eye.

He nods once, stiffly, and steps outside. The others scatter into the house behind him, searching for a landline, any sign of help.

Outside, it's dark but warm still. The smell of smoke hangs in the air, but it's fading, blending into the salt of the ocean breeze. Mason stumbles down the gravel path, phone clutched tight in his hand. He's still sweating. Still shaking. He doesn't know if it's the heat or the memory of what he just said. The words are playing on loop in his head—*five, ten maybe…*

The weight of his admission clings to him like sweat. He told them the truth. Or at least, his truth. What he remembers. What he let happen.

He reaches the edge of the road, just past the gate. It's so quiet out here now, the house a distant echo behind him. Darkness stretches out in every direction, broken only by the faint orange glow of a distant streetlight. He holds up his phone, the screen bright.

No signal.

He exhales shakily, dragging a hand through his hair, dizzy.

Then—one bar.

It flickers. Disappears. Then returns.

He spins to face the signal, raising the phone higher like some desperate offering to the gods of reception. His thumb hovers over the screen, shaky but ready.

That's when he hears it.

A shift in the air. A footstep. Too close.

He turns.

Too late.

A blur of movement. Cold metal.

Stab.

His breath catches in his throat.

Stab.

Pain blossoms through his stomach, sharp and burning.

Stab.

He drops to his knees, choking on air.

Stab.

"For Benny," the voice says.

Mason falls, mouth open, a silent scream escaping. His body hits the dirt with a thud, his phone slipping from his hand, tumbling just inches away. Blood spills fast, warm and endless, seeping into the gravel.

He can't move. Can't shout. His muscles won't respond.

The house is too far. The others won't hear him.

He lies back, face tilted to the stars, heart thudding a frantic, slowing beat. He reaches with trembling fingers toward the phone. Tries to swipe up. Nothing. The blood smears everything. The screen won't respond. His hand slips. The phone hits a rock, flips face-down.

He groans, flips it back over with the side of his wrist. Everything is spinning.

The phone rests beside him, glowing faintly in the dark.
He licks his lips, dry and sticky, and forces a breath.
"Hey Siri…" he croaks. "Call…"
His voice is barely there.
The phone lights up. A pause. Waiting.
Who should he call?
His eyes sting. His chest heaves.
"…Call Dad."

Chapter 57

MARTIN

Martin drives in silence, the road stretching endlessly ahead, the darkness slicing past in blurred streaks. The headlights cut through the night like blades, but his mind is somewhere else—back there, in the water, with Mason.

The image keeps playing in his head. Mason's hands, shoving him under. The panic. The pressure in his chest. The weight of water filling his ears. For a moment, Martin truly believed he was going to die—that his son was going to drown him. That he *deserved* to be drowned.

And part of him… still thinks he does.

He had left. Just disappeared. Walked away from a boy who needed a father and never looked back. He told himself that Mason was better off without him. But those were just excuses to hide his fear.

Mason was right when he called him a coward. That word had hit harder than the water, harder than anything.

A coward.

Martin grips the steering wheel tighter, his knuckles whitening. No more. He's done being that man. He's going to make this right. Whatever it takes, however long it takes—he's going to be the father Mason deserved.

He knows it'll be a long road, to rebuild that trust with Mason.

Especially after last night.

After Mason pulled him out of the water, there was a brief moment when they just stared at each other. As Martin was gasping for breath, his vision blurry still, he saw that look of fear in Mason's eyes, of what he had nearly done. Before Martin could say anything, Mason ran off.

Yes, it was going to be a long journey to a normal father-son relationship. He had thirty years to make up, but now, especially following Josh's death, still raw, his heart longed to bring his family back together.

His phone rings.

A number he doesn't recognise.

He thinks about letting it go to voicemail, but something tugs at him. He taps the screen.

"Hello?"

There's silence on the other end. Then, a voice—hoarse, shaking.

"Dad…"

Martin's heart skips.

"Mason?"

"I… I need help."

The world slows down.

"What, what's happened?"

There's a pause, heavy breathing.

"Mason?"

"I've been….stabbed."

Martin's entire body goes cold.

"What? Where are you?"

"A party… at a house somewhere…"

Martin's foot slams the accelerator. Greg's—it must be. "Is it a big house, by the beach?"

More heavy breathing, spluttering almost.

"…Yeah."

"I'm not far. I'll be there soon. Just hold on, son. I'm coming."

He swerves the car onto the next road, not caring about speed limits, not caring about anything but getting to Mason. His pulse is pounding in his ears.

"Have you called the police? An ambulance?"

"No… can't…" His voice is weak. Martin can hear him fading.

"Okay, okay—I'm hanging up and calling them right now—"

"No…don't….please. Just talk to me…"

"Mason, I need to call them now—"

"Please… Dad… I'm scared…"

Martin's throat tightens and against his better judgment stays on the line. "Alright. I'm here. I'm with you. Just talk to me."

There's a pause on the line. Shallow breathing.

"It was because of… Benny," Mason says eventually. "What happened…. What we did..."

Martin feels the weight of those words. He knows the name. *Benny.*

"Let's not talk about that now," Martin says softly. "Right now, I just want you to stay with me. Keep talking."

"I'm sorry…. about our fight," Mason breathes. "I'm sorry... I wish… you'd been in my life more," Mason's voice turns into a whisper

Martin wipes at his eyes, his vision blurring.

"I'm so sorry, Mason. For leaving you. I've missed you every day. Not a single one went by where I didn't think about you. I've regretted it every day. I swear to you, I'm going to fix this. Just hang on. Please, just hang on."

The breathing on the other end becomes faint. Barely there.

"Mason? You still with me?"

"…Yeah…"

His voice is fading.

"You're strong. You're my son. You've survived worse, haven't you?" Martin laughs through his tears, trying to keep him awake, trying to keep the world from slipping away. "You're tougher than me. Always were."

"…love you, Dad."

"I love you too. Just stay awake, okay? Talk to me. Tell me anything."

Silence.

"Mason?"

Nothing.

"Mason, please…"

He's a minute from Greg's house. With his heart thudding, he ends the call and immediately dials emergency services. His voice is frantic, stumbling over the address, shouting it into the phone. They say they're sending someone.

Minutes pass in a blur. Then he sees it.

Greg's beach house.

The driveway.

And Mason.

Crumbled in the gravel.

"No… no no no…"

Martin slams the brakes and throws himself out of the car. He runs—doesn't care about the pain in his legs or the scream in his chest—he runs.

He falls to his knees beside the body, already knowing the truth before he sees the face.

Mason.

Lifeless.

His eyes still open, staring at nothing. Blood soaks his shirt, his hands, the phone beside him like a useless relic.

Martin lets out a howl. Raw. Animal. He cradles Mason's body, pulling it into his arms like he's trying to piece him back together, trying to warm him, trying to bring him back by sheer force of will.

"I was coming," he sobs. "I was coming."

His tears fall onto Mason's face, mixing with the blood, smearing the lines.

"I'm sorry. I'm so sorry."

He kisses Mason's forehead, holding it there for a long time.

And then he looks up.

It was because of... Benny.

Mason's words.

Through the windows of the house, he sees a selection of faces. They don't see him, but he knows the one who is responsible for this.

Martin's grief turns.

Curdles. Becomes rage.

He lays Mason's body down gently. Brushing the hair back from his face, smoothing the blood from his cheek.

"I'll make it right," he whispers. "I promise you, son. I'll make it right."

Then, he stands.

His fists clench. His jaw locks.

And he walks straight to the house.

Vengeance is now on his mind.

Chapter 58

DAN

Everyone's looking for a phone.

Jessie's disappeared upstairs. Dito went into the basement. Hugo went to the dining room. I ran to look in the lounge.

The silence is tense, frantic. Like the house itself is holding its breath.

I search along the wall by the bar, dragging my hands over surfaces sticky with spilled drinks. No phone. No landline. Nothing but empties and ashtrays and the ghosts of conversations that feel decades old.

All I can hear is my own heartbeat. And in my head, that sick, looping replay of what Mason just told us.

A party that turned into a feeding frenzy.

I can't stop picturing it—Benny, wide-eyed, drunk, confused, surrounded. How scared he must've been. How alone. And they all stood there and did nothing.

It's like my stomach's been lined with lead.

Someone is out for revenge. It's obvious now. All those who died were involved somehow that night.

Jessie's voice cuts through the air like a blade. "Found one! Upstairs in the office! Calling the police!"

I exhale, just a little. Relief and fear tangled together like barbed wire.

Across the room, Hugo stands frozen by the fireplace, one hand gripping the mantel. His face is pale. His eyes fixed on something that isn't there.

"Hugo?" I move toward him, careful. "You okay?"

He blinks like he's waking up. "Yeah… yeah. Just…" He swallows, jaw tightening. "Hearing Mason tell the story… it's hard to stomach."

I nod, slowly. "Yeah. I know."

Hugo shifts, eyes flicking toward me. "Doesn't get easier to hear it."

His turn of phrase makes me pause.

"What do you mean?"

He looks at me. Doesn't answer right away. Just stares like he's figuring out what to say—or whether he should say anything at all.

"I mean… it's hard to hear."

"You said it doesn't get *easier* to hear it," I press. "Like you've heard it before."

He hesitates. His throat bobs. Then a shrug, but it's too casual. Too late.

"Hugo…" I lower my voice. "Did you know? What happened to Benny?"

He doesn't answer.

And in the silence that follows, I realise I don't need him to.

His expression says everything.

Chapter 59

BENNY

2 Years earlier

The lights are too bright. Or maybe they're too far away. They blur and bend like neon ghosts, sliding off the walls and into each other. The floor's cold. Benny's tongue feels like sandpaper. There's music somewhere. Voices. Laughter.

Where am I?

Still at the house.

And then, above it all, a voice.

"Just get rid of him."

Greg?

It slices through the fog.

Still faces around, but no longer focused on him.

Trying to move. His arms don't work right. They feel heavy, like they've been filled with wet sand.

The room keeps spinning, swimming.

Footsteps. Two shadows. One is Luca. The other one Benny doesn't know. His face a blur.

Hands grab him under the arms.

He tries to talk, but words melt out of his mouth.

Dragging feet. Weightless, floating, flying. No—being carried. Through a hallway. Down steps. Out into night air.

Then a car door slams.

The engine hums like a lullaby.

The road is a blur. Streetlights flicker past like stars he can't quite reach. Benny tries to speak, to ask where they're taking him, but can't form words.

His mouth doesn't belong to him anymore. Neither does his body. He's just watching. Like he's floating above himself.

The car stops.

The door opens.

And he's on the beach.

Dumped on the sand like garbage. Luca says something to the other man, but Benny can't hear it. The wind swallows it up.

Then they're gone.

The sound of the tide is louder now. Closer. It's coming in. Each wave a slow, wet heartbeat against the shore. And then—against him.

The water hits his legs first. Cold. Then his side. His arm.

I can't move.

Everything inside him feels shattered. Detached.

The tide hits his face. Salty, stinging. Benny gasps, sucking in air.

His phone buzzes in his pocket, deep and muffled.

His arm moves to his pocket, but it's too tight inside.

Can't reach it. No chance.

His wrist is alight.

His watch is flashing from the call. Dragging his other hand up like it weighs 500 pounds, so much effort, he just taps the green symbol on his watch and answers it.

He makes a groaning sound in place of a hello.

"Hey, it's me." Hugo's voice crackles through his watch. "I know I said I would give you some space, but I can't sleep, and I just wanted to clear the air."

"Hugo…" Benny's voice croaks, forcing the words out.

"Yes, it's me. Are you drunk?"

Benny can't reply.

"Benny?"

"They hurt me, Hugo," is all he can say.

"What? Are you okay? Where are you?" Hugo says, the concern rising in his voice.

"Beach…"

"Where on the beach?"

"They hurt me…" Benny whispers this time.

"What happened? Where exactly are you?"

"…Party… Greg's party…"

The tide hits his face again and he coughs hard, chest seizing.

"Who's Greg? What party?"

"Reece took me there…Tommy, Mason, Luca," Benny's voice slurs as he says the names.

"Benny, have you taken something?"

"Josh gave me something…"

"Josh? Okay, where are you? Which beach? Benny—tell me where you are!"

"Don't know… I don't…"

More water splashes over his face, harder this time, submerging his face for a moment, before gasping for breath.

His vision tilts.

"Hugo…" he mumbles.

The water laps over his mouth. He tries to turn his head, but it's too much. His body's too far gone.

Another wave.

Deeper this time.

Submerging his entire face.

His lungs scream. His ears fill.

He chokes.

Then another.

And everything goes quiet.

Just water.

Just dark.

Chapter 60

DAN

"He called you?" I say, staring at Hugo like I've just been slapped.

He nods, eyes distant, lips barely moving. "Yeah."

"And you didn't say anything?" My voice is sharper than I mean it to be, but I don't care. My whole body is tight with disbelief, anger, dread. "Hugo, why wouldn't you—?"

"I don't know, it was all…a lot," he says, quieter now.

"I don't understand why you wouldn't tell me?" I say, confused. After all the discussion we had around Benny this holiday, he never once even suggested he knew anything about it.

"Because when he needed me, I couldn't help him!"

We're standing at the bottom of the stairs. Half the lights are still off. Somewhere, someone's music is still playing faintly from a forgotten speaker. The scent of smoke still clings to the air from Greg's body.

"So….he drowned?" I ask. I'm trying to keep my voice steady, but it trembles anyway.

Before Hugo can answer, Dito and Jessie come rushing down the stairs. Jessie's out of breath, holding a dusty cordless phone in her hand.

"I got through," she says. "The police are on their way."

Then we hear it—a door slamming. Not from upstairs. From somewhere behind us.

We all freeze.

From the kitchen, a man steps into the hallway.

Older, heavyset, still in a white shirt soaked with blood. Eyes wild. In one hand, he's holding a knife.

None of us know who he is.

But he knows us.

"I know you killed him," he growls, stepping forward.

Jessie raises a hand, calm but cautious. "Okay, let's all just—just slow down, yeah? Who are you?"

"Mason's dead," he says, voice cracking. "He's lying outside. Bled out in the dirt like a fucking animal."

"Wait, what?" My stomach drops.

"He said it was because of Benny. I know you did it!"

"Wait—" Jessie starts.

"He was my son!"

There's no time to process that this is Mason's father.

The man lunges towards us.

The knife flashes in the light.

Jessie throws the phone at him, which he bats out of the way. A small distraction, but enough for us to turn and head upstairs.

We sprint, stumbling up the staircase, every step a thunderclap in my skull. I hear glass breaking, furniture scraping.

In the panic, we separate: Jessie heads off to the bathroom, while Hugo, Dito and I head to a room ahead of us. The house groans as we flood into the room—massive, ornate, French doors open to a wide balcony where the sea air hits my face. Must be Greg's bedroom.

Once we're in, I turn to slam the door shut as I see the man running at me. I try to close it in time, but I'm not quick enough. The man drives his weight into the door, forcing me back. Stumbling, I fall, cracking my head against a chest of drawers on the way down. Light explodes behind my eyes and the floor rushes up to meet me.

Everything goes muffled. Like I'm underwater.

Voices swirl around me. Screaming. Crying.

I force myself up, vision swaying.

The man's face is red, spit flying as he shouts.

"I knew it was you. I recognised you! You were there that night."

Dito and Hugo are backed onto the balcony by their assailant.

I'm trying to pick myself up but my head is banging.

"Okay, let's just calm down—" Dito says, desperate to defuse the situation, holding his hands up.

"Mason was a good boy! He didn't deserve this!"

Hugo steps forward. "Yes he did!" he screams, his voice cracking and raw. "They all did! For what they did to Benny! I'm glad they're dead! I wanted them all dead!"

Martin spins on him. "You!"

He charges, knife raised.

But Dito leaps forward, grabbing him by the shoulders, shoving him back—

Their attacker stumbles.

Loses his balance.

Slips.

And then he's gone, over the balcony.

The sound of his body hitting the ground below is a sickening crack.

Time stops.

For a moment, no one moves.

I pull myself upright, staggering toward the balcony. I grip the railing, eyes scanning the drive below.

Mason's father is lying there.

Still.

Twisted.

Dead.

A slow pool of blood spreading around his head.

"Oh my God," I whisper.

Then I hear it.

A choking gasp.

I spin around.

Hugo is on the floor, blood pouring from the side of his neck. His hands are pressed to the wound, but it's no use—the blood's seeping between his fingers, too fast, too much.

A nick from the knife in the struggle.

Dito's kneeling next to him, frozen in place, trembling.

"Call an ambulance!" I shout. "Now!"

Dito doesn't move.

I shove him hard. "Go!"

He snaps out of it and bolts.

I drop to Hugo's side, hands shaking as I try to put pressure on the wound. My palms slip, warm and slick with blood. Hugo's eyes find mine, wide with pain.

"You're okay. Help's coming," I say.

He smiles, faintly. Blood bubbles at the corner of his lips. "I just wanted them to pay…" he whispers. "For what they did to Benny…."

"You're going to be okay," I lie.

"I loved him, Dan." His breath is shallow now. "I loved him so much."

"I know," I say, voice cracking.

And then he's gone.

Just like that.

His eyes glaze over. His chest stops moving.

Gone.

I sit there, my hands still pressed to a body that's no longer alive.

Chapter 61

DAN

It's been over twenty-four hours.

Twenty-four hours since Hugo confessed, since he bled out in my arms.

But it feels like a lifetime.

I'm still numb, in shock. It doesn't quite feel real, that this would happen. That Hugo of all people would do something so horrific.

Hugo, my best friend for years, would seek such horrific revenge for a man he loved. Yet he did, he told me himself. He looked me in the eyes and told me he wanted them dead as he slipped away.

I'm sitting in the hotel reception, whirring the last couple of days through my head, trying to make sense of it. It's too hot to sit outside and I can't face going back to my room, full of Hugo's things, quite yet.

It felt like minutes after Hugo died that the police arrived and took us away for questioning. I vividly remember walking away from the house, seeing Greg's burnt corpse, the body of Mason's dad, who we later found out was named Martin, on the patio and Mason's body out front by the driveway. So much death in such a short space of time.

The police interviewed us for hours after they arrived—Jessie, Dito, and me—separately, back at the station, under harsh lights and too many questions. How Martin came at us with a knife, how we ran, how he fell. How Hugo bled out. They listened. Took notes. Nodded. But our stories all matched. Everything lined up.

I told them about Hugo's confession, about what I had been told about Benny, what happened that night. Part of me wanted to keep it quiet, protect Hugo's reputation and integrity, but there's been enough secrets, enough lies.

Enough silence.

None of which has ended well. So, I made the decision to tell the truth.

Unbelievable at first, the idea that Hugo could hurt anyone was insane, even after his death bed confusion. But the evidence kept coming. There was further CCTV of him walking up the steps towards Luca prior to his death, circumstantial yes. But the nail in the coffin was the knife that was found in a bin within walking distance from the Yumbo, covered in Tommy's blood, and a partial set of fingerprints that matched Hugo's. There was no denying Hugo's involvement after that.

They're still finishing the investigation, tying loose ends, chasing reports, but the general understanding is that they're content to write this off as Hugo's rampage. One man. One motive. End of story.

But they've asked us not to leave the country. They're still finishing the investigation, they say. Still tying up loose ends. It shouldn't take more than a few more days.

Opening my bag, I pull out a bottle of water. I remember I've got Hugo's phone with me. He left it in the hotel room when we went to Greg's. The police were looking for it and I had totally forgotten that he'd left it behind, only finding it charging when I got back to the room earlier. My intention was to take it to the police station later, but I can't face going back there just yet.

Holding the phone in my hand, I open it with his passcode, 240285, the same code it's been for years, his birthday. Flicking through the recent photos, there's some of us by the pool, having cocktails, some with him and Jessie, all smiles and laughter.

So much laughter.

Yet, all that rage was inside him, hidden away, and as his best friend I had no idea.

All I can think of is coming home. I called Alex earlier to talk it all through, but I still haven't cried, even after everything, replaying Hugo's last moments back in my head over and over again, not yet. Could I have done more?

From the other side of the hotel, Jessie and Dito appear. Throwing Hugo's phone back in the bag, they sit next to me, on the edge of one of those ugly floral couches, shoulders hunched, eyes shadowed. We're all dressed differently than yesterday. Showered. Changed. But none of us look like ourselves.

"Hey," I say.

Jessie lifts her head. "Hey."

No hugs. No tears. We're past that now.

"You alright?" I ask, though the question feels hollow.

"Just exhausted," Dito mutters.

Jessie nods.

The gruelling endurance test of the police interview has drained every last bit from us, when all we want to do is process and grieve.

There's a pause between us, thick with everything we don't say. The image of Greg's burnt corpse. Hugo bleeding out. Mason's body on the gravel. All of it burned into our retinas.

Still, there's something binding about it. Like trauma soldered us together. Three people who barely knew each other a few days ago. Now sharing a grief no one else can touch.

Jessie and I haven't talked about it properly. What Hugo did and why he did it. The fact that Hugo, my best friend, brutally killed her best friend Tommy, is not a topic that either of us want to discuss right now. Maybe we never will. Who knows if we will either stay in touch once we return home.

"Did you sleep?" I ask.

"A little," Jessie says.

Dito shakes his head. "I haven't even been to bed yet."

I nod. "I might take a walk later. Clear my head."

The police have visited Hugo's parents back home from what I hear. I know I should call them and offer my condolences, but I can't face having that conversation yet. They're on the next flight over here, the police told me.

Then my phone rings.

Jimmy.

I stare at the name for a second before I answer. "Hey."

“I heard what happened,” he says, voice low. Strained. “Are you okay?”

“No,” I admit. “But I’m managing.”

There’s a pause on the line. Then: “Can you come over?”

“Now?”

“Yeah. I—” He hesitates. “I’d like to talk to you. It’s important.”

And while I’m not sure what could be important at this point in time, I know Jimmy has connections with the police, so maybe it will be beneficial.

“I’ll be there soon.”

I hang up and look at the others.

“I’m going to see my friend. Jimmy.”

Jessie gives a slight nod. “I think I’m going to lie down for a bit.”

“Same,” Dito says. “I just need to… not be conscious for a while.”

And as tempting as unconsciousness sounds right now, I say my goodbyes and head out of the hotel.

*

Jimmy’s apartment is a twenty-minute walk away on the other side of town. Being mid-afternoon, it’s sweaty and uncomfortable in the sun. I’ve not put any sun cream on and I can feel the back of my neck starting to scorch.

As I arrive at Jimmy’s ground floor apartment, it’s quiet, with people sensibly taking shade.

The door is ajar.

Not wide open, just unlocked. Hanging, slightly, like it’s waiting for me.

I knock anyway. “Jimmy?”

No answer.

I hesitate for half a second, then push the door gently. It creaks open, and I step inside.

The apartment is dark. Too dark. The curtains are drawn tight, but one of them has slipped at the edge, and a thin shard of light cuts across the floor like a blade. It’s quiet—no music, no TV, just the soft hum of the fridge and my own uneasy breathing.

"Jimmy?"

I find him in the kitchen.

He's standing by the counter, half-lit by that narrow beam of light. Shoulders hunched. Eyes distant. His hands are flat on the counter.

He looks up to me. "Hey."

"Hey," I say back. I don't know why, but I was expecting a hug or some kind of relatively warm welcome more than this coldness, which unnerves me.

"I'm sorry," he says, voice low and shaky. "About Hugo."

I nod slowly. "Yeah. Me too."

"My friend at the police updated me," he says. "I told him about our conversations, about what happened that party a couple of years ago. I told them what I could." As he talks, his voice slurs, like he's been drinking. I hadn't picked up on it on the phone, but now I'm here, I can see his bleary eyes, in and out of focus, a slight instability to the way he stands.

"Okay, thanks," I say, acknowledging that the more people who corroborate my version of events, the more likely it is to wind this whole nightmare down.

He keeps staring at the wall like he's not really seeing it. Like he's looking through it.

I approach the kitchen table close to him and place the phone in my hand down on it.

"Jimmy, what did you want to talk to me about?"

He turns to look at me. "So many people have died," he mutters. "Because of that party. Reece. Greg. Mason. Now Hugo. All of it… all of it started there."

He's rambling. Shaky. I can see the sweat on his brow, the twitch in his jaw. My stomach tightens.

"Jimmy, what's going on?"

"I never thought it would lead to this," he says. "I wasn't thinking straight. I didn't know what would happen. I thought it would just… go away."

"What would go away?"

Jimmy turns toward me, eyes wide. "I was there."

My breath catches. "What?"

"That night. The party. With Benny."

He's trembling now. Gripping the edge of the counter like it's the only thing keeping him standing.

There's a knife resting next to him on the counter. I hadn't noticed it at first, but as I take a small step forward, the light reflecting on it catches my eyes and I stall.

"I was there," he says again, slower this time. "I didn't know what they were going to do. I didn't know how bad it would get. I was just helping Greg. Just driving people, picking them up. Greg asked me to bring some guys there. Luca too. He gave us money to bring them. That's all it was supposed to be."

I say nothing. I just stare.

"I took him away," Jimmy says. "Me and Luca. Greg told us to get rid of him. Those were his words. Get rid of him.

"We dumped him on the beach. He could barely stand. His head was rolling around. But he was alive."

My heart is pounding out of my chest. *Why is he telling me this?*

"The tide was coming in," Jimmy says, his voice cracking. "I didn't think it would God, I didn't *think*. He was right by the water. Luca said he'd be fine. I didn't…but I just left."

He looks up at me now, tears in his eyes.

"I went back a couple of hours later, I thought I would help him, but the tide was way in by that point. He couldn't have got away, he must have been swept away."

He stares me straight in the eyes.

"I left him there. I killed him."

There it is.

The room spins for a second.

I lean on the wall.

"Why are you telling me this?"

"Because I can't keep it in anymore," he chokes. "It's tearing me apart. So many people have died because of that party. I played my part.

"I deserve to die. Like the others."

I shake my head. I don't know what's happening. I don't know how to process this. My chest is tight and I can't tell if it's rage or grief or shock.

"Are you going to tell the police?" I ask.

Jimmy's eyes go flat. He shakes his head.

"No, no, I can't."

"Then I'll tell them."

His panic is instant. "Dan—no, please—"

He steps forward, hand reaching out—and then—

He grabs the knife.

I flinch back, heart leaping into my throat.

He's not pointing it at me. Not yet. But he's holding it. Tight. Like a lifeline. Or a threat.

"Please don't," he begs. "You don't understand what'll happen to me."

"I don't *care* what happens to you," I snap. "You left him there. You *let* him drown."

"I didn't know—"

He takes another step towards me, the knife directly pointing at me now.

"You *should have* known."

The knife glints in his hand, and for a moment I think—*this is it*. Another body. Another mess.

But Jimmy just stands there.

Broken. Frightened. Pathetic.

I walk toward the door, every muscle screaming. My heart pounding.

He doesn't follow.

I step outside.

My hands are shaking.

*

I've been walking for twenty minutes.

My brain is a blur of confessions and lies. Too much for me to handle. Too much in this heat. I just need to get home.

I'm nearly back to the hotel, when it dawns on me, I don't know where my phone is.

Shit.

I stop in the middle of the pavement, blinking dumbly like the thought just hit me from a great height. I reach into my shorts pockets again and again—nothing. I *left it*. On the table in Jimmy's flat.

"Fuck," I say aloud.

I spin around, already retracing my steps. I don't want to go back. I *really* don't want to go back. But I need my phone.

The last thing I want to do is go back and see Jimmy, but my hands are tied at this point.

I pick up the pace.

It takes less than 15 minutes to reach his place again. The door is closed now. Still, I knock. Not hard. Just a few quick raps.

"Jimmy?" I call out.

No answer.

I wait a beat.

Then another.

Nothing.

I try the handle. It's unlocked.

"Jimmy?" I say again, louder this time, pushing the door open a crack.

Silence.

The place is still dark. No lights. Curtains drawn.

I step inside slowly, the way you do when you know you're not supposed to be somewhere. My breath catches in my throat. The air feels colder. Thicker. Like something's settled in it.

Jimmy's probably passed out from the alcohol anyway. I'll just pop in quickly and grab it and run, a ten second job.

The hallway is empty.

I pass through into the kitchen.

Jimmy's there.

Sitting in a chair in the centre of the room. Facing away from me. Head tilted.

Relief flickers for a moment—until I see it.

The blood.

It's pooling beneath the chair.

Spreading across the tiles like paint.

I step closer, my stomach coiling into a knot.

His mouth—

There's something stuffed inside it. A towel? No—tighter. Coarser. Fabric of some kind, soaked in red.

His throat—

Cut open. A deep, brutal slash. So wide it looks unreal.

He's tied to the chair, his hands bound around the arms.

And on the floor—

Fingers.

Two of them.

Lying there like they've been casually dropped.

I stumble back, gagging, hand over my mouth. My brain is screaming at me to run, to leave, to *do something*, but I'm frozen.

Then I remember.

My phone.

I force myself toward the table, eyes darting away from Jimmy's body, searching—

It's not there.

I spin in a panic, heart hammering. I scan the counter. The floor. Nothing. Then I hear it.

A creak.

Behind me.

I turn.

There's someone in the doorway.

Holding my phone in one hand.

And a knife in the other.

"Dito," I say, a whisper soaked in confusion.

He smiles at me, nodding.

"I've never quite got used to people calling me Dito," he says casually. "My nan used to call me it because she never liked my real name. Benedito.

"But most people would call me Benny."

Chapter 62

MARTIN

2 years earlier

The beach is quiet this time of night.

Waves lap softly against the shore, and the world feels a little less cruel beneath the stars. Martin walks slowly, letting his busy mind settle. The last show at Rocky's ran late—drunk tourists, half-hearted applause, and too many hecklers in the front row had killed the energy. He gave them what they came for. As always.

But now he's alone.

Tired.

Thinking about Mason again.

He always does, after a show. When the makeup comes off and the applause fades, there's nothing left but him and the silence.

God, what a mess Martin's made of things. What a bloody mess.

If he could just speak to him. Just once—to say he's sorry. Try to make it right. But he's just left it far too long, something he will never forgive himself for.

A flicker on the water catches his eye.

Martin slows.

At first, he thinks it's seaweed. Or driftwood. Or maybe just the moon playing tricks on the waves.

But then—

A shape.

Limp.

Floating.

Human.

He runs to the water.

The water bites cold as he splashes in, stumbling over slick sand and breaking tide. The body bobs with the motion, face barely above water. A young man.

Martin grabs him under the arms and drags him back toward shore, heart pounding.

"Come on," he mutters. "Come on, come on!"

The body flops onto the sand, still. Pale. Unmoving.

Martin checks for breath.

Nothing.

He starts CPR. One, two, three—his hands press into the man's chest. He counts aloud, louder than necessary, trying to drown out the panic. Breath. Compress. Again.

And then—

A cough.

A violent choke.

The man jerks upright, coughing out seawater and bile, eyes wide with panic.

Martin kneels back, gasping with relief. "It's okay. You're okay. You're safe."

The young man blinks, chest heaving, face streaked with tears and seawater. He looks around like he doesn't know where he is. Like the world is too bright, too loud.

"You nearly drowned," Martin says gently. "I found you in the water."

He tries to speak but only gets out a rasp. "Where—?"

"You're on the beach. It's okay. Just breathe."

The boy nods slowly, shivering hard now. His lips are blue. His clothes soaked. He looks dazed, wrecked, like he's been through hell.

"What's your name?" Martin asks, voice soft.

"...Benny."

Martin exhales. "Benny. Okay. You're safe now."

But something in Benny's face shifts. His eyes narrow—not with suspicion, but with some buried memory. A wince. A flinch.

"Are you okay? Benny?" Martin asks.

Benny doesn't respond at first. He's still catching his breath. His eyes are glassy, trying to focus.

"They hurt me," he whispers.

Martin's heart skips. "Who?"

Benny's jaw clenches. "They hurt me," he repeats, like he's in some confused state.

"Where, what happened?

"At… the party…at the house…" he stutters.

Martin's stomach turns.

Greg's party. It was on tonight.

It *had* to be.

"I'm so sorry," he says, reaching out instinctively, his hand landing gently on Benny's shoulder.

But the second he makes contact, Benny flinches back like he's been burned.

"Don't touch me!" he shouts, scrambling to his feet.

Martin stands and steps back instantly, hands raised.

"Hey—it's okay. I'm not—"

"Just leave me alone!"

Benny's eyes are wild, darting everywhere, breath coming fast.

Martin doesn't move.

"I'm not going to hurt you. I just wanted to help."

But Benny's already backing away, staggering down the beach, soaked and shaking and lost.

Martin watches him go.

His silhouette disappears into the darkness.

And Martin stands there, chest aching, soaked to the skin.

He'll never forget that face.

Those eyes.

The young man with the deep, haunted stare and a scream trapped in his lungs.

The one he couldn't save—even after dragging him from the sea.

Chapter 63

DAN

"No."

That's all I can say.

I shake my head. "No," I say again. "You can't be Benny. I've seen pictures of him. Hugo showed me."

I feel sick. I try to picture Benny's face, from the few photos I've seen—big eyes covered by thick glasses, skinny frame, pale skin, wiry hair, soft features, the kind of shy smile you'd miss if you blinked.

Dito is muscular, solid, sharp.

They're not the same.

They *can't* be the same.

But something in his eyes—something deep—*is* the same.

"I couldn't be him anymore," he says. "After what happened that night. After what they did to me. I didn't want to be a victim. I didn't want to be someone people forgot. So, I became someone else."

He takes a breath, and for the first time, I see the weight behind his performance. The cracks.

"I don't understand. How?"

Dito smiles at me.

"New nose, chin implant, ears pinned back, bit of filler, hair system, among other things. Got rid of those God-awful glasses.

A personal trainer, a lot of hard work, a fuck-load of steroids. And here we are."

I can't process this.

"I come from quite a well-to-do family, you could say, so I had plenty of resources for what I needed."

"And the others never knew?" I ask.

"Don't be ridiculous, they couldn't have picked the original Benny out of a lineup. If it's not some hot six-packed stud, their eyes just gloss over. When I infiltrated my way into their friendship group last year, the new improved Dito, they were all over me. I just had to spend a bit of cash around Reece and his eyes lit up, then it didn't take long to meet the others. Or persuade them to book a holiday over here. It felt fitting that this should be the place to finish them off."

"So, it was you, all along?"

Dito's eyes flicker, just for a second.

"That night… it was like something infected my bones. The hands. The voices. The way no one stopped it. A lot of it's a blur, but I remember enough: Reece, Tommy, Mason getting me to go; they just saw me as a joke, some light relief at the party they could mock. Josh gave me those drugs. They all knew I shouldn't be taking that much, but I was naïve, an idiot, I let them talk me into it. I remember Greg on top of me, along with a bunch of faces. I still can't remember them all.

"Harry Shaw was a stroke of luck," Dito continues. "I saw him in the local paper the day I arrived, recognised him immediately. Wasn't hard to lure him up to the top of the Yumbo, and chuck him off. Then, Luca, who took me there, disposed of me on the beach like trash, along with this guy here." He nods to Jimmy's body on the chair in front of him.

"I wasn't quite sure what to do with Jimmy. I even thought about coming back another time for him, when things calmed down, but when he called you earlier, it just triggered me."

"Dito—" I start to say, not knowing where I'm going to go with these words.

"You have no idea the pain I've been through," he says firmly. "And not just physically. I mean getting fucked by ten guys without lube while your unconscious is no party, believe me. My insides were torn to shreds. It took months for me to get back to normal, if you can call it normal. And then to add to the humiliation, I caught syphilis, chlamydia and gonorrhoea when I got tested at the clinic after. A clean sweep! Can you fucking believe it? That was an awkward conversation."

I'm lost for words as Dito continues.

"The nightmares, the flashbacks, the panic attacks. I couldn't sleep or eat or move for months. But I was determined that it wasn't going to drag me down."

"Why didn't you tell anyone? The police?"

"Seriously, the police? To relive that over and over again. Do you think some guy high on ket getting fucked by a bunch of men at a party is news here. Fuck no."

"Dito, I'm sorry for what you went through. I really am. I can't imagine …" And despite the bloodshed that he has caused, I do feel for him—for what he must have experienced, the horror of that night.

"All I've thought about for the last two years is revenge. Coming back here and making them all pay for what they did. And I don't regret killing a single one of them."

My throat is dry. "So, Hugo didn't kill anyone?"

He shakes his head. "Of course not. The idea of Hugo killing anyone is ludicrous. But he did help me. A lot. I mean I couldn't have pulled Tommy's body up on the rope on my own, it was a two-person job.

"We arranged to stay at the same dates at the same hotel. He brought you; I talked the others into coming along. He befriended the group pretty easily, we knew he'd click with Jessie. Then he could be around them and keep an eye on everyone while I was disappearing off to do what I needed to do. His aim was to spend as much time with the group as possible. We shared our locations on our phones, so I always knew where he was, where they were, and when he was needed."

"Needed?" I ask. "Sounds like you were keeping control of him?"

"He didn't do anything he didn't want to do. He dropped a little something in Luca's drink while you were on your date to slow him down a bit. Made it so much easier to slip that noose around his neck."

I remember Luca suddenly turning that night, out of the blue. It's all starting to make sense.

"He told me about seeing Josh in the sling in Corruption. That was a bit of luck too. He didn't see it coming before I snapped his neck.

"He got rid of the knife I used to kill Tommy, not very successfully it turns out. Probably should have wiped his prints off properly, but criminal mastermind he ain't. He even kept a watch out while I smashed Reece's head in. Hugo was my eyes and ears."

"And he knew all along that you didn't die that night?" I ask, trying to make sense of it all.

"No, he didn't find me on the beach that night. He spent the night looking, but he had no idea where I was, thought I'd been swept away. He was wracked with guilt for a long time. It wasn't until about a year or so later, I tracked him down. Told him what happened, that I loved him, that I wanted to be together forever. That we could get revenge together then start our lives afresh."

"And he just agreed?"

"Eventually. Once I told him everything that happened, what went on that night, what they did, what they didn't do. He was horrified."

Although knowing Hugo, knowing how much he wanted love, how much he wanted to be with Benny, I can imagine when the new improved Benny turned up, promising him the world alongside the guilt he must have felt, Hugo would have agreed to anything.

"And did you have any intention of actually being with him once this was all over?"

"Hugo was very important to me," Dito says.

"Sounds like you just manipulated him into helping you. And now he's taken the fall for you too?"

Dito shakes his head. "I didn't manipulate him into anything. Yes, what happened to Hugo was tragic; it was never my intention for him to get hurt. Or Martin, it was never my plan to hurt him! I was thankful to him! He saved me that night on the beach, dragged me out of the water, the only person who looked after me that night. I owed him.

"But he recognised me, turned up waving a knife around. He wasn't coming for Hugo, he was coming for me."

Dito is still standing in front of me, knife in hand. And I have no idea how I'm going to get out of this alive.

"I don't think you'll be able to get away with this," I say. "If more people die, they'll know it isn't Hugo, they'll come looking for you."

Dito looks unphased. "As I said, I have very resourceful parents. I can disappear anywhere I want to. I'll be off this island before any other bodies are found."

The word 'bodies' causes me to take a sharp intake of breath.

"So now it's over, they're all dead. What next?" I ask.

"This isn't over!" Dito shouts. "There's so much about that night I still don't remember. Men whose faces are just a blur. Luckily, Jimmy helped me out; it took a bit of persuasion, but he gave me four more names of men who were there that night."

I look down at the severed fingers on the floor, well aware of Dito's persuasion technique.

"So, I have a new list to work through now. You could call it the sequel."

I take a breath. A real one.

Not the shallow, panicked gasps I've been sucking down since he closed the door. A real breath. Slow.

"Dito," I say. "You don't have to do this."

His jaw tightens. "Yes. I do."

"No, you don't." I step forward, just half a pace. Careful. "You think this is justice. That what you're doing is right. But it's not. It's just pain. The same pain they put you through, only now you're putting it on everyone else. Over and over again."

"They deserved it," he says, almost in a whisper.

"Maybe they did," I reply. "Maybe every single one of them deserved to rot. But I *do* know that this—*this*—isn't healing. It's not power. It's just more trauma. More bodies. More blood you have to carry."

He looks at me. Really looks. And I see him—*Benny*—for the first time.

The terror. The ache. The exhaustion in his bones.

"You think killing everyone who hurt you is going to make you feel better?" I ask. "It won't. And you know that. Because you've already done it. You've crossed every line, and look at you—you're still drowning."

He blinks. His hand holding the knife twitches slightly.

"I'm not saying what happened to you wasn't horrific. It *was*. It was unspeakable. And I am so, so sorry. For what they did. For what they allowed to happen. For every second you've had to carry it alone."

My voice breaks. I feel it in my throat.

"But this isn't the way. It's never been the way. You don't need revenge. You need help. You need someone to *see* you. Really see you. Not the version you created, not the armour, not the anger. *You.*"

His lips part. For a second, the mask slips. He looks lost.

"You don't have to be alone anymore, Benny," I say. "You don't have to keep punishing yourself, and everyone else, for what they did to you. Let this stop. Let *you* stop. Let someone take care of you for once."

Silence.

I take another cautious step close to him.

Holding out my hand.

Another step.

Then a tear slips down his cheek.

Just one.

"I'm sorry it came to this, Dan," he says, and although it feels genuine, I've misinterpreted what he's sorry about.

The knife thrusts into my stomach.

Once.

Twice.

Three times.

Each one a searing agony ripping through my inside.

My knees hit the floor. My hands go instinctively to the wounds—wet, warm, slick with blood.

He steps back, breathing heavy, eyes wide.

"I'm sorry," he says again, but it sounds so far away now. Like he's underwater. Or I am.

He turns and walks out. Calm. Quiet. Like it's done. Like I'm already gone.

The room tilts. The walls feel like they're closing in. I press my palm hard against the worst wound, but the blood's seeping fast. Too fast. I'm dizzy. My limbs feel heavy.

No. Not here.

I crawl.

Every inch hurts. My vision pulses, narrows. The kitchen floor is streaked behind me now, smeared with red handprints and drag lines. I don't even know how I make it to the door.

But somehow… I do.

I push it open with what little strength I have left. The light from outside nearly blinds me. I squint.

I collapse onto the pavement.

All energy gone, it's like I've given up the fight and my body just relaxes, as I accept my inevitable fate.

Lying back, letting the warmth of the sun seep into my skin, my body sinking into the ground like it belongs here. Above me, the sky stretches out, impossibly blue, the kind of blue that feels endless, untouched, a colour that only exists in places like this.

The clouds move lazily, slow and unbothered, drifting without purpose, without urgency. I watch them shift, morphing into soft, shapeless figures that my brain half-heartedly tries to turn into something recognisable.

The heat is perfect, that deep, golden warmth that makes everything else fade away. My limbs are heavy, my breathing slow.

I close my eyes for a moment, feeling the weight of the sun pressing down on me, the lazy hum of summer wrapping around my body like a second skin. When I open them again, the sky is still there, still endless, still moving in its own quiet rhythm.

There's noise nearby, chatting maybe, I can't quite tell.

Such a peaceful day.

The kind of day I came on holiday for.

So calm.

So relaxed.

My palms are damp, but not from sweat.

No, it's from the blood that covers them.

A reminder of what's really happening.

I hear more voices around me.

I can't open my eyes, they're too heavy.

But I feel at peace, I feel my life draining away from my body, as I take that final breath.

Epilogue

ALEX

The hospital smells like bleach and heat and something Alex can't quite name. Something metallic. The kind of smell that settles in your throat and stays there, no matter how shallow you breathe.

Sitting in a hard plastic chair in the corner of the waiting room, sweat is clinging to his back, his shirt damp. The air conditioning hums faintly above him but does nothing to cut through the sticky warmth.

He's been here for what feels like hours. No one's told him much. A nurse at reception asked for his name, his relation to Dan. Then they asked him to wait. Not in the main area—no. They led him through a back corridor, into a smaller room. Quieter. Out of the way.

Too quiet.

Alex stares at the scuffed floor tiles, eyes unfocused, heart beating too loud in his chest. His legs are jittering. His hands won't stay still.

The silence is suffocating.

He tries not to let his thoughts spiral. But it's hard not to. He flew out here the second he got the call—he had to be here. Dan's parents are on their way too. A few hours behind Alex on a different flight. He had to be here for them.

He's had no time to process what he was told, still in disbelief that it has ended like this.

Footsteps echo in the corridor.

A nurse appears at the door. She looks young, tired, and like she's been working this shift far too long.

She says something in Spanish, slow and gentle. He only catches a few words. Something about *tranquilo*. Something about *ahora*.

Then she nods at him, her face soft with sympathy.

The kind of look he doesn't want to see. The look he doesn't want to think about.

Alex stands, legs like lead, and follows her.

They walk in silence. White walls. Bright lights. A corridor that seems to stretch forever.

Outside one of the rooms, the nurse stops and reaches into a drawer. She pulls out a small plastic envelope. Inside—a phone. Wallet. Blood-streaked sunglasses. Must be Dan's belongings, but again, he doesn't want to think about it.

She says something again as she presses it gently into his hand.

Alex swallows hard.

The nurse opens the door and steps aside.

Alex enters slowly.

The room is quiet. Too quiet.

And there he is, in a way Alex would never want to see his best friend.

It knocks Alex for six.

Dan lying on the bed, face to the ceiling, arms by his side. White sheets pulled up to his chin. Eyes closed. His skin is pale, lips slightly parted. The whole room feels still. Reverent.

Peaceful.

Alex stands at the foot of the bed.

Just staring.

His throat tightens. A lump rises he can't swallow down.

"I'm here," he whispers.

Alex clenches his fists, willing himself not to fall apart, forcing back the tears.

And then—

Dan's eyes flutter open.

Slowly. Groggily.

Blinking against the light.

"…Alex?" he croaks, voice like gravel.
Alex stares.
Then chokes out a breath that's part-laugh, part-sob.

DAN

Waking up feels like surfacing from underwater.

Slow. Heavy. Like the world's wrapped in cotton. My body aches in a way I can't begin to describe—deep, throbbing pain stitched through every nerve ending. But I'm here. I'm *awake*. Which, if I'm honest, surprises me.

The ceiling is white and too bright. There's a steady beep next to me, a soft mechanical rhythm keeping time with my heart. I turn my head—barely—and I see him.

"Alex?"

Sitting by the bed, elbows on his knees, hands clutched together like he's been praying or trying not to fall apart. His eyes are rimmed red, but he's smiling. Just a little.

"Hey," he says softly, like if he says it too loud I might disappear.

I try to speak, but my throat's dry, my voice barely a croak. "Hey."

"You scared the shit out of me," he says. There's a breath of laughter in it, but it's broken.

"I am pretty scary," I nod.

Alex leans closer. "You're going to be okay. Doctors said you lost a lot of blood, but no major organs were hit. Lucky bastard."

"The three knife wounds in me beg to differ."

I close my eyes for a second. It hurts. Not just my body. All of it. Everything.

"How long have I been out?"

"About a day and a half."

I nod, though it feels like moving a mountain.

"I'm sorry," Alex says suddenly. His voice is low. Raw. He places his hand on mine. "About Hugo. I can't even imagine what that was like."

I open my eyes again. There's too much I could say. Too much I *should* say. But I don't.

"Yeah," I whisper. "Thanks."

He doesn't push. Just nods. "There's a lot to catch up on. But now's not the time."

He reaches down beside him and lifts a small plastic envelope.

"Some of your stuff," he says, handing it over. "They gave it to me earlier."

Looking in the envelope, I see the phone.

"That's not mine," I say, confused.

"What?"

"My phone was still at Jimmy's place. I never got it back. Police said they'd look for it."

Alex takes the envelope back from me and frowns. "Then whose…?"

"That's Hugo's," I say, realisation washing over me like cold water. "He left it at the hotel that night. I found it earlier. I was supposed to drop it off to the police. It was in my bag."

"Oh," Alex says.

We both fall silent.

I look away, swallowing hard.

"Any word on… Dito?" I ask, though I hate the sound of the name in my mouth now. Benny. *Benny.*

Alex shakes his head. "They think he's already left the island. Ferry or flight, maybe under a fake name. There's nothing concrete. He's gone."

And while that should give me comfort, it doesn't. Knowing that he's still out there, that he could come back at any time makes me feel sick to my stomach.

"Maybe he'll never be found."

"Maybe," Alex says. "I don't think he'll want anyone to know where he is."

"No, I'm sure he doesn't."

Then it hits me. Hugo did. Hugo always knew.

"Give me the phone," I say to Alex, who hands it over, a slight look of confusion on his face.

I unlock the phone, as I've done many times before, with the familiar passcode. Hugo's birthday.

We shared our locations on our phones, so I always knew where he was and when he was needed.

That's what Dito had said.

I pull up the Find My Friends app, and there he is, a little blue dot, on the coast of Morocco.

It says: Benny's phone.

I've found him.

Coming Summer 2026

Death at the Yumbo Centre

Part 2

If you enjoyed **Death at the Yumbo** centre,
why not delve into Dan's first mystery…

FOLLOWERS

Be careful who you follow… because not everyone is who they seem.

Dan, a single gay man nearing 40, finds himself stuck in a cycle of doom scrolling and self-doubt, which do nothing but fuel his own insecurities.

Following a not-so chance encounter with a charming local influencer, Dan finds himself drawn into a mystery surrounding the sudden death of his handsome insta-famous neighbour.

What begins as harmless curiosity quickly spirals into obsession, as Dan delves into this alien world of picture-perfect facades. Armed only with his stifling social anxiety and a penchant for sarcasm, the deeper he digs, the more he risks—because in a world where nothing is as it seems, the truth might just kill him.

OUT NOW

ACKNOWLEDGEMENTS

I've been to Gran Canaria more times than I can count over the past decade—drawn back each time by the sun, the fun, and the sheer chaos of the Yumbo Centre. It's a place that's seen many nights of laughter, frolics, and questionable decisions. But it was during one particularly memorable trip at the end of 2024, holed up in an Airbnb just a stone's throw from the Yumbo with my friends Ash, Jon, and Stephen, that the idea for this book was born.

Somewhere between my Strawberry Daiquiri obsession and our daily mental unloading in *Wellbeing Corner*, I announced—probably with more confidence than was warranted—that I was going to write a Yumbo-based murder mystery, which led on to much brainstorming of *Final Destination*-style holiday deaths—most of which were far too horrifying, impractical, or just plain ridiculous to include here (though a few came dangerously close).

Still, that holiday was the start of it all, and I'll always be grateful for the laughs, the inspiration, and the occasional "absolutely not" that helped steer this book toward something at least halfway sensible-ish.

Once again, my plan was to bring together some relatable, flawed, and messy characters and catapult them into a delightfully loopy murder mystery. Hangings and stabbings aside, a lot of this story stems from my own experiences—the nights of excess, the on-demand sex, the overstimulation, and the gloriously messy judgment calls that probably shouldn't have been made after 2 a.m. So, I hope a certain demographic will see their own experiences within these pages.

Anyway, onto the thank-yous.

Ash, Jon, Stephen—my GC gang. I imagine we'll be back there together sometime soon to make more ridiculous, wonderful memories. That week away with you lot is one of my favourite times of the year.

Thanks to Richie from More Visual for whipping up another brilliant cover design for me, just like he did with my first. He'll most probably never read this book or even know he's mentioned here, but he still gets a big thumbs-up from me.

To Michelle, thank you for being my longest and dearest friend. Our annual holiday is my *other* favourite time of year—admittedly a very different vibe to GC: still cocktails and books, but swap the drag shows and darkrooms for chocolate pudding and temporarily adopted German children. Thank you for being my makeshift editor and spellchecker, and for reminding me that *wandering* and *wondering* are clearly different words.

To Emma, my other dearest friend, a massive thank-you for being my biggest supporter (alongside my mum). You can find her being endlessly bookish and fabulous at @emieloulovesbooks.

And finally, a big thank you to *you*, for taking the time to read this book. It means the world to me, and I hope you enjoyed it. If you did, leaving a lovely review would be most appreciated!

I will raise my next Strawberry Daiquiri to you all.

ABOUT THE AUTHOR

Darren is a web analyst by day and a budding novelist by night, loving a good book and a pivot table in equal measure.

He lives in Bristol with his two cats, Nelson and Erin.

Death at the Yumbo Centre is his second novel.

You can follow him on Instagram **@dmpickersgill.books**

Printed in Dunstable, United Kingdom

79901299R00180